P1

LET'S PLAY MURDER

'Brilliantly executed with unexpected twists and turns, *Let's Play Murder* is like the best, most carefully crafted mystery mixed with classic video games. It will keep you guessing until the very last page … the chilling thriller you don't want to miss'
Alison Weatherby, author of *The Secrets Act*

'I just couldn't put it down – Kesia's writing was so immersive, and she's taken a very unique concept and created such a gripping story with very distinctive characters'
Aneesa Marufu, author of *The Balloon Thief*

'*Black Mirror* meets *One of Us Is Lying*. *Let's Play Murder* had me racing to finish and questioning everything right up to the explosive conclusion'
Amy McCaw, author of *Mina and the Undead* and *Mina and the Slayer*s

'*Let's Play Murder* is unputdownable, immersive, edge-of-your-seat excitement. If you're looking for a thrilling blend of thriller and horror to set your pulse racing, plus a truly shocking, gasp-worthy twist, this is the book for you'
Katharine and Elizabeth Corr, authors of *The Witch's Kiss* and *A Throne of Swans*

'A fast-paced mystery that keeps you guessing until the very end. *Let's Play Murder* is like a dark, twisted escape room for your mind. The ultimate combination of fun and fear'
Fran Hart, author of *The Other Ones*

'I rattled through it in a couple of frantic nights' reading as I couldn't wait to get to the end! I loved the twisty mash-up of virtual reality and old-school murder mystery; it was delightfully creepy and atmospheric'
Andreina Cordani, author of *The Girl Who …* and *Dead Lucky*

'Talk about twists and turns – this book had me gripped and guessing all the way through. Everything about it was wonderfully dark: the secrets, the intricately drawn setting, the shadowy characters. I've never been so desperate to get to the end of a book'
Molly Morris, author of *This Is Not the End*

'*Ready Player One* meets Agatha Christie. I gulped down this thrilling, mysterious and highly original read, and I defy anyone to guess the ending'
Anna Day, author of *The Fandom* and *The Fandom Rising*

'A fast-paced, tense read that combines murder mystery with a sinister VR world – a thrilling ride!'
Ravena Guron, author of *This Book Kills*

'A nightmare VR escape room brilliantly combined with a gripping murder mystery – I was hooked from the first page and tore through *Let's Play Murder*!'
Tess James-Mackey, author of *Someone Is Watching You*

LET'S PLAY MURDER

LET'S PLAY MURDER

KESIA LUPO

BLOOMSBURY

LONDON   OXFORD   NEW YORK   NEW DELHI   SYDNEY

BLOOMSBURY YA
Bloomsbury Publishing Plc
50 Bedford Square, London WC1B 3DP, UK
29 Earlsfort Terrace, Dublin 2, Ireland

BLOOMSBURY, BLOOMSBURY YA and the Diana logo
are trademarks of Bloomsbury Publishing Plc

First published in Great Britain in 2023 by Bloomsbury Publishing Plc

A catalogue record for this book is available from the British Library

ISBN: PB: 978-1-5266-3546-4; eBook: 978-1-5266-3545-7;
ePDF: 978-1-5266-3568-6

2 4 6 8 10 9 7 5 3

Typeset by RefineCatch Limited, Bungay, Suffolk
Printed and bound in Great Britain by CPI Group (UK) Ltd, Croydon CR0 4YY

To find out more about our authors and books visit www.bloomsbury.com
and sign up for our newsletters

For Zöe

Thanks for taking a chance on me

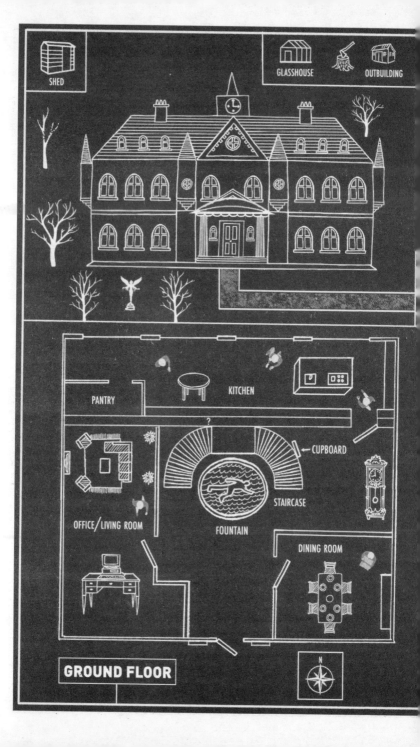

SHED

GLASSHOUSE   OUTBUILDING

PANTRY   KITCHEN

?

← CUPBOARD

STAIRCASE

OFFICE/LIVING ROOM   FOUNTAIN

DINING ROOM

GROUND FLOOR

N

FIRST FLOOR

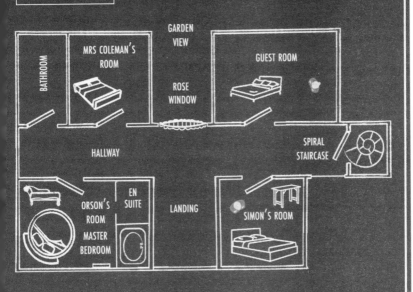

BATHROOM

MRS COLEMAN'S ROOM

GARDEN VIEW

GUEST ROOM

ROSE WINDOW

SPIRAL STAIRCASE

HALLWAY

ORSON'S ROOM

MASTER BEDROOM

EN SUITE

LANDING

SIMON'S ROOM

BUTLER'S ROOM

PETER'S ROOM

STUDIO

SPIRAL STAIRCASE

SPIRAL STAIRCASE

SECOND FLOOR: THE 'GALLERY'

The Players

Veronica

Charlie

Nate

Yasmin

Aaron

NPCs (non-playing characters)

The Colemans

Orson Coleman – *the deceased*

Grace Coleman – *his wife*

Peter Coleman – *Orson and Grace's oldest son*

Simon Coleman – *Orson and Grace's youngest son*

Anne Coleman – *Orson's mother*

The servants

Rita – *the maid*

Ned – *the gardener*

Madame Dubois – *the cook*

Mr Inglesby – *the butler*

Other

Esteban – *Orson's friend and business partner*

Game Guide

Angel

POSTED ON YOUTUBE BY 'THE GAME'

9 billion views

A girl stands in a snowscape, staring directly at you. She's young – a teenager, you'd guess. Tall – enough that it ought to be awkward. But this girl stands with her shoulders squared. With a confidence that, on second glance, makes her seem older. The snowflakes land, catching in the curls of her hair – but she's not bothered. She isn't wearing a coat – but she doesn't look cold.

Perhaps that's what makes this feel like a dream, you think.

'Everyone wants an escape,' she says, her voice low, private. Even though the line feels rehearsed – the first line of a speech or a screenplay – it sounds like she's talking to you and you alone. 'Why do you think virtual reality is so popular? There's something in VR for all of us: from addictive puzzle games where you can distract yourself with a world of

1

abstract colour, music and wild pattern; through fantasy role-playing games where you can wield unimaginable powers to fight – or even be – evil; to real-world games that feel a lot like life except you can be, and be with, anyone you want … Trust me, there's a VR world out there just for you.'

A sly, slight smile as she walks towards you.

'And somewhere on the dark web, there is a VR world that trumps them all. It's not a game you can choose to play. It's a game that draws you in from other VR worlds like the extending tendrils of a spider's web and keeps you there, captive, until the game is done.' The snow swirls around her face. 'Have you heard of it? Most people have, by now. They call it the Game. *The* Game. It's a game that has the power to change your life – your real life. Because in the centre of its web, if you can make it, there's a prize. What is it that you most desire? If you win the Game, it is yours.'

She opens her hands wide and, though the space between her palms is empty, you feel yourself start to fill in the gap. What is it that you want? What is it that you need? You know. You see it now.

She drops her arms down. You refocus on her eyes. She's close now, a little too close, for a stranger. 'Perhaps, if you can win, you won't need VR any more, you won't need to escape,' she says. 'You could create the reality you really want. You could change the hand you were dealt.'

She smiles.

'You'd like that, wouldn't you?'

Her eyes gleam as she finally draws to a halt, her face mere inches from yours.

'So keep your eyes wide open when you're in VR. A door might appear in the fabric of your world, one that doesn't fit. Open it if you dare. If it's the Game, you'll know it by the snow.'

And with that, the snowstorm swallows her whole.

LEVEL ONE

1

Coldness whispered on her cheeks, tickled her eyelids. A heartbeat sounded in her ears, fast, heavy and ponderous – her breath hitched as if she'd been running. The girl blinked, opened her eyes. Snow drifted down from an iron-cloud sky. For a moment, she was peaceful. Blank. But cold. Then the questions started.

Where am I?

She tried to raise herself on to her elbows to find out – but her body refused to obey. That worried her. That, and the fact her memory was fogged – non-existent, even. Who was she? What was the last thing she remembered? Disconnected images flashed through her mind – white sheets, a red cloak, a forest, golden light – and she didn't feel so peaceful any more. *Why* couldn't she move? Then a single word screamed through her like a siren.

Veronica!

That was her name. She knew that much at least. And this word, this *scream*, was the last thing she remembered.

Panic raced through her body. She pushed herself away from the ground again, successfully this time, her head spinning as she forced herself up to a seated position, snow fluttering down around her.

Then, other phrases roared at her through the cloud of her mind, as if in moving she had dislodged an avalanche.

Veronica, help me!

It's happening again.

Her heart lurched as fragments of memory surfaced.

'Max?' she called. Her voice was croaky; her breath plumed into the air, ghostly against the dark charcoal lines of trees beyond the small clearing in which she lay. She sat up abruptly and stared at the pale skin of her hands in confusion. 'Max!' she tried, louder. 'Where are you?' Her brother had been right next to her, hadn't he? Right there under the white hospital sheets? But where were the sheets now? Where was Max? ... And where was she?

White sheets, white snow ...

And then ...

Her neck prickled; she had the strong sensation she was being watched. She scrambled to her feet and spun around. A small, sad shed stood behind her, stacked with logs – but it was obviously empty of anything or anyone else. A broad stump with an axe lodged into its top stood nearby – someone had been chopping wood, but not recently. Two inches of snow already lay on top of the stump like whipped cream on a hot chocolate.

She stumbled to her feet, her heart pounding so hard it felt like it was trying to escape. She scanned the rustling fir trees. Her mind was running in overdrive now. *I've been abducted*, she thought wildly. *Abducted and brought here, perhaps to be killed. Whoever it was, they must've drugged me – that's why I can't remember anything.*

I have to get out of here.

'Haven't you figured it out yet?'

Veronica spun around so violently she slipped over on the icy ground, falling hard on her hip. The pain shot through her like a warning – but what was worse was the screeching sound in her aids as she hit the ground. She lifted a hand to her left ear. The aids felt bulkier – their normally familiar shape now alien to her touch – which was confusing. Even weirder, her hair – normally a wavy, puffy mess – felt as if it had been curled. *Permed?* But she didn't have time to ponder the bizarreness of someone perming her hair while she was unconscious.

An extremely pretty Asian girl around her age had walked out from between the trees. The kind of pretty that belonged in advertisements, or between the pages of magazines. The girl was wearing a yellow plaid skirt suit with wide shoulders and thick-soled platform boots. Her sleek black hair was pulled into a ponytail, not a single strand out of place. Veronica relaxed slightly. The girl was intimidatingly put-together, but she didn't look like the kind of person to drug her, bring her to the middle of nowhere, perm her hair and kill her.

But then, does anyone really look *like a killer?* she pondered, before shaking the thought away.

She was thinking like her dad, dreaming up one of his murder mysteries in the garden shed. Back when her mum and dad were still together, Veronica had sat with him sometimes, curled up on a beanbag pretending not to watch him. Sometimes, even though she was only little, he'd run something by her, asked for her input. She'd liked that. But this wasn't fiction. Right now, she had to focus on what was important.

'Who are you?' Veronica managed, scrambling to her knees. 'And what's going on?'

'I'm Charlie.' The girl stared at her coolly. Her voice was rounded, plummy. A posh accent – posher than Veronica's anyway. Like the girls in Veronica's class nowadays, since her dad had hidden her away in private school. The girl didn't offer to help her up, or ask her if she was OK, or even answer her second question. 'And you are?'

'Veronica,' she mumbled, wincing as she forced herself on to her feet again. Only then did she finally notice the clothes she was wearing: a multicoloured jumpsuit with a drawstring waist under a red puffer jacket. Bright colours. Not her clothes. Not any clothes she recognised. She felt chilled to the core at the thought of someone undressing her and redressing her without her even having woken up. Even changing her hearing aids. And ... she lifted her hands to her face. Yes, her glasses too. They felt huge.

They'd changed everything on Veronica's body, as if she were nothing more than a doll.

What was more, she stood out against this monochrome world like a target. She swallowed, feeling doubly vulnerable. These days, she dressed to blend in. She didn't like feeling conspicuous. *Be calm, deep breath in ... and out.* 'Do you know what's going on?' she asked Charlie again, in what she hoped was a rational tone. 'Who brought us here? I ... I can't seem to remember.'

Charlie met her eyes. 'You really *haven't* worked it out yet. We're in the Game, Veronica,' she said, her eyes sparkling.

Veronica felt as if she'd been thrown off balance – she reached out for the shed, felt the grain of its wood against her hands, rough and pitted and oh-so-real.

'What game?' she managed.

'You know, *the* Game – the one everyone's been talking

about,' Charlie said, her left eyebrow arching. 'The viral YouTube video game. VR? The real-life actual game.' Annoyance rang through her voice when Veronica's face displayed no signs of recognition.

Veronica shook her head. 'Can't be VR,' she whispered. 'I don't play any more. Plus it feels …'

'So real?' Charlie's impatience was starting to show in more than her tone. She tapped one of her platform boots against the ground in annoyance. 'You must've been playing some kind of VR game before you came in here. That's how you get drawn in – through other games. Do we really have to go over this? We need to start playing.'

Veronica closed her eyes and breathed deep. What was the last thing she remembered, really …?

She'd been sent to fetch the coffee from the vending machines for her stepmum Nyra and Dad, who'd been sitting with Max when she left. The rubber soles of her trainers squeaked across the floor as she carried the brimming cups from the kitchen. Except, when she returned to the spot outside Max's room, the door was open and they weren't inside. Max's eyes were shut – he'd fallen asleep. He did that nowadays: wide awake one second; flat out the next.

Voices drifted from a small consulting room across the hall. She stepped closer.

'There's nothing we can do. I'm afraid we're looking at a matter of months.'

Her stomach suddenly screwed itself up into a tight, tangled ball. She dumped the coffee cups on a table beside her, hands shaking. She missed whatever her dad said next because her ears were ringing. She lifted a hand to adjust her aids, but they were fine – the noise was something her brain was producing. The consultant was speaking again, her voice professional but gentle.

'… an experimental treatment. But the cost is in the millions. The NHS won't cover it. You'd have to fly out to the treatment centre in California.'

'V? Are you out there?' Max's voice.

She stepped quickly away from the consulting-room door, attempting to compose her face. She breathed deep, then poked her head around Max's door.

'Hey, you! You're awake,' she said.

'There's a VR set in here!' Max was rummaging in a box one of the nurses had left by his bed. 'Look!' He pulled out two chunky VR headsets.

She'd noticed how the paediatric wings of hospitals were filled with junk from well-meaning people. Books. Old tech. Soft toys with plastic fur. And Max's room … well, he was one of the really sick kids there. So naturally, his room had turned into a charity shop.

'Wow, those look old,' she said with a smile.

'I want to play,' Max had said.

She hated VR. She hated the way it pretended to be real, but wasn't. Hated how sometimes VR could be more real than reality itself …

'Please,' said Max. 'I know you don't normally play, but just this once? Mum and Dad never let me, the nurses are too busy, and the other kids here are all losers.'

'Hey, that's not nice,' she said.

He shrugged. 'So, will you? Pretty please? I just want to try it. All my friends play all the time.'

She thought of the bad news she'd overheard outside and swallowed her 'no'.

'Are there even any games in there?' she asked.

'Just one. Hide and Seek. The original version. Is that OK?'

Of course. Of course it's Hide and Seek, she thought. She'd played a later version, once – two years earlier, in fact – on super fancy equipment. The original would be as dated as the headsets: at least ten years old. Subpar visuals, tinny sound effects, unrealistic gameplay. Still, she was reluctant. 'I don't know if it's a good idea. You're supposed to be resting.'

'They wouldn't have given it to me if it was a risk,' Max argued.

He had a point.

It won't feel real, she'd told herself. *Not this time.* 'OK, just one round, Dad and Nyra won't like it.'

'Awesome,' Max had said, handing her one of the headsets.

Hide and Seek was as simple as it sounded, except you could choose any setting you liked – some harder than others. Veronica removed her hearing aids and placed them on the bedside table. Then she pulled on her headset and scanned the menu. Max was full of enthusiasm.

'How about the under-the-sea one?' he suggested excitedly, his voice muffled. 'Or, look, the old creepy mansion!'

'No,' she'd said quickly. 'Not that one.'

They'd settled on the forest.

'I'm hiding!' Max shouted, as he ran off between the semi-pixelated trees, his avatar cloaked in bright red as he was swallowed into the leaves. And she had started counting ...

Veronica shook herself out of the memory. A small amount of tension unfurled from her shoulders as her mind gathered itself together. At least she remembered that, yes, she *had* been playing a game.

That game.

She shouldn't have agreed to play it. Not again. But Max had begged her. And it was hard to refuse your sick eight-year-old brother.

So Charlie was right. This *was* VR. And whatever tension had started to unfurl now returned, double the strength.

Because being here was literally her worst nightmare.

'Remember now?' Charlie said, half sighing with impatience. 'I've heard this kind of thing can mess with your head. What were you playing? How did it happen?'

Veronica swallowed. 'I was playing Hide and Seek with my little brother. I was the seeker. I was searching for him and then, out of nowhere, there was this … door. In the middle of the forest. It didn't even look like it belonged in the game – it was too realistic. I reached out to open it …'

'Then you were here.' Charlie nodded. 'Right, you've got it at last. You're in the Game. *You'll know it by the snow* – blah blah blah.' She gestured round at the snowy woodland clearing, palms spread. 'So if you don't mind, I'm going to have a poke around.' She headed for the shed. 'There might be something important here – something we can use later on. I wonder if it'll be a racing game? Doesn't seem like it. Maybe a first-person shooter? Or some kind of RPG?'

As Charlie continued to rant about everything this game might or might not be, Veronica stared at the forest around her. *White sheet, white light, white snow.* She felt the snowflakes falling across her cheeks and the backs of her uncovered hands, cold and feathery. It didn't feel like a game. It looked and felt *totally* real. She stared down at her hands – normally a dead giveaway – but they were perfect. Right down to the small mole on the back of her right hand. She'd been using a really shitty old headset – was it even capable of these kinds of visuals? Even the sensation of the freezing air in her lungs was totally authentic.

She thought back to how pixelated the forest had been in the early version of Hide and Seek she'd been playing with Max – the way the game hadn't been totally immersive, so she'd still been able to hear some of the sounds of the hospital in the background, even without her aids: the footsteps scuffing the linoleum floor outside; the muffled sound of voices – perhaps from the room opposite, where her parents were trying to figure out what the hell they could do to save Max's life, or where they had already started to grieve. She shook away the thought.

Charlie continued to speak, now stalking around the perimeter of the woodshed '... This whole thing is pretty insane, isn't it? I haven't heard any real clues about what the prize is, not a single one, though plenty of speculation ...'

No sounds intruded, here, past the snowy silence and Charlie's constant chatter. Even the newer version of Hide and Seek, the one she'd played a couple of years earlier, hadn't been this convincing. This was the most immersive VR she had ever experienced.

Charlie rattled around inside the woodshed, as if anything interesting might be hiding between the logs.

'How does this work?' Veronica interrupted in a hollow voice, stopping Charlie in her tracks. 'How does it feel so real?'

Charlie's face turned serious for a moment as she walked out of the woodshed, resting her hand gently on the tip of the axe jammed into the log. 'You're right – I forget sometimes, but it's pretty bloody amazing, actually. This isn't just great graphics and stuff, though that's part of it. For a while now, they've been perfecting this technology where our actual consciousness is uploaded here. *We're* here. Our avatars are like perfect digital replicas of our actual bodies. And this ... The games I play are always convincing, but *this* is next level.' She brushed the snow off the axe handle with her hand then wriggled her fingers, as if contemplating the sensation. 'You really haven't experienced this before, huh?'

'Once before,' Veronica replied quietly. 'But not this good.'

She felt queasy at the thought of her consciousness – her very *self* – being literally uploaded into a VR world, a place she had no control over. Then she remembered: if you wanted to leave VR, you only had to ask.

'I want to leave,' she said, her voice coming out strangled

and trembling as she lifted her face to the sky. Nothing happened. She screwed her eyes shut and clenched her fists. 'Hey, computer, get me out of here!' Her voice cracked. 'Game over, OK? I never consented to this!'

'That's not going to work, dummy,' said Charlie, who was now curling her fingers around the axe's handle.

'This is VR, right? So why won't it let me out?' Veronica said. 'I have to go. My brother—'

'It's the Game, Veronica. I've said it, like, twice already.' Charlie stared at her, her hands still wrapped around the axe's handle, and Veronica stared back. 'You can't just *get out* of the Game.'

Veronica had no idea what she was talking about. She could barely focus on Charlie's words over the sharp ring of a flatline in her imagination. Max had called for her, like he was in pain, or in trouble. His voice had been ringing through her head as she'd arrived in this place. He could be having one of his episodes. The ones that could ultimately kill him. She imagined herself out cold with a VR headset on, lying beside her brother, useless. She tried to calm herself, but her thoughts were spiralling now. The last moments she could ever spend with the one member of her family who actually cared about her, wasted in a stupid dream – some ridiculous game she'd never asked to play. Why hadn't anyone removed the headset?

A short, sharp laugh rang through the clearing, breaking Veronica's cycle of panic. 'Whoa … OK, I finally get it. You've actually never heard of the Game, have you? That's … really crazy. Where have you even *been*?' Charlie pulled sharply on the handle. The axe lifted free of the snow-covered stump and she held it up to the light admiringly.

Veronica felt her cheeks colour. Didn't Charlie understand how little this mattered? 'I—'

'Listen to me. You've got to hear this before you say or do anything else. OK?' Charlie didn't soften her tone one bit – she stalked towards Veronica at a steady pace, her voice brash and confident, snow crunching under her heels, the axe dangling from her right hand. 'It's not *a* game; it's *the* Game. The legendary virtual world hosted on the dark web – it's, like, the most incredible game ever created … or so they say. Only a few people have ever played it so far. You've really never heard the phrase "You'll know it by the snow"? It's been everywhere for ages.'

Veronica's eyes widened slightly. She *had* seen the phrase – graffitied around town or carved into the doors of the women's bathrooms at the hospital. And, now she thought about it, she might've even heard about the Game on the news. But it was probably the sort of thing she would've switched off anyway. 'So … let me get this right. We've basically been digitally abducted and the

Game won't let us out? And we're now trapped in the dark web?'

'You make it sound so *bad.*' Charlie scuffed the snow with her boot, scanned the woodshed. 'This is an opportunity, V.'

Veronica bristled at Charlie's use of the nickname. Max called her that – but this girl, she hadn't earned it.

'Look, legend has it that some shadowy coder created this place. I've heard rumours he's a rich guy with an insane inheritance and he decided to give it all away … to those who win. He planted gateways to it inside other games. Even Hide and Seek, apparently, for some unknown goddamn reason,' Charlie said. 'That game is for little kids.'

Max's shrill scream rang again through her mind. *I have to get back,* Veronica thought. 'Why hasn't someone just removed my headset?'

Charlie looked at her like she was insane. 'You can't do that, obviously. Pulling someone out of VR like that is super dangerous, but especially if they're in as deep as we are. The more convincing the VR world, the more dangerous it is to be jolted.'

'Jolted?' Veronica repeated.

'That's when you're pulled out of VR without your consent,' Charlie replied. 'It would be really dangerous if that were to happen to you. Your entire consciousness is here, you know? … Whatever,' she added, obviously tired of Veronica's questions. 'We're wasting time. I've heard about the people who've played the Game already. They're all rich now. We should get a move on if we want a chance to win.'

'I don't want to win – I don't want any of this. How do I get out?' Veronica could hear her voice rising with panic now. 'Oh my god …' She doubled over, visions flashing through her mind – a hospital monitor flatlining, Dad and Nyra's horrified faces, Max's cold, pale body. *And Em's body, two years ago.* The edges of her vision were blurring. She was shaking all over. 'Let me out!' she shouted at the sky. 'Let me out!'

Charlie dropped the axe, stepped up to Veronica and jerked her upright with both hands. Then, without hesitation, she drew back her arm and slapped her once, hard, around the face.

Veronica wanted to object, but she was actually speechless. She touched her stinging cheek mutely.

'Get it into your head, V: you can't leave,' Charlie said, her voice perfectly calm and cold as she picked up her axe again. 'I'm pretty sure the only way out is to play it through until the end. Got it?'

Veronica clenched and unclenched her fists. Her eyes felt prickly, but she didn't want to cry in front of this girl. She knew her type from school – from Em too. Showing weakness never ended well. 'Trapping us here can't be allowed,' she said, her voice thick.

Charlie shook her head, a low chuckle leaving her lips. 'Hey, this is the dark web. The whole thing isn't technically allowed.' She scanned the path behind Veronica, snaking off into wherever they were headed.

'So will the police—' Veronica ventured, but Charlie cut her off.

'Oh my god. Do you have to be such a wet wipe?' Then she snorted. 'Whatever. Who cares? Let's be real – we don't know each other, and we're not going to get to know each other. I have literally no interest in you. We're both playing for ourselves. If you want, you can go it alone – what do I care? You'll probably lose anyway, since you have about as much spine as a banana. But, if you can get a grip, staying together would be good. Alliances are good. Especially for you. So if you're smart, which I think you are, you'll want to come along with me. And you're going to have to stop with the "I need to get out" crap, OK? You're a player now. So play.'

For some reason, despite Charlie's attitude, the thought of being alone here among the silent snow and trees actually filled Veronica with horror. So, she bit her tongue. Charlie was right – she was clueless about this place, about anything to do with gaming. So she'd stick with the girl, however much she disliked her – until she could find a way to leave. Her eyes fell to the axe hanging from Charlie's hand. She didn't seem like someone Veronica would want to cross.

'Well, if there's firewood, there's got to be a house,' said Charlie. 'I'm freezing my tits off. Let's go.'

She didn't wait for Veronica before setting off down the snowy, winding path through the trees.

2

Veronica clutched the unfamiliar red puffer jacket closer around her shoulders as she followed Charlie's wide-shouldered suit, her teeth chattering as smears of snow obscured her glasses and wind crackled in her subpar hearing aids. The snow was already deep enough to seep over the edges of her high-tops. Her cheek was still stinging from the slap. She couldn't believe Charlie had actually hit her. Who did that – even if it was VR?

'You know what the worst thing about all of this is,' Charlie was saying. 'I can't even access my actual NFT wardrobe. Like, a checked skirt suit? Seriously? *This* is what I'm wearing in the Game?' She rolled her eyes, barely pausing for breath. 'I've got serious designer shit in the wardrobe – like, custom stuff. That crap is *expensive*.' She drew out the word. 'And the whole point is you're meant to be able to wear it anywhere – virtually, of course. Guess that doesn't apply to the dark web though. What a joke.'

Veronica had literally no idea what she was talking about, but she wasn't about to ask. She trotted to catch up with Charlie, who walked nearly as fast as she spoke. 'How did *you* get here?'

'I was playing Faster.' Charlie barely slowed her pace. She was a good two inches shorter than Veronica, even in her chunky-heeled boots, but somehow covered twice as much ground.

'Faster. Right …'

'You don't know what that is either, do you?'

Veronica shook her head. 'I don't play VR, like I said. I mean, before my little brother roped me in to Hide and Seek. Haven't done for years.'

'What kind of freak our age doesn't play VR? I mean, how old are you anyway? Are you one of those weird twenty-something-year-olds who looks sixteen?'

'Seventeen,' Veronica muttered, cheeks burning.

'OK, whatever. Faster is, like, the biggest racing game in the world. I like racing games – I'm good at them too. I'm consistently top ten on the scoreboard. Worldwide.' She paused as if to leave time for an impressed reaction.

After a few beats, Veronica said a bit robotically, 'Wow, that's great.'

'Sure is.' Charlie nodded, apparently not picking up on her sarcasm – or not wanting to. 'Anyway, there was an unfamiliar tunnel on the racetrack. The back of my neck prickled – I knew it was special, you know? So I went for it. Gave up my biggest win yet for this. Better be worth it.' She glanced over at Veronica. 'So, if you don't game, what do you do for fun, V?' Her lips curled slightly. 'Do you, like, bake cookies? Or read books? Wait, let me guess – you probably watch old TV shows and love black-and-white movies and fantasise about time travel. You look like you might be the type. Am I right?'

Veronica shrugged; she could feel her cheeks colouring. Charlie was kind of spot on, except the cookies – she'd never been able to bake anything without burning it. But there was a hard, mocking note to Charlie's tone that Veronica didn't like. She was wise enough to know that answering yes to questions like that was social suicide. Experience had taught her the best defence was often silence or neutrality. Blend in. Don't be noticed.

That's what Em had told her – before things got really bad. She remembered her standing at her bedroom door, the one they used to share. Her voice had been exasperated, not cruel. Not yet.

'If you just tried a bit more to fit in, things wouldn't be so bad for you at school.'

The hammer strikes the nail that sticks out.

Luckily, at that moment, they turned a corner into a wide clearing and Veronica's jaw dropped open, saving her from answering the question.

'Holy shit,' Charlie said.

The building in front of them was monstrous, towering, bloated … bizarre. Veronica's eyes were drawn to a variety of colours – a peachy stone predominated, with accents of alternating grey-blue and mottled beige on what she thought might be pseudo-turrets high up on the roof. The windows were surrounded by a kind of smoothed-out nod to Romanesque arched windows – curved macaroni shapes with little adornment. There were pillars everywhere, but they didn't seem to be holding anything up – and circular windows here and there, which Veronica couldn't imagine looked out on anything.

The whole thing was shiny and new – and every single window blazed with yellow light.

'It's like someone had a bizarre fever dream of a castle?' Charlie breathed. 'I kind of love it.'

Veronica wasn't so sure. She craned her neck. A massive clock tower with cartoonish blue and red baubles on the hands loomed over everything with an air of menace, though the snow was falling so heavily Veronica couldn't read the time.

'Actually, it's like someone ate and then regurgitated the whole of postmodernism,' Charlie said thoughtfully. 'Like, it's so playful. They've thrown absolutely everything at it – it's like one massive fuck you to sleek, understated modernism.'

Veronica stared at her.

Charlie scratched the back of her neck a little sheepishly. 'My mum's an architect. Can't help picking this stuff up.'

The front door, covered by a moon-shaped awning, was reached by four shallow steps – and under the awning, a dark-clothed figure stood, head bowed. A boy. He was peering down at something in his palm.

Charlie and Veronica headed over, their footsteps squeaking through the snow and crunching on the gravel underneath. Veronica's socks were now soaking where they peeked out of the top of her high-tops.

'Player or NPC? What do you think?' Charlie asked under her breath.

'NPC?' Veronica asked. 'What's that?'

Charlie glanced at her sidelong. 'Oh, my sweet summer child – you have so much to learn.'

The waiting boy glanced up, slipped whatever he'd been looking at quickly in his back jeans pocket – the hems, Veronica noticed, had been rolled up to reveal chunky leather boots – and stepped down from under the awning. He was tall and gangly, dark-skinned and wore an enormous *E.T. Come Home* hoody and a woolly hat. The googly-eyed alien on the front of the hoody had one ginormous green finger extended into space.

'Hey,' he said. 'I'm Nate.'

'Yeah, hi. I'm Charlie. This is Veronica.' She gestured at herself and Veronica in turn. 'Can we go inside? It's fucking freezing,' she added, stomping up the steps.

'I hear you. But the door's locked and no one's answering,' Nate said.

He had a sharp, clipped American accent – maybe East Coast, Veronica thought, remembering how her dad's US editor had sounded on the phone. Nate too had an air of quiet confidence. Unlike Veronica, he didn't appear to be panicking – and unlike Charlie, he didn't seem overly keen or excited. He was patient. In control.

'Are you serious?' Charlie said. She tried the big brass handle, confirming Nate's information, then gently kicked the bottom of the door. 'I'm literally on the edge of hypothermia. Why would anyone build this kind of discomfort into VR?' She gazed at the axe in her hand contemplatively, then up at the door. 'Maybe I should just …'

'Whoa whoa whoa …' said Nate, holding up his hands. 'There's no need for that. Where did you get that thing anyway?'

'Found it by the woodshed. Figured it might come in handy.' Charlie turned away, swinging the axe in experimental arcs as if testing its heft.

Nate caught Veronica's eye. She shrugged slightly. 'OK, well ...' Nate continued. 'My hunch is the door opens when all the players are here. So I guess we wait for the others.'

'How long have you been here?' Veronica asked, wiping the snow off her glasses on the cotton lining of her puffer jacket and pushing a tight curl out of her face.

'I don't know. Five minutes? I spawned right over there, conveniently.' He pointed to an ornamental statue on the front lawn – an angel with outstretched wings covering a small circle of grass, like it was protecting it from the snow. The snow was falling so heavily now though that even the protected patch of lawn was speckled white. The angel looked oddly out of place, Veronica thought, like it belonged to a building that was no longer here ... Her eyes slid back to Nate's.

'Spawned?' she asked.

Charlie rolled her eyes. 'So, the first thing you need to know about our friend V, here, is that she doesn't know jack about gaming, like, she's literally been living under a rock for years,' she said to Nate. 'It's kind of annoying. Kind of cute, I guess, if you like that sort of thing.' Then, turning to Veronica, she added, 'Look, in a game, wherever you start out is where you "spawned". So you spawned out by the woodshed, OK? I spawned in an old glasshouse, literally had a spider on my face when I woke up.' She shuddered. 'Whoever's running this place has a sick sense of humour, I'll tell you that.'

Veronica felt her fists clench slightly at Charlie's patronising tone, especially since she could still feel the sting of her slap on her cheek, but she simply nodded. Nate glanced between them, obviously sensing the tension. He didn't appear fazed by it – if anything, he was coolly disinterested. Like he was just … getting the lay of the land. Then he smiled.

'So, it's great to meet you guys,' he said, holding out his hand.

Veronica took it but paused mid-shake, blown away by the realistic sensation of her hand in his. Was this *really* just a game? She continued to stare at their joined hands for a few seconds after she ought to have let go. 'Are you sure this isn't real?' she said quietly, then quickly released his hand when she realised how long she'd been lingering. 'Sorry, I just …'

Nate met her eyes, smiled. He might be cool, Veronica thought, but he was kind too.

'The graphics and sensations really are next level,' he said. 'Best I've ever experienced, and I've played the best games on the best gear. It's like real life, right? But yeah, I'm sure.'

Veronica returned his smile. Then Nate turned to Charlie, hand outstretched.

'For fuck's sake, I'm not shaking hands with you. Who the hell does that? It's not 1950, people.' Charlie arched an eyebrow and ignored the proffered hand. 'You two are nerdy as hell.'

Nate dropped his arm, shrugging – her words sliding off him like water.

Veronica felt her cheeks colour and wished she could be more like him. She'd never been able to take teasing – or criticism. Both felt equally like failure. The mere thought of a B grade was enough to bring tears to her eyes.

'Always been nerdy and proud,' Nate said, smiling good-naturedly.

'Hey,' said a voice from behind.

Veronica turned around. A brown-skinned girl was tramping noisily across the snow-crusted gravel, clutching the sleeves of a leather jacket over her hands, the furry collar turned up to protect her neck. Veronica felt the back of her neck tingle, her stomach twist. The similarity … God, she looked a lot like Em from a distance. She shook herself. Why did she keep thinking of Em here? She tried not to. Tried to focus on the future, not the past.

As the new girl got closer, the spell broke down, bit by bit – her eyes were set wider, her nose snubbed rather than ski-sloped, her chin a different shape. Her hair was similar in colour and texture – but it wasn't long, styled in an up-do as Veronica had first thought. Instead, it was shorter, stylish, a curly quiff drooping down over her forehead. Then, she started speaking in a broad Australian accent and the tension in Veronica's shoulders unravelled.

'So, this is the Game, huh?' The girl smiled. 'I am *so* excited.' Her dark brown eyes shone with enthusiasm as she climbed the steps to the porch. 'I'm Yasmin.'

'Yasmin?' Charlie asked, stepping out from behind Veronica and staring at the girl, her voice suddenly lighter. 'Is that actually you?'

Yasmin stopped in her tracks. 'Charlie?'

'What the actual shit!' Charlie bounded forward and, after a moment's hesitation, wrapped Yasmin in a huge hug. Yasmin quickly reciprocated. As they pulled apart, their eyes met and Veronica watched as a faint blush rose up Charlie's cheeks before she quickly broke eye contact with the other girl. 'God, this feels a hell of a lot realer than the Faster forums, doesn't it?' She laughed. She was like a different person from the mean girl who'd slapped Veronica by the woodshed – warm, happy, softer edges. Charlie liked Yasmin, Veronica realised. *Liked* her.

'You two know each other?' Nate asked, frowning.

'Only virtually,' Yasmin said a little breathlessly. 'Wow, this is insane.'

'We live on opposite sides of the world, but we've gamed a lot,' Charlie said.

'I've got insomnia,' Yasmin explained. 'We race against each other all the time in Faster.' She half smiled, dimples appearing on her cheeks. 'Sometimes I even win.'

Charlie turned back to her. 'So how did you end up here? … Did you follow me in?'

'I was right behind you, didn't actually see you go in – but, yeah, there was this weird tunnel,' Yasmin said. 'Wow, this is insane.' Her eyes flickered down to the axe Charlie was carrying. 'And of course, you already found a weapon. That is *so* you.'

Before the two could continue enthusing at one another, more footsteps crunched on the gravel. Everyone stopped to see who else had arrived. Veronica's eyes slid past Yasmin to a tall boy with light brown skin in a red 1950s-style sports jacket. He approached, up to a point, but then hung back from the group, leaning against one of the pillars at the bottom of the steps, his hands jammed deep in his jacket pockets. He didn't look uncomfortable or shy though – only kind of moody, like he didn't have any interest in the rest of them. He didn't even look cold, although he must've been, the thickening snow not appearing to bother him in the slightest.

He had luscious black hair, heartthrob eyes and serious

young Elvis Presley vibes, like the framed black-and-white poster Veronica's nonna had had on her kitchen wall. Nonna would definitely have called him 'dishy' or a 'dreamboat' and said embarrassing stuff like, 'If I were forty years younger, eh?' He was one hundred per cent picture-perfect, standing there like he was posing for an album cover. Veronica was mortified to feel heat rise in her cheeks and dropped her gaze to the ground. *Seriously? Get a hold of yourself.* But since no one else said anything, staring, maybe they were all thinking the same.

'Hey,' he said kind of scratchily, scanning the group.

'Hi,' Veronica managed when no one else replied. 'I'm Veronica.'

'Aaron,' the new boy said without looking at her. In fact, he was staring at the house behind everyone as though he couldn't give less of a crap if anyone remembered his name.

Everyone else introduced themselves – only Nate appeared unfazed by Aaron's too-cool-for-school demeanour; he even offered Aaron his hand, which he stared at until it dropped.

'Anyone know how to get out of this place?' asked Aaron, breaking another tense silence. 'I need to get back.' His accent was American, but different from Nate's. Softer – maybe Southern, Veronica thought.

'You want out? Of the Game? THE Game?' Charlie's voice rose in disbelief. 'You're as bad as V.' She put on a whiny voice. *'This can't be allowed! We've been digitally abducted!* Guys, come on – this is the opportunity of a lifetime.'

Veronica bristled again at Charlie calling her V. Why did she think she had the right?

Aaron didn't crack a smile. 'So you don't know then. Great, super helpful, thanks.'

Veronica couldn't help glancing at Charlie from the corner of her eye. She had a feeling she wasn't used to being spoken to like that, and the expression of pure outrage on her face confirmed the hunch.

'I need to leave too,' Veronica mumbled, feeling hot and uncomfortable. 'I mean … my little brother … he's sick. Actually, I'm pretty sure he called out for me just as I … I don't know, entered this place. I think he's in trouble. I tried asking to leave, but it wouldn't let me go.'

'Me too,' Aaron said, his eyes meeting Veronica's for the first time. 'Digitally abducted is right. This is ridiculous.'

She felt absurdly pleased that he'd acknowledged her but hoped it didn't show.

'Abducted? Ridiculous?' Yasmin shook her head. 'No way, guys – the only thing that's ridiculous about this is its total awesomeness! I'm with Charlie on this one. Do you know what kind of prizes players before us have won? They're millionaires, at least! If we win, this could be life-changing.'

Charlie chimed in. 'Right? That's what I've been trying

to say. It could be, like, crazy money. Or property. Or some kind of business thing. I heard someone won a private island.'

'Oh my god, no way! Not my style though – if I win, I'm definitely going to Conservatoire!' Yasmin said, spinning round excitedly. 'Juilliard, if I can get in. I'll buy a loft in NYC. *And* buy my parents a *massive* house. And, um, give a lot of money to charity,' she added a little bashfully.

'I'm going to stick it to my damn parents,' Charlie said. 'When I win, I'll buy my own house, thanks, complete with a pool, a state-of-the-art gaming suite and a cinema. And *you* can come and stay for as long as you like,' she said to Yasmin with a slight smile. 'The rest of you, you're on probation.'

Yasmin laughed, but no one else did. *When I win.* The girl was definitely confident.

'So you're excited to be pulled, unsolicited, into some psycho's game you can't escape based on … rumours?' Aaron shook his head and muttered something Veronica thought sounded suspiciously like 'dumbasses'.

Charlie's mouth opened again in outrage, as if she was about to snap his head off but was frozen by a mixture of extreme anger and disbelief.

Veronica pushed her ginormous glasses up her nose. 'He's got a point. How do you know there really is any kind of prize? It's not like we signed a contract.'

'*Everyone* knows,' said Charlie. 'Well, everyone who knows anything at all about gaming. Like, how could so many people be wrong?'

'Yeah, because if enough people agree on something, it must be true?' Aaron muttered.

'What about you, Nate?' Yasmin asked, pointedly ignoring the conversation's sniping tone, her voice bright. Veronica had the sense that Yasmin wasn't a fan of conflict. 'What do you think?'

'Well …' He glanced around at the others. 'I've been looking into the Game for years. It's real, all right. Real prizes, real stories.'

'See?' Charlie said, her eyes fixed on Aaron, who simply curled his lip.

Nate continued. 'But to be honest, it's not the prize that interests me. I'm more excited to find out about this elusive game than anything else. Like you said, there's so many rumours swirling around. I'd love to know what this is really all about.'

'Wait, you'd rather just play the Game than win millions?' Yasmin's eyes glowed with humour. 'That's wild. Does that mean you'll let us win?' Her voice was light, joking.

'I wouldn't go that far.' He smiled. 'Winning would be a pretty big bonus. But being here is already the prize for me.'

Veronica raised an eyebrow. Really? She liked Nate but wondered how truthful that could be.

'You're a total gaming fanboy, aren't you?' Charlie said, rolling her eyes. 'I know your type. Hanging out on all the forums for a scrap of a clue. Connecting all the dots on a crazy pinboard like some kind of conspiracy theory maniac.'

Charlie had a bad habit of summing people up in an instant, thought Veronica. And once she thought she knew you, she wasn't interested in digging deeper.

Kind of a dangerous habit, if you thought about it.

'I mean, you're not wrong,' Nate said mildly, 'though that's a bit rich coming from someone who dedicates half her life to the scoreboard on Faster.' Her words didn't appear to bother him in the slightest – but she coloured at his response. 'But, yes, I've been following news of this game for ages.' Nate glanced at Veronica as if expecting her to speak next. 'What about you?' he asked gently.

She bit her tongue, eyes dropping to the cold stone beneath her feet. 'I can't even think about winning, or even playing whatever this is. Like I said, I just really need to get back ... My brother, he's ... he's in hospital. I'm so worried.' From the corner of her eye she could see Charlie start to pull a face of exasperation, but then—

'Hey ... I'm sorry,' Yasmin said, and Charlie's face froze in a kind of half-grimace before quickly settling back to neutral. Yasmin reached out for Veronica, pulling her into a quick one-armed hug. 'That sucks.'

Although she didn't know Yasmin, the warmth felt genuine. That didn't make the brief hug any less uncomfortable to Veronica. It wasn't just her appearance; Yasmin reminded her so strongly of Em's character – well, of how she'd been when they were younger. That was what had been so difficult about how everything had changed: Veronica *knew* Em had it in her to be kind.

'Let's see what we can figure out when we get inside, hey?' Yasmin continued. 'Maybe there is some way for you to leave, as it's an emergency.'

'Thanks,' Veronica murmured.

'Aaron, I know you don't believe in any of this, but what would you do if you won?' Yasmin asked him, perhaps sensing how little Veronica cared for the attention.

'I'm already rich. And I hate VR,' said Aaron. 'I just want to go too. I don't want to play.' He glanced around as if he half expected the Game to release him, now he'd supplied a reason. But nothing happened.

'Speaking of playing,' Charlie said, 'it's been great getting to know you all, but can we get the hell inside before I freeze to death? I don't think anyone else is coming.'

41

'OK, let's go!' Yasmin replied, punching the air. 'I can't wait.'

Once again, Charlie turned the brass handle carefully and pushed the door. This time, it wasn't locked – in fact, it swung wide open, the hinges perfectly oiled, into a cavernous space. So, Nate's hunch that it would open once all the players had arrived had been right.

They all stepped inside. The first thing Veronica noticed was the huge stained-glass rose-shaped window, set over a sweeping marble staircase. The glass of the window was an array of pinks and reds – beautiful, but it filtered the dim light from outside in a way that felt menacing. Then her eyes drifted down. The ostentatious marble staircase split in two, surrounding a fountain as if in a cold, stony embrace. The fountain itself wasn't running, although it had four round, marble tiers like a cake stand and was wafted by fronds of fern-like houseplants. Finally, her eyes hit the rippling fountain water.

Veronica wasn't sure what she'd expected to find inside the building, but it wasn't this.

'Shit,' Charlie cursed.

'Oh my god.' Yasmin's voice was shaky.

A dead man floated in the shallows, sprawled face down with his arms askew. Red coiled in the water in viscous clouds, dripped over the marble fountain sides in long vivid streaks. Veronica raised a hand to her mouth – for a moment, she forgot this was only VR. It was completely realistic – right down to the wet-iron smell lingering in the air. Her lungs felt tight as she traced the details. A wound gaped in the back of the dead man's head. His legs were at a weird, unnatural angle – like his back was broken.

Her digital heart was beating so loud, so fast, it was hard to believe it too wasn't real. She raised a hand to her chest. *Breathe*. But it was like something was caught in her throat, stopping the air well before it could reach her lungs. She felt her legs buckle and she dropped to her knees.

She blinked, but when she opened her eyes, the light was a deeper, darker red and nobody was around. The light was low and long shadows surrounded her, yawning across bare earth. Her vision sharpened and she realised she was standing in a forest. The forest from before, from the game she'd been playing with her brother. Hide and Seek. The trees were crude, as they had been before – their pixels clearly visible against Veronica's hyper-realistic hand as she lifted it in front of her face.

What was happening?

Snowflakes drifted down, light as dust, brushing against her face like hundreds of tiny fingers. And between one blink and the next, the fountain from the house appeared – white and clean and extremely out of place in the forest. Oddly pixelated leaves floated on the surface of its water ... and something else too: a dark, rippling shadow.

She felt herself drawn forward, as if the darkness were a magnet, and she a thing of iron.

The shadow grew, lengthened. Tendrils like strands of pondweed splayed out in the clean water, which – as Veronica approached – was suddenly lit up by bright swimming-pool-aquamarine light under the surface.

Veronica stopped. She felt her heart pounding – so hard it felt like it would burst from between her ribs, panic pushing waves of adrenalin through her body – but she had nowhere to run and no one to fight. Where had everyone else gone? Where was the house, the man's body she had seen moments before? And what was *this*?

You know what it is, her own sly inner voice whispered.

She didn't dare move, though her mind was screaming at her to run.

A snowflake landed on the back of her neck, sending a shiver spiralling through her.

As she watched, a black stain started to bloom out of the shadow, reminding Veronica of how condensation spreads when you breathe on a freezing cold window. Veronica's mouth felt cold, prickly.

The water was all black now. And, as if that had been a signal, the water started to grow restless, lapping and spurting up like the edges of the sea. Bubbles rose in a whispering string, floating to the surface. Veronica felt the strength drain from her legs. She dropped to her knees.

But wasn't she *already* on her knees?

The world was loud, a roaring sound in her ears. Colours and shapes rushed through her head in a psychedelic torrent. And then she passed out.

3

'Veronica?' Yasmin's voice – her face, blurry against the red-tinged air but sharpening.

'Don't sit her up too fast,' said another voice – Aaron's. 'She'll just faint again.'

'I didn't even know you *could* faint in VR,' said Charlie from somewhere further back, her voice dripping with barely concealed disdain.

'Me neither,' Nate said more seriously.

Veronica blinked. Slowly, everything shifted into focus and the others' voices sounded less like they were reaching her from underwater. She was back in the house. The fountain. The pink-and-red window with its abstract patterns of glass. The bloody water.

Bloody, not black. Not rotten.

'Are you OK?' Yasmin asked, her kind eyes fixed on hers. 'You went down pretty hard there.'

'Yeah,' Veronica managed, her voice hoarse, though she wasn't sure it was true. 'Did any of you ... see that?'

Nate frowned. 'See what?'

'The forest ... the black water.' She heard her voice shake and cursed her weakness.

The others shared a glance that told Veronica all she needed to know. The vision, if that's what it was, had been all her own.

'Take it slow.' Aaron's voice again, surprisingly gentle, from slightly behind her. She felt warm arms helping her to a seated position. Her ears rang, but the faint didn't rush back.

When she had sat up, she noticed somebody else was standing in the shadows beside the fountain. The back of her neck prickled.

'Who's that?' she asked shakily.

The others followed her eyes, clearly as startled as she was.

'Welcome,' said a voice. The slender figure stepped into the light. 'Welcome to the Game.'

The figure was wearing a petrol-blue boiler suit and had eyes to match. Black hair. The clearest alabaster skin Veronica had ever seen. Sharp cheekbones. A slightly mocking quirk to their smile.

'My name is Angel, and I'll be your guide.'

Veronica stood up carefully, and met Angel's gaze – which quickly passed on to the next player, then the next. They held Nate's last – and perhaps for longest, though Veronica couldn't be sure.

'Our … guide?' Charlie said, her eyebrows raised. She folded her arms over her stomach as if in appraisal.

'Your guardian angel, if you will.' They had a truly wicked gleam in their eyes. In fact, they couldn't have looked less like an angel if they tried. 'I've been watching carefully so far and, well, I'm sure you all have a lot of questions,' Angel said. 'Now's your chance.'

'You've been watching us?' Charlie said, snorting. 'Wow, kind of creepy for a guardian angel.'

Veronica swallowed. She did have a lot of questions … too many, perhaps. Where to start? The room smelt like death, a sour blood smell mixing with humidity unpleasantly. *A game. It's only a game.* The shadow on the water flashed through her mind, raising her heartrate again. *What was that strange interlude? Was it part of all of this, or was I really dreaming?* That's what she really wanted to ask, but already the others were jumping in with questions of their own.

'Are you an NPC?' Nate said, stepping forward, his tone curious.

'He's a fucking AI,' growled Aaron, clenching a hand in

49

his floppy dark hair, tension visibly rippling through his body.

'No, I'm not an AI or an NPC – although you'll find plenty of NPCs around. More on that soon. I'm not a player either. I'm a moderator. A real person who has entered this game just like you have – except, I'm not playing. I'm here to help and guide you all. Hence the name.' Angel smiled, but their eyes were cold. 'And I prefer they/them pronouns, Aaron, if you'd be so kind.' Their voice was icy.

Aaron's eyes dropped to the floor.

'What's an NPC?' said Veronica in a small voice. Charlie had mentioned the acronym outside too, so she figured it had to be important.

Angel's attention shifted to her again – she found herself uncomfortably pinned under their gaze. 'NPC stands for non-playing character,' they said. 'They're artificial characters generated by the Game, who exist only inside the Game – rather than real-life players like you, or real-life moderators like me.'

'So … Angel isn't your real name?' Yasmin asked.

'No. And this isn't what I really look like either,' Angel said.

'So who are you really?' Charlie jumped in.

Angel smiled. 'I won't be telling you that.'

Veronica inhaled. What did any of this matter? She had

to get back to the hospital; she had to make sure Max was OK. She stepped forward, tried to keep her voice steady. 'Angel … I can't stay here. Something happened to my little brother just as I entered the Game. He's only eight, and he's sick. In fact, he's in hospital – and he needs my help. Can you get me out of here, please?'

'And I don't want to play,' Aaron said, from the back of the group. He was leaning on the door frame, hands jammed into his pockets. 'I need to go too.'

'I'm sorry, Veronica and Aaron, but this is out of my hands. There's no escaping the Game now, until you finish it.' Their bright eyes met Veronica's again. 'No exceptions, even though I sympathise with your position.' Their voice, despite their words, was neutral.

'This is bullshit,' Aaron said, stepping forward, colour rising in his cheeks as he drew his hands from his pockets. 'My mom's one of the top attorneys in the country. If you don't let me go, right now, I can guarantee she'll sue the shit out of you on my behalf.' Veronica watched his fists clench at his side. So, he wasn't simply a statue simmering with suppressed annoyance. He had real emotions too.

'If she can find us, Aaron, she can have every penny. But I assure you my employer is untraceable.' Their tone was completely businesslike. 'And remember – the quicker you win the Game, the quicker you get out. Perhaps with a prize that will change your life forever … and –' they turned to Veronica – 'maybe your brother's too. And isn't he in the best place already after all? What could you do that the doctors couldn't?'

Veronica swallowed the lump in her throat. Angel was right. Max couldn't be in a better place, or in safer hands. But Veronica was his sister: after everything that had happened to Em, through the messy, tear-filled arguments, and the loaded, tense silences, sometimes they'd only had each other. Max, he'd always treated Veronica exactly the same – even when Dad and Nyra had grown sad and weird. She needed to be there for him. But it sounded like she was going to have to suck it up and play, whether she wanted to or not.

And maybe she *should* want to.

'*Perhaps with a prize that will change your life forever … and maybe your brother's too.*' That line stuck in her mind.

She remembered the conversation she'd overheard from the hospital corridor, the one between the consultant, her dad and her stepmum about the expensive treatment that might be her brother's last hope. If she won this money, perhaps she could give Max a second chance.

What's more, perhaps Nyra and her dad would leave her alone – stop gazing at her across the dinner table like she was a changeling, stop sending her to the therapist every week where she stared at her folded hands and spoke about the feelings they felt she should be feeling, stop whispering about her behind their bedroom door where they thought she couldn't hear.

Suddenly, all of this sounded a bit like a shot at something pretty big. Something that could change her life.

'So what do we have to do to win this thing?' Charlie's eyes were fixed on the body floating in the fountain. 'Solve the murder?'

'Correct,' said Angel. 'Let me tell you the basics. This unfortunate victim is Orson Coleman. And the date is Saturday 2nd December 1989.'

'That explains the clothes,' muttered Yasmin, glancing down at her baggy acid-wash high-waisted jeans and wide-shouldered, cropped leather jacket.

And the hearing aids, Veronica thought, the bulky devices cracking as she adjusted them slightly under her tightly curled hair.

Angel continued. 'This is Coleman's house. There was a castle here before, a faux-gothic mansion built in 1895 – but it burned down in the 1960s. Orson decided to rebuild it … with a twist. He incorporated the original plans into what you see today – a modern castle for a modern king, ruling over a vast media empire. His fantasy home.'

Angel stalked over to the nearby wall, where dozens of framed newspaper front pages were arranged in neat military lines. 'He was a newspaper man – owned a famous tabloid, first and foremost. More recently, he acquired a publishing house or two, a TV studio, a handful of other businesses. People thought he was invincible. But here he is, thirty-eight years old and murdered … and by someone in this house. Someone he trusted implicitly.' Angel stalked around the fountain, carefully avoiding the patches of pink-stained water splashed on the tiled floor. 'The snowstorm has cut off the landlines – and there's no way anyone could get here in this weather anyway. But the good news is, no one can leave – so the killer, whoever it is, is trapped here too. And you five plucky outsiders, stranded here in the storm, are the perfect team to investigate.'

'This is BS. Why was I chosen for this anyway?' Aaron was glancing around as if he were trying to find someone or something to punch. 'Surely the bare fucking minimum would be to make sure everyone who's brought here actually has an interest in any of this crap. I hate VR.'

'You've already said you want to leave, several times,' Nate said, his voice tight. 'But you must've been playing a VR game to be here, so you can't hate it that much.'

There was a short, uncomfortable silence.

'I didn't have a choice about playing that one either,' Aaron snapped, at last, 'not if—'

He broke off, then rubbed his temples with one hand.

What did he mean by that? Veronica wondered. Aaron had turned his back on Angel, marched a few paces towards the door.

'But there's an extra incentive,' Angel continued.

Charlie's eyes glowed. 'The prize?'

'It's the biggest we've ever offered. A cash prize.'

Angel pulled a slip of paper, something Veronica recognised as an old-fashioned cheque, from the pocket of their boiler suit and presented it to the group. The cheque grew in their hand until it was comedy-large, like the kind lottery winners pose with for the press when they choose to go public. Veronica blinked – it was the first time anything in this VR world had felt less than real … Well, except for her bizarre, terrifying vision. The name was blank, but it had a very long number written on it in black pen and it was signed with a scrawl. The words under the signature, where a name would normally sit, were simply YOU'LL KNOW IT BY THE SNOW. But she suspected no one else was looking at that.

Yasmin gasped at her side. Charlie's face spread into a wide grin. Nate barked out a surprised laugh. Veronica felt her heart beat faster. *'An experimental treatment. But the cost is in the millions,'* the consultant had said.

Even a bestselling writer like her dad didn't have that kind of money. Very few people in this world did. This … well,

Veronica would have plenty left over after saving her brother's life.

She shut her eyes for a moment, her dreams flashing before her eyes. Max cured. Veronica starting a life of her own. Nyra and Dad off her case forever.

All of that was possible; this game could make her a billionaire.

'So … how do we win?' Charlie said, her voice slightly breathless.

'Now that's the question.' Angel's eyes glowed. 'Listen carefully. There are three floors in this house: this, the ground floor; then the first floor; then the gallery. After that, you'll find a staircase up to the clock tower. The clock tower itself has two floors, but we'll get to that in a minute. On each floor – except the clock tower – you'll find one major clue. And by interviewing the NPC inhabitants of this house, you'll also find one piece of vital information per floor. Understood? Three clues, three bits of crucial information in total. But then, just to make it fun, there are a host of other small things you may or may not spot which could lead you to the answer … or send you in the wrong direction entirely.'

Everyone except Aaron nodded. He stood glowering at the marble floor, his shoulders visibly tight with anger. Veronica wasn't even sure he'd turned around to glance at the figure on the cheque.

'Once you have collected all the major clues and information, you should be able to piece together three facets of this murder mystery: who did it, why they did it, and how they did it. The first person to speak aloud all three solutions *in the lower floor of the clock tower* will be the winner – you'll know you've won because the door to the upper floor will open and, up there, you will receive your prize and exit the Game. Please be advised, it'll be next to impossible for you to guess the full answer without having collated all of the crucial clues. Understood?'

'Couldn't we share the prize?' Yasmin suggested, smiling round at everyone else. 'Like, if we work together. That kind of money is more than enough to go round.'

Veronica wondered if that was the case, for her at least. She knew how quickly private healthcare could eat through a fortune; when her nonna had gone into a hospice, they'd had to sell her house. Splitting the money five ways would seriously reduce it. Charlie squirmed where she stood, as if she was considering contradicting Yasmin but couldn't quite bring herself to do so.

But Angel was already shaking their head. 'There can only be one winner, Yasmin. Otherwise, what would be the fun in the Game? You could, of course, give up the prize to another player, if you wish. But the winner takes it all.'

'Why does whoever it is do this?' Veronica blurted. 'I mean … what's in it for them?'

'Now that's a question the whole world would like an answer to.' Angel smiled slightly. 'The truth is, I don't know. But here's what I think – why does anyone play games, Veronica? For fun, of course. See, you can work together to gather the clues and information – in fact, I recommend you do. But at the end of the day, you're all playing to win. And that … that is interesting to watch.'

Veronica's throat was dry as she scanned the room, half expecting to glimpse a pair of eyes shifting in the walls. Who was behind all of this? Were they really here just for someone else's entertainment? Her spine tingled with the remnants of the vision – the forest glade, the blackening water, the horror creeping over her skin. Already, this didn't feel like fun to her.

'More importantly,' Angel continued, 'each of you has been gifted a special object to help you solve the mystery. Charlie, you should find yours in your suit pocket.'

Charlie patted the upper pocket of her yellow checked suit and pulled out a pair of metal-framed aviator glasses. She inspected them with a grimace – they looked like the kind of glasses someone's grandpa might've worn. 'I don't have to actually *wear* these, do I?'

'Not all the time. But they may help lead you towards

the clues. Nate, you've probably already noticed your device.'

'Yeah – this ... err ... phone? Right?' Nate reached under his hoody and lifted a phone the size of a brick from a kind of holster on his belt. Veronica watched carefully but couldn't see the smaller object she'd spotted him holding previously. Perhaps *this* was the object he'd been peering at after all, when they'd first seen him in the porch ... but she was almost certain it had been something different ...

'Correct. With that phone you can contact any of the other players at any time during the Game via the landlines in every room. Yasmin, your trainers have a special power too. Rock back on your heels and see what happens.'

Yasmin bounced on her toes then leaned back on to her heels. Two bright red lights flickered on panels in the trainer heels. 'Whoa, they flash! Check it out!'

Aaron scoffed. 'I thought this was supposed to be 1989. They didn't make flashing sneakers till the early 90s.'

Charlie put on her aviators and a nerdy voice. '*Err, guys, actually, they didn't make flashing sneakers till the early 90s,*' she mimicked.

Yasmin snorted quietly but noticeably into her hand. Veronica frowned – she expected Charlie to be mean, but Yasmin? She glanced over at Aaron, whose expression was hard – though he said nothing.

Angel smirked. 'Just a little artistic licence, Aaron. But, Yasmin, that's not all. If you tap one foot on someone else's shoe and then another on the floor, you'll be able to see the traces of any of their footsteps from the last twenty-four hours.'

'Coooool!' Yasmin leaped over to Veronica, tapping her shoe against Veronica's high-tops before jumping enthusiastically on the marble floor. Sure enough, a trail of red glowing footsteps led out the front door before fading, step by step, as Veronica watched.

'The steps are less bright the older they are,' Angel explained.

'Gotcha,' said Yasmin.

'Now, Veronica,' Angel said. 'Check the inside pocket of your jacket.'

Veronica drew out something she didn't recognise – a rectangular plastic device with a series of chunky buttons along one side. 'What's this?'

'A Walkman,' Aaron muttered, drawing closer to the group apparently in spite of himself. 'It plays cassettes. See?' He reached out and took the Walkman from her hands. Then, he pressed what must've been an eject button, and the front popped open, revealing an old-fashioned tape inside.

'Oh, right. You have one of these?'

His face flushed and he didn't reply, though he kept hold of the Walkman.

'Dig a little deeper in that pocket, Veronica,' Angel said.

She reached further into the deep pocket and found a pair of collapsible bright red foam headphones. She felt a flush of annoyance. How was she supposed to use these with her aids in? Was this some kind of joke?

Aaron hadn't noticed her reaction – he was still staring at the device itself. 'This has a recording function,' he said, his finger hovering over a button with a red circle.

'That's right,' Angel replied. 'But you don't need to press any buttons for this to work – it will simply record the Important Information on each floor as you hear it, which you can then rewind and listen to as much as you like. Very helpful in identifying *what* information is important.' Angel turned to Aaron. 'Finally, Aaron, the watch you're wearing.'

Aaron handed Veronica back her Walkman, then tugged the sleeve of his sports jacket to reveal a large black digital Casio. 'Yep. What does this piece of crap do?'

'This is perhaps the most valuable gift of all. The watch has the capacity to rewind game time by up to thirty seconds – you simply press the button to the left of the screen and hold. I'm sure it'll come in handy.'

'Unless it can teleport me out of here, I don't think it'll come in handy at all,' snapped Aaron, tugging his sleeve back down over the watch and drawing back from the group, as if suddenly remembering he wasn't supposed to be one of them.

'Can we swap?' said Charlie immediately.

'*The most valuable gift of all*,' thought Veronica. Of course hyper-competitive Charlie wanted it.

Aaron glared at Charlie but didn't reply.

'Whatever. It's not like you care about winning anyway.' Charlie fiddled unhappily with her aviators.

'That's it from me, for now,' Angel said, already walking behind the fountain, from where they'd appeared. 'I'll be around – just call my name if you need me. Oh – and one last thing: you *really* don't want to be down here when the windows fill up with snow, so you'd better get investigating. We've been talking so long, we've lost track of time; they're already a quarter full.' They smiled slightly. 'Happy playing – and good luck.'

And Veronica blinked as, sinking into the shadows, Angel disappeared as completely as if they'd never been.

4

The five players were left in the hall, where the shimmering water reflected pink light-shadows across the fronds of the pot plants and dappled on the stairs. Pretty, until you realised the pink was down to the blood. Somewhere in the house, music was playing – a drumbeat and whining synths that set Veronica's nerves on edge.

'Screw this.' Aaron scuffed his shoes against the marble then stalked towards the front door, grabbed the handle, turned it and pulled. Then pushed.

The door was now locked – but Aaron didn't give up. Everyone watched in silence as he rattled the handle, then pounded his fists against the wood fruitlessly. Again and again, until Veronica was sure he was bruising his fists. Yasmin caught Veronica's eye and raised an eyebrow.

'Cut it out,' said Charlie, her voice bright with annoyance. But his fists continued to pound the door, drowning out the faint music from upstairs.

Nate approached, put a hand on his shoulder. 'Hey—'

But instead of calming down, Aaron pushed him backwards with one arm and kicked the door so hard Veronica was sure she felt the whole building resonate. She had never seen anyone so uncontrollably angry – except, maybe, herself the day she found out Max was really, really sick. She'd screamed so loud, someone next door had called the police.

Nyra would never forgive her for that either. *Explaining your temper tantrum to the police was the last thing I needed, after … after everything we've already been through,* she'd hissed, her brown eyes brimming with tears.

'Did you actually just *push* me?' snapped Nate, gazing down at his hoody and back up at Aaron in disbelief. When he spoke again, his voice was sharp. 'Shit, I hate people like you. You've made it clear you've got money. You've also got a mom. That's two things I haven't got. Now, you've also been given this amazing opportunity. But it's not enough for you, is it? You still have to throw your pointless tantrum.'

Aaron glowered at him but didn't reply.

'Well, I've got news for you. Mommy's not coming to save you, not this time.' Nate's voice dripped with bitterness – and something broken, something like jealousy, hitched on to the word *Mommy*. 'The only way out of here is through.'

'You sound like my damn therapist,' Aaron said quietly, but finally he stopped.

At least someone else here has a therapist, thought Veronica.

Aaron leaned against the door, sank down to the floor, burying his face in his hands. They were trembling, as if barely containing the raw energy under their skin.

'If you don't want the money,' Nate said, his voice calmer now, 'at least try to win the prize and give it to people who need it. It's not all about you.'

Aaron glared up at him. Nate held his gaze – and Aaron looked away first.

'Screw that,' Aaron said, staring at his own clenched fists. 'I didn't ask to be here, so I'm not fucking playing. We'll see how fun that is for this sicko to watch.' He gazed up at the ceiling. 'You hear me? I'm just going to sit here until you let me out.'

Nate made a small noise of disgust and stalked away, his shoulders hunched. He'd been so totally cool against Charlie's barbs, Veronica was surprised at how Aaron had clearly got to him.

'Aaron, think about this. I don't—' Veronica started.

'I'm not playing,' Aaron said, cutting her off. 'I refuse to do anything against my will for this psycho's entertainment.'

'Whatever,' Charlie said, shrugging. 'Play or don't play – what do I care? You're just one less person for me to beat.' And she walked after Nate, the axe swinging from her hand.

Yasmin hesitated a little, catching Veronica's eye again in something like exasperation. Veronica squirmed slightly. But ultimately, Yasmin sighed, shook her head and turned back to the fountain.

Aaron hadn't exactly endeared himself to the group, Veronica thought; they didn't really want him to play anyway. Charlie was right – it just meant less competition, didn't it? One less player meant one less obstacle to the prize.

Veronica's throat felt dry. A part of her thought, as everyone else clearly did, that Aaron ought to get over himself; besides, as far as she knew, it wasn't like anyone *he* loved was dying.

And then there was the part of her that agreed with Aaron. Why *should* she play? Why should any of them play? They hadn't asked for this – it *wasn't* right. And the last time she'd played a game, well, it hadn't exactly ended well. This might not be real, but the consequences could be.

That was exactly why she *had* to play – for Max. For change. She squashed down her fears.

Focus. If I win this prize, he could recover. If I win, I could save his life ... and mine.

Aaron continued to sit motionless, head bowed in determination – clearly unwilling to discuss the matter further.

'Come on, V,' Charlie said, calling her over. 'What're you waiting for?'

After one final glance at Aaron, Veronica joined the others by the fountain where, for a few moments, they all stared down at the grisly corpse face down in the water.

'Well, I'd say the head wound was the cause of death,' Nate offered.

Veronica nodded. 'I suppose technically he could have drowned and *then* had his head caved in …' *But if that were the case, he wouldn't be floating. His lungs would have been full of water, so he'd have sunk.* She was about to tell Nate but he had started to wander off, heading round the other side of the fountain.

'Oh god … I might actually vom,' said Charlie, though she kept staring at the corpse. 'Is that his brain?'

Veronica glanced at Charlie's axe. Could it have been the murder weapon?

'I guess there might be clues on the body?' suggested Yasmin, who also appeared to be genuinely struggling with nausea, judging by the thickness in her voice.

Veronica's eyes drifted over the water and caught on something else, floating a few metres away from the corpse. 'Hey, look,' she said. 'It's a bottle.'

Charlie walked over and peered at it. 'Dom Pérignon. Nice.'

'Maybe he was carrying it when he died,' Veronica said. 'Which means ... he could have been drunk.' She gazed around the hall and then up at the banisters above.

'You think he could have fallen?' Charlie asked.

Veronica considered the question. 'I mean, it looks like he could have – doesn't it? If he'd stumbled into the fountain from ground level, would he really be floating around like that, in the middle of the water? Also, look at all the water over the floor. It's soaked. If he'd fallen, that would've caused a huge splash.' She gazed at the landing above. 'But Orson would have needed a big push to fall over those banisters, even if he was drunk. They're pretty high.'

'Him being drunk would have made it easier to push him though ...' Charlie trailed off. 'And he's face down. Whoever did it could've just pushed him in the back.'

'Actually, being face down doesn't signify much,' Veronica said. 'Corpses tend to float that way – it's the weight of the arms and legs.'

From the corner of her eye, Veronica spotted Charlie and Yasmin exchanging a glance.

As she continued to scan the room, she noticed something else: a dark stain on the edge of the middle tier of the fountain. 'Look, I think that could explain the head wound,' she said. 'He fell ... or was pushed ... and hit his head.'

'Right. Well, he would have to have been pushed, right?' Yasmin asked. 'This is a murder mystery after all.'

But Veronica stared contemplatively at the bottle of Dom Pérignon. 'Probably ... unless there was another cause of death. Something that made him fall. Poison?'

'Holy shit,' Charlie said. 'Really? All of this fountain and head-wound stuff is one big red herring?'

'I don't know. I just don't want to jump to conclusions. It's really important to be guided by the evidence, not the other way around.'

'Huh,' Charlie said, before falling silent.

'Charlie,' Yasmin said, 'why don't you try those glasses – maybe you'll see something?'

Charlie slipped the aviators on with a shudder. The old-fashioned frames totally dwarfed her face. Then, she approached the fountain, arms outstretched as if she was walking through darkness.

'Whoa ... these have an insane prescription.' She turned her head slowly from left to right, scanning the room, holding the glasses against her face with one hand to prevent them sliding down. 'Where's the body? OK, OK.' She stared down into the water. 'Ew, right, dead body ... At least it's less gross with these on. What am I looking for? ... Oh, wait.' She crouched down carefully, reaching out with one hand to point at the breast of the suit. 'There *is* something glowing here … Do I really … ? Oh god, oh god … It's under the water. There's no way I'm touching that.' She snatched her hands back from the pink-stained pool.

Veronica walked over, her high-tops splashing in the narrow bloodstained puddle at the base of the fountain. She might not know much about VR, but at least she wasn't squeamish. 'Where is it exactly?'

'Front pocket. Right there,' Charlie pointed.

Veronica leaned over the water, barely reaching one of the corpse's shiny leather shoes. She pulled the body closer to the edge of the fountain and rotated it carefully, water sloshing on to the knees of her jumpsuit. Then she reached into the stained water and slipped her fingers into the upper pocket of the body's suit – which was double-breasted, she saw, with large gold buttons. She eased out a folded piece of sodden paper. 'This?'

'Yeah – well, it's glowing when I wear the clue-finding glasses, so I guess so.' Charlie slid the glasses off her nose and blinked. 'Can you open it, even though it's wet?'

'I think so.' Veronica glanced around, her eyes settling on a small side table containing a shiny, boxy landline. She carried over the paper – Charlie and Yasmin following close behind, Nate joining them from where he'd been searching the other side of the hall.

'Our first clue?' he asked.

'Yup,' Charlie said.

Veronica set the wet paper on the side table and carefully eased it open. Luckily it had been thick, expensive-looking paper – the kind you didn't really see any more, not in the real world – and the writing had been in pencil, so hadn't run, though the words were faded. 'It's a handwritten note.'

'Read it out,' said Yasmin, drawing closer. So she did, carefully holding it up to the light.

Dearest,
Meet me in the studio at midnight.
I need to see you.
E x

'It's a *love* note,' Nate said. 'May I?' Veronica allowed him to lift the paper from her hands. 'Whoever wrote this must know something.'

'No shit, Sherlock,' Aaron muttered from the shadows by the front door. 'Wouldn't be a clue if it didn't lead somewhere.'

'I thought he wasn't playing?' Nate murmured, irritation in his voice.

'It's pretty minimal evidence. So he had a girlfriend,' Charlie said. 'Whatever.'

'Or boyfriend,' Yasmin interjected. 'But why communicate like this? It seems weirdly secretive, right?'

71

'Maybe not for the 1980s,' Veronica said quietly. 'No internet. No smartphones.'

'I mean, it was the 1980s though, not the 1890s,' Charlie said, frowning, and looking suddenly interested. 'Couldn't they have just called each other?'

Nate brandished his brick-sized phone. 'I think Yasmin's right – it must've been secretive. Look at this thing – it was either this or the house phones. I mean it's hardly subtle, is it?' As he hitched up the hem of his hoody to replace the phone in its holster, Veronica watched closely – sure enough, there was definitely something peeking out of Nate's back pocket. She blinked. A wallet, maybe? But that would certainly be out of place here – the rest of them didn't appear to have anything but the clothes they were standing in and the single item allotted them by the Game.

Nate appeared to notice the direction of her gaze and lowered his sweater unhurriedly, holding eye contact and cracking a small smile.

She shook her head slightly. He wasn't acting like he had anything to hide. Perhaps she'd imagined the whole thing.

Veronica walked back to the fountain and knelt on the fountain ledge beside the body again, peering at it closely. She happened to be a fan of murder mysteries – as her father's daughter, she hadn't really had a choice – and she knew the number-one rule was to examine the corpse thoroughly. She leaned her head down to peer at the dead man's face, which was submerged.

'What are you doing?' said Charlie, her voice laden with disgust. 'How come you, like, literally fainted when you saw the body earlier and now you've gone all Agatha Christie?'

'Agatha Christie was an author, not a detective,' Veronica said automatically, immediately feeling her cheeks redden. *'Why do you have to be such a know-it-all?'* Em's voice rang through her mind.

Charlie stared at her with utter disdain. 'Sherlock bloody Holmes then,' she growled. 'Question stands.'

Everyone was staring at Veronica curiously – even Aaron, from his shadowy sulking spot by the door.

Veronica held out her hands. 'Look, I'm not actually squeamish – that wasn't what that, um, faint was about. I spend half my time in hospitals, watching doctors stick needles into my brother Max – trust me, I'm not fazed by blood. I don't know what happened earlier.'

There was a short silence.

'Max – he's really sick then?' Yasmin asked quietly.

Veronica nodded shortly, not turning towards her. She didn't want to go into details. She might have a way to actually help Max – so right now, she just wanted to focus.

'The fainting episode is bugging me. What game were you playing?' asked Nate, walking over. He'd been wandering around the room – perhaps searching for other clues. 'I mean, when you entered this game?'

'Hide and Seek,' Veronica replied. 'The original version.'

'Whoa. Is that version even still available?' Yasmin asked, her eyebrows quirking. 'I played it when I was little. I didn't think headsets supported that kind of software any more.'

'We were playing on some donated headsets – they must've been ten years old at least,' Veronica explained.

Nate stood up straighter, as if he'd realised something. 'OK … That must've been the reason for your faint,' he said. 'It all makes sense now. Your old tech was cutting out – these kinds of graphics, real-life sensations … normally it would take a full-body device, which is what I'm using.'

'Of *course* you are,' muttered Charlie.

'Oh, like you're not?' Nate replied, his voice mild. 'Didn't Daddy buy you the best gaming hardware on the market?'

Charlie's lips tightened. 'Whatever, Nate. At least I'm not a nerd about it.'

Nate returned his attention to Veronica. 'I'm not even sure how you're here, to be honest. Your consciousness has been uploaded, same as everyone else's, but the graphics and VR sensations are relying at least partly on your old tech. It's no wonder you're having technical difficulties.'

Veronica wouldn't have described what she'd seen as

technical difficulties … Wouldn't that have been more like a glitch? A blankness or a darkness rather than the 'other place' she'd experienced – a place that felt like somewhere she'd hoped to never be again? But even if Nate was wrong, she felt a little better knowing the episode might have a rational explanation. The rest was probably her imagination and being freaked out at playing VR again.

'The point is, we really should examine the body properly,' Veronica said. She reached out, pressed her hand into Orson's, attempting to move his fingers.

'I get that you aren't squeamish but … what *are* you doing?' said Yasmin in a curious tone, crouching down beside her.

'He's pretty stiff but not totally so.' She tried his elbow too, to be sure. 'And he's not quite as cold as the water.' She let go of the hand, gently placing it back into position. 'As a rule of thumb, I think that means he's been dead between three and eight hours.'

The others stared at her except for Aaron, whose eyes were fixed on his shoes. 'How do you know all this stuff?' asked Yasmin. 'About dead bodies floating face down … and now this …'

'You know, all the murders I've committed,' Veronica said, deadpan. Everyone stared at her until she cracked a slight smile.

'Wow, you almost got me,' Yasmin said, giggling. 'But seriously, you are way too good at this.'

Veronica cleared her throat and explained. 'My dad's a crime writer – books and TV. I've read a lot in the genre – and we used to watch loads of shows together.' *Used to.* For the past two years, he'd hardly seemed to want to spend time with her at all, if he could avoid it. But if she was honest, she'd felt the same about him for even longer. Things just hadn't been the same since him and Nyra got together. 'Time of death is important. It'll help us place the killer – and Orson.'

'Three to eight hours is a pretty wide bracket,' Charlie pointed out. She nodded towards the ornate clock on a side table. 'It's eight fifteen in the morning now. So you're saying he could've died anywhere between quarter past midnight and five fifteen?'

'Whatever happened during that time, he would probably have had time to meet "E", since they suggested midnight,' Veronica said. 'It might've even been right before he died. We should find this E and see what happened.'

'I guess that means we should start exploring,' Yasmin said. 'Shall we try that way first?' She pointed to a door to her right, next to the entrance.

Nate nodded and headed over, scanning the hallway as he went. Charlie squeezed Yasmin into a half-hug and followed.

Veronica was last, lingering to stand by Aaron, still sitting there, hugging his legs tightly to his chest. Suddenly he looked very young – just a little boy who'd been left out of the playground games. He looked cold too, shivering slightly under his sports jacket. Part of Veronica, the bizarre and stupid part, wanted to stoop down and hug him. Another part wanted to shake him by the shoulders. She did neither.

'Sure you don't want to come?' Veronica said gently.

'No way. I told you – I'm not playing,' Aaron muttered. 'I'm no one's toy.'

As she turned away, she caught a glimpse of her reflection in a big mirror by the door. She was in silhouette, the rose-shaped window behind her, catching in her lusciously curly hair – if she was honest, she didn't hate the perm. Her face appeared smaller by comparison, her features delicate. She'd always had good skin too. She adjusted her hearing aids and her chunky-framed glasses, grimacing at the unfamiliar weight of both on her ears. She was turning away when she caught a glimpse of someone behind her, a figure standing halfway up the stairs, their face in shadow. But it looked like …

'Angel?' she said hopefully, her voice hoarse. She spun around.

But the figure had disappeared.

5

Veronica followed the others inside the room. Her heart was pounding after her glimpse of a figure on the stairs – but she told herself she'd been gazing in a mirror, in the half-light, and it was perfectly possible that she hadn't really seen anything at all. Or perhaps it was another glitch, due to the age of her headset. She shook the feeling off and took in where she was now.

Charlie and Yasmin were waiting in front of the room's large double doors. Nate had already wandered further inside. And nearby, a woman she'd guess to be in her early seventies sat behind a huge desk positioned in front of a trio of arched windows with their playful chunky surrounds, which were filling up with snow like hourglasses. She appeared to be deep in concentration; she didn't glance up when Veronica entered.

'What took you so long, V?' Charlie said. 'Still trying to convince your boyfriend to join us?'

Yasmin giggled.

Veronica cast her eyes to the floor. Yasmin was nicer than Charlie, but she was still willing to laugh at her mean-spirited jokes. 'He's not—' She cut herself off, shook her head. She should know by now that answering back didn't work. Lingering behind for Aaron had been stupid, since no one else had.

The hammer strikes the nail that sticks out.

Instead, she ignored Charlie and gazed around the room. The space was enormous and interspersed with huge windows looking out over the snowy gardens. Three fireplaces easily large enough for Veronica to stand in dominated the hallway side of the room, each one of them with colourful, cartoonish geometric mantelpieces.

'Yeah, this dude really went all in on postmodernism,' Charlie said. She wandered over to a framed photo above one of the fireplaces, showing a plump man in front of a large house with Tudor vibes. A blond child stood stiffly at his side.

'Could that be Orson and his father?' Veronica wondered aloud.

'Well, if so, he definitely did the exact opposite of his childhood home,' Charlie replied as Yasmin joined them both. 'I don't know what that says about him.'

Veronica continued to examine the room. The flagstone floor was scattered with gaudy rugs – and ostentatious furniture shone with polish. More tall houseplants stroked the walls and the shelves of bookcases stuffed with glossy-spined hardbacks. A large boxy TV sat on a wheeled golden stand in the far corner, bookshelves full of plastic boxes behind it. *Video cassettes*, she thought, remembering the old home videos they'd found in Nonna's garage. Chintz sofas in floral patterns were scattered throughout the room, interspersed with glass-topped side tables with elaborate gold legs. The whole room was a weird mix of traditional grandma-ish stuff and wildly imaginative takes on what could even be considered furniture, like a chair that was made of several different blobby colourful shapes stuck together.

The woman stood up at last, deigning to be interrupted from her work. A handkerchief – cream, printed with a gold-chain pattern – was clutched in her hand, as if she was prepared to or expected to cry, but her make-up was flawless. She had been seated in front of an old-fashioned cube with a screen, which Veronica realised was probably an early computer. She glanced at the screen, which was angled to one side – lines of green numbers glowed and flickered slightly against a black background.

The woman had iron-grey hair, short and blow-dried into a large 'set' style Veronica recognised from pictures of her own grandmothers when they had been young – and from a photograph of Margaret Thatcher turned face-out from the desk. The woman wore a beige trouser suit, pearls shining around her neck.

'What is the meaning of this intrusion?' she snapped. 'Get out at once!'

Veronica was startled by the realism of the reaction – she'd expected the NPCs to be a bit robotic. She blushed, instinctively starting to turn around and leave, but Yasmin put a reassuring hand on her shoulder.

She was the first to pipe up. 'I'm sorry to disturb you, but we'd love to ask you a few questions, if that's OK? My name is Yasmin, and these are my, err, associates. Charlie, Nate and Veronica.'

'I am Mrs Anne Coleman and, no, I do not wish to answer your questions. My son is dead.' For the first time, her voice shook slightly, as if she was holding back tears. 'Now is not a good time.'

Charlie picked up where Yasmin left off. 'But that's what this is all about. We're here to help, Mrs Coleman.'

Mrs Coleman's eyes shifted from Charlie to Veronica, who tried a small, kind smile.

'We want to find out what happened to Orson,' she said, her voice sounding stiff and false. 'Will you please answer some questions for us?'

Mrs Coleman lifted her chin. 'Thanks to my son's death, running the family business falls to me – so I have rather more important things to do than answer questions from a group of impertinent children. It would be far more prudent to wait for the police.'

Yasmin and Charlie glanced at each other doubtfully, but Veronica was good at dealing with adults – apart from Max, her life had been dominated by them for two years. Teachers, psychiatrists, counsellors, and Max's doctors and nurses … they had peopled her life nearly exclusively.

She nodded slowly. 'I completely understand. But by the time the police make it through the snow, we'll have wasted many crucial hours of investigative opportunity – plus, we'll be giving the murderer a chance to escape. Right now, your son's killer is trapped in this house. And we are outsiders – perhaps with our fresh perspective, we can help.' She smiled again, brighter this time, trustworthy. 'That's all we want to do – help.'

Mrs Coleman sniffed, dabbed her already immaculate face, then sat down in the chair behind her desk. 'You have five minutes.'

Veronica felt the tape recorder in the inside pocket of her puffer jacket click into action. Angel had said it would automatically record Important Information of its own accord, but part of Veronica wished she could record everything and decide herself what was important. *You're enjoying this too much*, a small, needling voice inside her head told her. *Try not to forget why you're here: for Max.*

Charlie and Yasmin drew closer, but no one spoke, appearing to accept Veronica's lead. As for Nate … he was exploring the room, wandering down to the opposite side. But now wasn't the time to get distracted. Veronica cleared her throat, wishing they'd had an opportunity to discuss questions in advance. *Start simply*, she thought.

'Please can you tell us when and how you discovered your son was dead?' she started.

Mrs Coleman's jaw visibly tightened. 'I wake early, around six generally, but I tend to stay in my room for around an hour while I prepare for the day. I was fully dressed and about to go down for breakfast when I heard a scream …' She stopped, swallowed, but maintained her composure.

Veronica was struggling to believe she was computer-generated. 'And what time would that have been?'

'Around seven, or just after,' Mrs Coleman said.

'What did you do when you heard the scream?'

'I rushed out of my room, down the hallway and to the top of the stairs. It was then that I saw the body. Our cook, Madame Dubois, was the one who had screamed. She had discovered Orson. She was standing right by the open front door, as if she'd just walked in.'

So the cook had discovered the body, Veronica noted, filing the information away until later.

'What happened next?'

'I told Madame to call the police. She picked up the hall phone, but the line was dead.'

'Because of the snow?'

'I presume so. Then I asked Mr Inglesby to set out in the car, but by the time he had started it up, the drive was impassable.'

'Mr Inglesby?'

'My son's butler.'

Veronica tapped her fingers against her knee. 'The cook and the butler, do they live here too?'

'Madame Dubois lives in the village – as do Ned, our gardener, and Rita, our maid. Madame Dubois generally arrives first – at seven to prepare breakfast – and leaves last after preparing dinner, around seven thirty in the evening. Mr Inglesby has a room upstairs.' She had a precise, sharp manner of speaking – as if she were cutting all her words out with a pair of nail scissors.

'Right. So apart from you, Orson and Mr Inglesby, would there have been anyone else in the house last night after midnight?'

'Ordinarily Orson's wife, Grace, but she spent the night in town and isn't expected back until this afternoon. We haven't, of course, been able to contact her due to the phone lines.'

So, he has a wife – and she clearly wasn't the "E" who signed the love note.

'And my grandsons, Simon and Peter. Simon has recently turned thirteen and is home from school for the holidays.' Veronica noticed an indulgent tone to her voice. Then Mrs Coleman continued, 'Peter is sixteen and bedridden.'

'Bedridden?'

'Is this relevant, young lady?' Mrs Coleman said testily, but answered the question anyway. 'He has an autoimmune disease. He's very sick.'

Veronica felt her stomach lurch in empathy but filed that away for reference too. So far, she had to speak to Madame Dubois, Mr Inglesby, Ned, Rita, Simon and Peter.

A knock sounded on the door.

'Ah,' said Mrs Coleman. 'And this will be our guest, who also stayed here last night. You may come in, Esteban.'

The door opened to reveal a handsome man in his early forties, the hair around his temples silvered. He was brown-skinned and although dressed in a smart grey suit and pressed white shirt, he was obviously dishevelled, his eyes rimmed with red. Yasmin nudged Veronica quite hard in the ribs and mouthed, *'Esteban.'* Veronica's eyes widened and she nodded slightly. Could he be the 'E' in the letter?

Mrs Coleman's face was pinched with dislike as she watched him walk inside.

'Ah, apologies. Am I interrupting something?' His voice was lightly accented – Veronica was strongly reminded of her nonna, who never lost the rolling Italian consonants of her youth, even after fifty years living in London.

'Not at all, Esteban. These children are rather unconventionally attempting to solve the mystery of my son's murder before the arrival of the police.' Her voice was hard. 'I'm sure they'll have questions for you too.' She turned to Veronica. 'Esteban is – was – my son's business partner. He stayed last night after a meeting with my son ran late.'

Esteban stepped forward, extending his hand to Veronica, who shook it – his grip was warm and firm, and his eyes met hers sincerely. 'Thank you for trying then,' he said, offering a grateful glance to Charlie and Yasmin too. 'How can I help?'

Veronica tried to focus. 'Can you tell us a little about your relationship with Mr Coleman?'

'We are … were … friends, at first. But we've worked together for a decade. It was difficult,' he said bluntly. 'We met at Oxford, around fifteen years ago. I was in my final year of economics. He was starting out on his English literature degree. We were opposites, but we struck up a friendship. I left and didn't hear from him for some time.

Then, after he graduated, he was in touch out of the blue. He'd bought a newspaper with money he'd recently inherited from his father, he said. I was back home in Mexico – but he lured me to London with a job offer and we've worked together ever since.'

'Mr Suarez is the brains behind my son's operation,' Mrs Coleman said. 'And I am the backbone. My son had little of either.'

Veronica was surprised at her disparaging tone.

'Orson was a creative,' Esteban said. 'He was more interested in the stories we were printing than the numbers.'

'You said your relationship was difficult?' Veronica prompted.

'Ah, yes. They say you should never mix business and friendship.' He glanced at Mrs Coleman, who nodded slightly. 'Mixing business, friendship and family ...'

'What was the meeting about?' Charlie asked.

Esteban and Mrs Coleman exchanged another glance.

'That's sensitive information,' Mrs Coleman said tightly. 'My son, Esteban and I met in private in this very room, that's all you need to know.'

Interesting, Veronica thought. *Probably important.* But she decided not to lose her momentum – she'd press on, for now.

'The meeting didn't go well?' Veronica prompted.

'No,' Esteban said, 'you could say that. We talked late into the night.'

'How late? When did the meeting end?' Charlie asked.

'Eleven?' Esteban said uncertainly.

'Eleven thirty,' Mrs Coleman supplied.

'And how did you feel about Orson after the meeting?' Veronica asked.

'I won't lie, I was in a pretty foul mood. I would go so far as to say I was angry.'

Yasmin cleared her throat. 'But … you didn't hate him *that* much?' she said, raising her eyebrows meaningfully.

'I didn't hate him at all,' Esteban said calmly. 'I said I was angry. But I would never kill Orson. I was readying myself to leave for Mexico this morning.'

'And you, Mrs Coleman? How did the meeting make you feel?' Veronica asked.

Mrs Coleman stared at her coldly. 'What exactly are you insinuating?'

'I wasn't insinuating. I was asking,' Veronica said, matching her coolness. Then, she glanced between Mr Coleman and Esteban. 'And neither of you saw or heard anything in the night?'

'You don't think I would have mentioned if I had?' Mrs Coleman snapped.

Veronica was losing her.

'I heard nothing untoward,' Esteban said. 'Even though I didn't sleep. This house – it creaks and cracks all the time. It's new, of course, but it often acts like an old house. Perhaps it is its size. Sometimes, with the wind, it even moans.'

'Can you think of any reason anyone in this house would want Orson dead?' Veronica asked.

Mrs Coleman was silent, fixing Veronica with a withering stare. She stood up and her voice was tight as she replied, 'My son was a powerful man, who had many enemies. But this house was his sanctuary. He was safe here – or he thought he was. Now, I'd thank you to leave me alone.'

She sat down pointedly and stared at the computer screen.

'Come,' said Esteban to Veronica, Charlie and Yasmin. 'I have a little more to tell you.'

He drew them down to the opposite end of the room, where Nate appeared to have been fiddling with the TV set. What had he been doing all this time? Veronica wondered with mingled annoyance and curiosity. He stood up quickly as they approached.

'Another of your associates?' Esteban asked.

'Yeah,' Charlie said, shooting Nate a *What the hell?* glance behind his back.

Esteban sat down on one of the plump, uncomfortable-looking chintz sofas. Veronica took the seat beside him, while Yasmin and Charlie perched on the overstuffed arm. Nate hung back, leaning on the back of an armchair, although this time he appeared to be listening.

'What else is it you'd like to tell us?' Veronica prompted.

They were far enough from Mrs Coleman that it'd be nearly impossible for her to hear – such was the size of the room. Even so, Esteban lowered his voice. 'I've told you of my frustration surrounding my friend's business decisions. But there was more. I have no reason to hide anything from you – I am not the murderer – but I can see how it could look should you stumble upon this information later.' He paused, breathed deep.

Veronica held her breath. Could he really be the 'E' in the love note?

'I had feelings for Orson,' Esteban confessed with a sigh, as if he'd been holding back the information for a long time. 'Once, when we were at Oxford, he felt the same – or I thought he did. Then, he broke it off with me after I graduated – he said it was his family; they would never accept us. I returned home, heartbroken. I heard of his marriage via a mutual acquaintance and I thought that was truly the end of it. Then his father died. When he contacted me again, I couldn't help but hope …' His voice was trembling – he was staring at his hands. He didn't continue – Veronica thought, perhaps, he couldn't. *But*, she thought, *people often tell one big secret to hide others, don't they?*

'We found a note on Orson's body,' Veronica said. 'From someone with the initial "E". Can you … shed any light on this?'

The question appeared to shake Esteban out of his grief. 'What did it say?'

'It arranged a meeting in the studio,' said Charlie. 'It was clearly a love note.'

Esteban shook his head. 'No. That wasn't from me. From time to time we still … He kept my hope alive. But never here … never …' He sighed, massaged his temples. 'I am sorry. This is difficult. You are all strangers.'

'It's all right,' said Veronica gently.

'Last night, after the meeting, I stayed behind. I told Orson that I had always loved him, and that if he did as he planned, he would never see me again. I begged him to change his mind. He didn't.' Esteban rubbed the back of his neck.

'It would be really helpful to know what he had changed his mind about,' Veronica said. 'Why did he call this meeting? Please, Esteban,' she added, when he started to shake his head.

Esteban sighed. 'He had … he had decided to sell the business.'

'Really?' Charlie glanced over at Mrs Coleman. 'Bet that didn't go down too well with Mrs I'm-so-bloody-important over there.'

'No, it didn't. Orson was born rich. His father had never worked. Last night, Anne said something about him turning out just like her husband: a disappointment.' He met Charlie's eyes. 'Orson had spent his whole life trying to please his mother – thinking about it, this was really the first time he made a decision on the basis of what *he* wanted. But for all that, I can't believe Anne would kill her own son.'

'Why did he want to sell the business – did he say?' Yasmin asked.

'He said … What was it? He said that it was time to do right by the people in his life.'

'What did that mean, do you think?' Veronica asked.

Esteban shrugged helplessly. 'He certainly wasn't doing right by me – or his family. So I don't know which people he was talking about. Perhaps this other "E" in the note?' His voice was tinged with something sharp – like jealousy, or regret.

'What time did this conversation occur?' Veronica leaned forward slightly, her mind racing to connect the dots.

'Shortly after eleven thirty, if Anne was right about when the meeting ended. We spoke alone for a matter of minutes. He opened a bottle of champagne as I stood up to leave.' He shook his head. 'He was actually *celebrating*.'

The champagne. Veronica remembered her earlier theory about the poison. But if he'd opened the bottle in front of

Esteban, the chances of the bottle having been tampered with felt slim.

But before she could ask any further questions, the large black phone on Mrs Coleman's desk started to ring. 'That'll be the stakeholders,' she called to Esteban.

'Apologies,' Esteban said, standing up. 'As you can imagine, we have much to deal with.'

The four players filed out after Esteban towards the grand doors as Mrs Coleman answered the phone.

'Goodbye,' said Esteban as he took a seat at the desk. 'And good luck.'

'Well, that's ... a lot to unpack,' said Yasmin as the four of them walked back out into the entrance hall. 'Anyone else think Orson's mum didn't seem very ... upset? At least not upset enough. I'd be in pieces if my son had just died.'

'Maybe she just wanted to put on a brave face,' Charlie suggested. 'She's a powerful woman in a man's world. She can't show any signs of weakness.'

Veronica glanced across at Charlie – her beautiful face was uncharacteristically sad.

'Or is it suspicious that she's not upset enough?' Yasmin asked. 'I mean, we have to keep an open mind. Remember what Angel said about red herrings? I don't think we can really trust any of the NPCs. Besides, she did say disparaging stuff about Orson and the business. Perhaps she thought she could do better?'

'Enough to kill her own son?' Charlie asked. 'I don't buy it. She might not have been in floods of tears the whole time, but she was definitely grieving. Ever heard of denial? It's one of the first stages of grief.'

Yasmin nodded thoughtfully. 'And what did you think about Esteban, Charlie?'

'Honest. Came right out and said he could see why we'd be suspicious of him. There's no way he did it,' Charlie said. 'Whoever the killer is, they wouldn't be that straightforward.'

'Unusual though, isn't it,' Yasmin continued. 'Orson getting married to a woman then having an affair with a man.'

'Different times,' said Veronica quietly. 'And sounds like Orson's dad was super traditional.'

Veronica's gaze wandered towards Aaron, who was still sitting in front of the door; knees up, head bowed. Except, he was different somehow. Tenser, more tightly curled in on himself.

'Aaron?' she said. She walked a little closer, her footsteps hesitant. He was so … still.

'Yada, yada, Aaron hates this "dumbass" game and

doesn't want to engage, we get it,' Charlie said, muffling a yawn. 'Let's keep our eyes on the prize; he's not worth worrying about.'

Aaron didn't react – either to Veronica's approach or Charlie's words.

She frowned, stepped closer. 'Aaron?'

No reaction.

Gently she touched his hand; it was ice cold, way colder than the room. But he wasn't shivering. That was bad, wasn't it? Panic clutched her chest. She shook his shoulders – he didn't even raise his head.

'Something's wrong,' she called to the others, her voice unintentionally hushed – a rough whisper – as if part of her was afraid of disturbing something. In the brief second she turned away, Aaron slumped on to his side with a muted thump, his eyelids flickering.

'Shit,' Yasmin said, running over, crouching down and resting her own hand against his cheek. 'It's like he's got hypothermia!' She shrugged off her leather jacket.

Veronica leaned down, holding her ear against his face. She could feel the rush and tickle of his breath. 'He's breathing,' she said, 'but it feels weak.'

Yasmin laid her jacket over him, her hands fretting anxiously as she tucked the material under his body.

'I don't think that's going to help,' said Nate, his voice calm.

'Why are we all fine when he is so cold?' Veronica said, her heart racing. She'd not known Aaron long, but seeing him like this … it felt like an invisible hand was scrunching up her heart, knotting her throat.

'I think it's because he chose not to play,' Charlie said, after a beat.

'I'd guess this is his punishment,' Nate added, nodding in agreement. His voice was carefully neutral – but Veronica had the sense he didn't much care that Aaron was suffering.

'That's sick,' Yasmin said shakily. 'He's in pain.'

'There was a fire or two in the big room, right?' Charlie said. 'Perhaps we should take him in there?'

'I don't know. Nate's right, I don't think we can fix this with fires or blankets,' Veronica said hoarsely, wishing there was someone she could ask for help. Then she remembered there was. 'Angel,' she whispered. Then, she called out, 'Angel!'

'How can I help?' They stepped out from behind the fountain as before, laconic and calm.

'Something's wrong with Aaron,' Veronica said. 'Please, what can we do?'

'Ah yes,' Angel said, stepping over with far too little urgency for Veronica's liking. 'The Game doesn't like it when players don't want to play.'

So Charlie had been right. 'This is the consequence for refusing to take part?' Veronica asked, her voice tight. She felt her hand wrap around Aaron's, which felt icy and totally bloodless. 'Being frozen for the rest of the Game?'

'Yes. It's poetic justice, in a way,' said Angel. 'See, he's getting his wish: he wanted out. He didn't want to play. Now he can't: he's literally frozen here while the rest of you enjoy all this world has to offer.' Angel spread their hands in a wide-armed, exaggerated shrug. 'When the Game ends, he'll be let out like everyone else … but he won't have a very interesting story to tell.'

Yasmin shook her head and stood up, her hands balled at her sides. 'Why didn't you tell us this would happen?' she said, her voice infused with real – and somewhat unexpected – heat. 'The whole thing is messed up. Look, I know this isn't real, but we can still feel in this place. Keeping Aaron like this is a form of psychological torture. That kind of thing can have real-life impact.' Her hands were shaking. Charlie tried to snake an arm around her shoulder, but uncharacteristically Yasmin shrugged her off. 'You should stop it. Right now.'

'I can't stop it,' said Angel simply and without sympathy.

Veronica felt her eyes sting. Yasmin was right. She didn't know Aaron, but she did know something about the real-world effects that VR could inflict. 'Then how do *we* stop it?'

'It's simple. You just need to get him to play, that's all.' Angel turned around, heading back towards the fountain and the shadows. 'I would hurry up. Once he's totally frozen, that's it. I'd say you've got thirty seconds, max.'

'Totally frozen?' Veronica asked – but even as she watched, they disappeared.

Veronica turned to Aaron and with Yasmin's help, manoeuvred him on to his back. Ice crystals had formed on his eyebrows and frost speckled his jacket. Perfect snowflakes were caught in his long, dark eyelashes. Cold prickled up Veronica's spine. He was indoors, in relative warmth, but Aaron looked like he was outside in the dead of an Arctic winter. Impossible. *But then, nothing is impossible in this place*, she thought. 'Aaron? Aaron?' She shook him. 'Listen, you need to agree to play!'

To her relief, he groaned. He was half conscious. There was hope.

'Hang on,' Charlie said, stepping forward and rolling up her sleeves. 'This'll sharpen him up.' She pulled back her hand and slapped him once, hard, around the face.

She enjoyed slapping people around the face a little too much, Veronica thought – but this time, it worked. Aaron blinked, groaned again.

'Aaron, listen to me,' Veronica said. 'You need to agree you'll play the Game, or else you'll be frozen like this the entire time.'

Aaron's eyes sharpened. 'I don't want to—'

'Aaron, darling,' Charlie said sarcastically, shaking her head. 'Not that I give a shit what you do, but it's literally so not worth it. You might as well play.'

'Just say it. Say the words "I'll play",' Veronica said. When he didn't reply, his eyes rolling back in his head as if sleep were dragging him down, she leaned down until her face was inches from his ear. She could hear the thin rasp of his breath in her hearing aid. Then, she spoke only for him. 'Please, come on. Don't leave me with these gamers. I'm going to need your help.' The words that followed arrived in her mouth reflexively. 'My little brother needs our help.'

As she drew back, Aaron blinked slowly. 'Fine,' he whispered. 'I'll play.'

'He said it,' Veronica shouted at the room, at the Game itself. She was surprised at the relief she felt, the warmth rushing through her. 'He said he'll play!'

Even as she spoke, the ice crystals melted from Aaron's brow. He started shivering. 'Oh my god.' He rolled on his side, face pressed against the tiled floor.

'Thank you,' Veronica said quietly.

'Fucking hell,' said Charlie, rolling her eyes. 'He's back.'

Yasmin appeared nearly as relieved as Veronica, her shoulders sagging as she turned towards the staircase. Veronica could have sworn she spotted Yasmin raising her sleeve as if to dab away tears.

'God,' Yasmin said. 'That brought back memories.'

Charlie tucked a strand of hair behind her ears. She looked sheepish. 'Err … sorry. Want to talk about it?'

Yasmin shook her head. 'Only, I've been in therapy for years because of something that happened to me in VR. It's why I only play fun games now. Races and dancing.' She spread her hands. 'I kind of thought this was fun, the fake murder aside. But it feels … darker now. I don't think whoever made this game is a good person.'

Veronica couldn't help but agree – especially as she thought back to the vision … and the figure she'd maybe, just maybe, glimpsed on the stairs. *But what makes someone good or bad?* While Charlie comforted Yasmin, Veronica glanced over towards Nate, noticed how he was hanging back again from the group; how he was wandering around the room, like he had before, as if searching for something. She remembered again how he'd been gazing down at something in the porch – something that couldn't have been the brick-like phone. *He's definitely up to something – does he have his own agenda here? He did say he was more interested in the Game than he was in winning … but if so, why?* Then Aaron was stirring, drawing her attention away.

'Are you OK?' Veronica asked him as he lifted himself to his elbows.

'Yeah. Well, no – it feels like I was hit by a really cold truck, but I'll be fine. Thanks, I guess,' he said, but softened his words with a half-smile that set Veronica's pulse racing. 'I don't want to play but … it wouldn't have been fun to spend the whole game frozen like that. I guess I just have to give in.' He clenched and unclenched his fists in annoyance. 'I just wish there was a way out of here. I know you do too.'

'Actually … I've come round to the idea that we might as well just … play,' she said a little shamefully.

He held her gaze for a beat, then glanced away, pulling himself up until he was cross-legged on the tiles, his dark hair flopping over his forehead. 'Really?'

'Look, I don't want to be here either,' she said distantly, annoyed at how weak at the knees she felt as his dark brown eyes locked on hers again. 'But for one thing, I really don't think there is another way out. We need to put all our minds together if we're going to leave anytime soon.'

Aaron's gaze softened slightly. He shook his head, even so. 'But this is all pointless. All this working together. Why even pretend we're a team? Only one of us can win. Do you really think Charlie won't screw us over as soon as she can? And what's Nate even doing here? He's more interested in snooping around than being a team player.'

So he'd noticed too.

'That leaves Yasmin, and is anyone really that nice?' Aaron continued. 'If you ask me, she's a little too good to be true.'

Veronica nodded. He had a point. Em had been nice at first too. And when Charlie had cracked a mean joke about Aaron being her boyfriend, Yasmin had giggled – in truth, she was laughing at Veronica as much as Charlie was; at least Charlie was honest about it. People like Em and Yasmin, they knew how to play nice. You just had to watch out for when they stopped deciding to pretend.

She met Aaron's eyes. She felt warm at the fact he appeared to implicitly trust her – like it was already the two of them against everyone else. But she pushed the thought aside. She had to be clear-minded.

'OK, I take your point. We can't all win – that's true. But we can form an alliance and whenever any of us wins, the Game will end and we'll be out, right? We've been told we can't leave until that happens.' Veronica half shrugged, feeling a strand of hair fall in front of her face. 'Though I'm not going to lie, I would actually like to win. I could really use that money.'

'This money … it can't be legal though, can it? This whole place is off the grid.' Aaron rested his elbows on his knees and put his head in his hands. 'I just really hate VR,' he said.

Veronica shifted gingerly on her knees. 'Did something happen?'

A long pause, then Aaron sighed. 'My best friend Zara … she's a VR addict,' he said quietly. 'When we were little, we'd

103

spend loads of time together. But as we got older, things got hard for her at school. She was transitioning, you know?'

Veronica nodded slowly.

'So … she retreated into her games. Now, she barely spends time outside of them. IRL, she's wasting away. If I want to see her, I have to play Other Life. She's some kind of billionaire playgirl there. That's the reality she wants. That's how I got in here, trying to spend time with her … trying to get her back, though I've tried a million times to talk to her and she never …'

Veronica noticed his jaw clench angrily.

'I hate it.' He shook his head. 'All of this crap, it's just lies – distracting us from what's important. From what really matters. Since when did we get to decide not to be part of the real world? The world that's literally dying around us while we use its last gasps to power servers that send us someplace else?' His voice was breathless, passionate. His shoulders were tight and he didn't meet Veronica's eyes, as though he were afraid to look at her. 'I don't need this prize, but I wouldn't take it even if I did.'

Veronica was silent for a moment, processing everything he'd said.

Aaron let out a long breath through his teeth. 'Fuck, sorry. I know I can get … intense.'

'Don't apologise,' said Veronica. 'You're right – it is wrong.

And I know how hard it is to see someone you love waste away.' She thought of the thinness of Max's wrists, the way his eyes looked like the eyes of a grown-up, sometimes, and shook her head. 'I'm sorry that's happening to you too.'

Realisation dawned on Aaron's face. 'Your brother. Man, that sucks,' he murmured. 'That's ... God, my thing feels trivial now. At least Zara's not actually physically sick. It's her choice.'

'No ... your thing sucks too. Really bad stuff doesn't make other stuff less bad ... you know?' Veronica shook her head – this was why she didn't usually talk to people about Max, on the rare occasions anyone actually encouraged her to open up ... well, anyone who wasn't a therapist. The truth made them awkward, and it made Veronica sad and angry that she couldn't talk about Max without feeling like she was stepping on everyone else's toes.

'What's wrong with him?' Aaron asked a little hesitantly.

Something about Aaron's tone urged her to continue, even though she was uncomfortable. 'A hereditary condition. To do with his heart. No one really gets what it is, except there's this really expensive treatment available.'

Aaron's eyes widened slightly. 'It could save his life?'

'Yeah. His granddad died from it ... and ...' She swallowed, her mouth dry. 'In fact, our older sister, Em ... she died of it two years ago. She had just turned fifteen.

Doctors say he's not got long to live, if we can't get on the programme.'

Aaron's face was grave. 'But *you* don't have it?'

Veronica shook her head. 'He's my half-brother – we share a dad, but he got the condition from his mum's side. His mum and my dad … they, um, got together when I was nine.' *Got together* didn't feel like the right phrase, so incongruous and neutral. But she pressed on. 'The age gap … I guess I always felt super protective of him.' She glanced over at Aaron, smiled slightly. His shoulders relaxed. 'Look, this may be just a game, but it could change a life. *Save* a life. But please know, I hate VR as much as you do. My stepsister …' She puffed out a long breath. She hated talking about Em. About what had happened.

'I'm sorry to hear she died,' Aaron mumbled – though his face was puzzled as he tried to understand the link. 'That must've been tough.'

'Yeah. She … she actually died in VR. That was the last time I ever played – before the one that got me into this mess, I mean.' She rubbed her eyes. 'That's why I hate it so much.'

'Oh man.' Aaron shook his head. He lifted his hand and – to her surprise – clasped hers in his briefly, warmly, before dropping it as if he'd touched hot iron. 'I'm … I'm really sorry.' He sounded like he meant it.

Now that she'd started, Veronica found she couldn't stop.

'We were at a birthday party at this super advanced arcade, state-of-the-art equipment – they had Hide and Seek, a newer version, and we were playing it in teams. Me and Em, I don't know how, but we ended up playing against each other. I was seeking her.' She sniffed, trying to keep her voice steady. 'Em was super competitive – and she always felt like she had a lot to prove. Especially against me. We played the old mansion setting. She found the best hiding place – of course she did. She was good at everything.' Veronica felt a tear trail down her cheek, swiped it away with the back of her hand. 'She hid in the old lake house. When I found her finally, we had a blow-out argument. She slipped, fell into the lake.' She took a shuddering breath. 'When you die in VR, it's usually fine – right? Game Over, but life goes on. But there are effects on your body too. Raised heart rate, adrenalin. On some level, your body thinks it's real. For Em, when it was Game Over that time, she really died. We didn't know VR could do that to her. We didn't know about her heart. I didn't know.'

The pause that followed was heavy. 'Damn, Veronica. I don't know what to say.'

'I'm sorry I just unloaded that on to you,' she said quickly, afraid he felt overburdened by her sudden show of emotion. 'I know it's a lot. I'm having a lot of therapy.'

'No, don't be sorry. But … why did you play it again? Hide and Seek?'

'Max ... he really wanted to. I'd just overheard some really bad news and ... I couldn't bear to say no.' She smiled a trembling smile. 'It was an older version and we played the forest, not the mansion. I thought it would be different enough.'

Aaron took a deep breath. 'Veronica, if I win, I'll give you the money. I promise. I don't need it, and if by some miracle it's actually legit, I'd like to help.'

Her whole body fizzed warmth. 'That's kind but ... I couldn't ask you to do that.' She pushed her glasses up her nose. 'But I'd love to work together. We can look out for each other. Keep an eye on the others.'

'Well ... OK. We'll work together.' Aaron's mouth tugged into a small smile. 'Sucks that we're both so shitty at games, huh?'

She laughed, exactly as Charlie, Nate and Yasmin walked over.

'Hey, V, you got Aaron to crack a smile?' Charlie said, sliding her long dark ponytail over her shoulder. 'Holy crap, I didn't know that was possible. You guys are cute together.'

Veronica squirmed but, out of the corner of her eye, she watched Aaron blush right the way up to the tips of his ears. She was somehow comforted by the realisation that he was as embarrassed as she was. He acted hard, but you didn't have to dig too deep to find his soft, squishy centre.

Aaron stood up and rammed his hands in his jacket pockets, avoiding everyone's eyes. Veronica stood too, glancing at him sideways. She hadn't felt a connection with anyone except Max in a long time. It felt good to have what felt like a friend. That conversation ... it had been short, but it had really meant something. To her, at least.

'Hate to interrupt this whole high-school-crush situation, but remember what Angel said about the windows filling up?' Nate raised an eyebrow as he glanced towards the arched windows on either side of the door. 'Well, thanks to Aaron's drama – no offence,' he added in a tone that somehow conveyed that offence was intended – 'they're nearly three-quarters full. We should get moving.'

Charlie huffed out a sigh. 'Much as I hate to agree with Aaron on any level, this game *is* totally lame,' she said, her voice bitter as she scuffed at the tiles with her boot.

Veronica didn't buy it. Ten minutes ago she'd been enthusiastically discussing motives. Charlie was the queen of cool, but Veronica was starting to think it was an act.

'Clues and information, really?' Charlie shrugged. 'I'm rubbish at this stuff. If it was a race ... or a first-person zombie apocalypse shooter ...'

'Like Dead Stars?' Yasmin snorted. 'Be careful what you wish for! These graphics are insane. Can you imagine shooting a zombie in here? It'd feel one hundred per cent legit.'

'Awesome,' Charlie said dreamily, swinging her axe in lazy arcs.

'Psycho,' Yasmin said with an affectionate smile.

'Guys?' Nate interrupted. 'Seriously, we need to hurry. Let's split – looks like there are two rooms left on this floor. Charlie and Yasmin, you pair up and interview whoever's in there.' He pointed at one of the doors, the one on the opposite side of the hallway to the huge office. He was officially taking charge, Veronica thought, which was weird, considering he didn't seem that focused before. 'Then me, Veronica and Aaron will go into the other room.' He pointed to a door at the back of the hall, behind the staircases and fountain. He slid his brick-phone out of its holster and waved it. 'If we need to contact you, I'll call you. Got it?'

Charlie visibly bristled at his tone – the colour rising in her cheeks – but ultimately shrugged. 'Fine. I still don't *quite* get how that's going to work, since we don't have anything to call,' she said.

'Landlines, Angel said,' Nate said shortly. 'There's one in every one room. And of course, we'll all share the "information" we discover.' His eyes were already drifting towards the door he'd picked for himself, Veronica and Aaron. 'Let's go.'

Veronica narrowed her eyes, thinking through Nate's probable reasoning. Aside from herself, Yasmin was the closest they had to a team player. He might not trust Charlie as far as he could throw a cat, but he trusted Yasmin would tell him if they heard or saw anything important – though Veronica wasn't sure that was wise. Or maybe there was something else going on. In any case, with her babysitting Aaron, and questioning whoever they found in the room, Nate could focus on, well, whatever he was focusing on … because he sure as hell hadn't been interested in the mystery since the second they'd started investigating. The thought made Veronica's heart squeeze strangely in her chest. If he didn't want the prize, then what? What was he really after?

'OK!' Yasmin said chirpily, bouncing over to Charlie. Her curls drooped down over her forehead, and now she brushed them away a little shyly as she reached out for Charlie's hand. 'Advance, compadre!'

'Cool,' said Charlie, smiling broadly. Not a snarky comment in sight. Then she shot the other three a glance over her shoulder. 'See you suckers later.'

6

Once Charlie and Yasmin had disappeared through their door, Veronica shared a quick glance with Aaron, then followed Nate, who was already heading through the other door, the one at the back of the hall.

Nate pushed it open into a long kitchen dominated by floor-to-ceiling glass windows gazing out over the gardens – which, at the moment, were merely a mass of white, the lumps of trees, bushes and even a distant shed barely distinguishable from the snowy haze. In fact, three-quarters of the glass was entirely blocked out by snow, exactly as the windows were in the hallway – although, of course, snow would not behave in such a uniform and predictable way in real life.

Veronica wondered what would happen when they filled up completely. Angel had said they really didn't want to know – and based on the horrifying punishment meted out to Aaron when he refused to play, she was inclined to agree.

Besides the three of them, there were three other people in the kitchen.

Sitting at the breakfast table, a tanned white man, who looked to be in his mid-twenties, sat cradling a steaming cup of coffee. He was broad-shouldered and wore dungarees over a threadbare jumper with the sleeves rolled up. Judging by this, plus the brown under his nails, Veronica guessed this was the gardener. *Ned*, she remembered.

Chopping a carrot at the worktop while sobbing was a tall, painfully pale girl in her late teens. She stopped for a moment to dab her eyes on her sleeves. *Rita*, Veronica guessed – the maid.

Next to her, along the counter, a light-brown-skinned woman, who Veronica placed in her late thirties, was chopping an onion – she appeared so absorbed in her work that she hadn't noticed the three teens enter. Her eyes were brimming with tears – but was it the onion or something more?

'You must be our visitors,' said Ned, the first to notice the three players enter the room. 'Crime-solving teens, eh?' He offered a wry, slightly mocking smile, cradling his mug.

'That's us,' said Veronica. 'You must be Ned.' She glanced over at the two women. 'And Rita ... and Madame Dubois?'

Rita nodded, cracking a small smile through her tears. 'Isn't it awful?' she said. 'He was in this room only yesterday, having breakfast … and now …' She choked back another sob.

Madame Dubois set down her knife and stroked Rita on the back. 'It's all right, love.' Her voice trembled slightly, undercutting her words. 'Look, why don't you fix yourself another cuppa, eh? And maybe a round for our guests, while you're at it?' Veronica had been expecting a French accent, but Madame Dubois spoke with a London drawl.

Rita nodded wordlessly, clearly holding in another sob as she clattered around the kitchen.

'Thanks,' said Veronica. 'That's nice of you.'

'That's all right, love,' said Madame Dubois. 'It's teas all round at times like this. I'll get on with lunch until you need me.'

She sounded kind but professional. Veronica couldn't help noticing that her shoulders were tight as she turned away and scraped the onions into a pot on the hob.

'Your name's Ned?' Aaron said to the gardener – then glanced away when the man's eyes fixed on him, as if he was uncomfortable with the attention. 'I mean … isn't that short for Edward?'

'That's right,' said Ned, glancing between Aaron and Veronica. 'Why d'you ask?'

Edward. E. Veronica felt her spine tingle. Aaron was right to notice … Could this man be Orson's lover? If so, and he was the true author of the note, the young man was a good actor. Of the three servants in the kitchen, he appeared the least bothered by Orson's death.

As ever, Nate hung back, this time by the patio doors, his eyes combing the room, exactly as he had done before. 'Hey, Nate,' Veronica called, annoyed. He turned, eyebrow raised. 'Want to get over here and help?'

'You got this,' he said, brightly but firmly. 'I'll have a look around for clues.'

She wanted to tell him they'd already found the important clue for this level – the pencilled letter on Coleman's body – but could tell it wasn't worth it. She clearly wasn't getting anything out of him now. Besides, they had to hurry. The snow wasn't going to wait.

She pulled one of the chairs out from under the table, signalled for Aaron to join her. 'Mind if we ask you a few questions, Ned?'

'I'd say I haven't got all day,' he replied, 'but being a gardener, in this weather … well, you can take your time.' He smiled a charming half-smile. 'How can I help?'

'Would you mind describing your relationship with Orson?' Veronica said.

Ned shrugged. 'He was my employer. Not the outdoorsy

type either.' Veronica studied his face carefully for signs he might be lying – but Ned returned her gaze coolly as he continued. 'We didn't have much of a relationship at all. What did you say your name was?'

'I didn't, but I'm Veronica. This is Aaron … When you say you didn't have much of a relationship,' she asked, following a hunch, 'did you mean to imply you didn't like him?'

Ned sipped his coffee, then glanced over at the cook and Rita – as if checking they were out of earshot. 'If I'm being honest … he was pretty full of himself. Just like his mother.' He shrugged. 'Rich people aren't generally very nice to the likes of me though. That didn't bother me.'

Veronica sensed he was holding back. 'But something else did bother you?'

'He'd be away on business a lot – or when he was here, up in his studio, painting. It annoyed me that he had this beautiful wife –' Ned's cheeks coloured slightly – 'and two boys, and this incredible house, and he never seemed to do anything but escape from it all.'

So, Orson was an artist. And Ned had a crush on Grace. 'What is your relationship with Grace Coleman?' she asked.

Ned snapped back, 'Not sure I like this line of questioning, Detective Inspector Veronica.'

Veronica's muscles tensed. She'd pissed him off. If she

lost him completely, she might miss out on crucial information. 'I'm not implying anything,' she said, her voice sounding calmer than she felt. 'I just want to know.'

He rubbed his temples. 'She's nice, that's all. She cares. Not like him.'

She allowed her shoulders to relax a little. She hadn't lost him yet. 'What about the two boys?'

He shrugged. 'I don't know them well. Younger one, Simon, he's just like his dad. Full of himself. High achiever. He's away at some fancy boarding school most of the time – home for the Christmas holidays now. Peter, the older one, he's sick. Spends all his time in bed, except when his mum helps him on to the porch right here in the summer.' He gestured out at the veranda beyond the kitchen doors. 'Sometimes he asks me about the flowers. He seems more like her. Nice kid.'

Veronica nodded, changed tack – useful as the context was, she had to remain focused on the murder itself. 'Mrs Coleman said you live in the village. What time did you arrive this morning?'

Ned was visibly relieved to be returning to practical questions. 'Just before eight. By which time, she –' he jutted his chin at the cook – 'had found the body and the snow was coming down thick.'

'What happened then?'

'Straight away Mr Inglesby – that's the butler – told me to help him with the car. The phone lines were down, so he was going to drive to the police station. I shovelled snow off the drive until my arms good as fell off. But it was no use. The younger Mrs Coleman had taken the Range Rover to London – and the Ferrari is useless in rain, let alone snow.' He shrugged. 'That's about it. No chance of me getting home in this weather – so I'm waiting it out in here.' He lifted his mug. 'At least there's coffee, eh?'

Just then, Rita brought over a tray of rattling tea, setting down a pot and three cups and saucers for Veronica, Aaron and Nate, her face red and puffy.

'Thank you,' said Veronica, 'and why don't you sit down a minute? We'd love to talk to you too.'

'All right … I'll just go and get my tea,' Rita said, wiping her nose on her sleeve.

As she walked off, Aaron asked Ned, 'Did she know him well?'

Ned snorted. 'She's only been working here three weeks. He barely nodded at her if they passed in the hall. It's *her* you'll want to talk to.' His eyes shifted over to the cook.

'Madame Dubois?' Aaron asked.

'That's right. She and Mr Coleman would sit here for ages talking. They've known each other for years too – her mum was the cook before her, so she grew up here.' Ned stood up, drained his coffee cup. 'I'll leave you to your tea,' he said. 'Can't stand the smell of the stuff. And I should check if there's anything Mr Inglesby wants me for.'

When Rita sat down, it was quickly clear Ned had been right – she knew very little about Mr Coleman and corroborated Ned's story entirely. She had arrived a couple of minutes after he had, Madame Dubois greeting her at the front door and walking her round to the kitchen from the outside, to spare her the shock.

'It's just so awful,' Rita said, blowing her nose. 'He's dead, right there in the hall, and now thanks to the snow, I'm trapped in this big haunted house with all its draughts, ghosts and secret passages and horrid empty rooms with a literal dead person.' She glanced fearfully around the kitchen as if expecting a ghost to pop out of the fridge.

'Wait … secret passages?' Aaron asked. 'And ghosts? Isn't this place basically brand new?'

'Simon told me it was built on the foundations of this old house that burned down,' Rita said, leaning in closer. 'Mr Coleman even used the original floor plan, Simon said, right down to these hidden passages that had been built into the walls. Simon said that the night of the fire, a maid got trapped in one of the passages and burned alive.' Her eyes were wide as saucers. 'He said if you listen at night, you can sometimes hear her screaming.'

Veronica lifted an eyebrow. Rita was her age, but she was as gullible as Max. 'I think that's all we need to know,' she said. 'Thanks, Rita.'

The girl blew her nose again enthusiastically, offered Aaron a weak, rather dreamy smile and picked up her tea.

'Come on,' said Veronica, as she drew Aaron away from the table. 'We need to talk to the cook.' She searched the room for Nate, finding him rummaging through the pantry, a small separate room with a high window off the back of the kitchen. She pushed down her irritation. Did he think he could get one up on the rest of them by finding the minor clues Angel had mentioned?

The cook was now chopping a head of cabbage. She was entirely focused on her task and when Veronica offered a gentle, 'Madame Dubois?' she started, losing her grip on the knife, which slipped and sliced her thumb. Vivid red bloomed on her skin. 'Shit,' she cursed, running over to the tap to wash the wound. 'Sorry, I was miles away.'

Veronica spotted a roll of patterned kitchen towel and brought over three clean sheets to the cook, who accepted them gratefully, pressing them against the cut. 'I'm sorry for your loss,' Veronica said softly. A shiver ran through her like a premonition as blood bloomed against the white paper, spoiling the blue and orange ink of the design.

'Thank you. What a day, what a day.' The cook's eyes

were raw and Veronica was now certain she hadn't only been crying because of the onions. 'Hard to believe he's gone,' she added in a small voice.

'We figured we could maybe help find out what happened,' said Veronica, 'since we're objective outsiders. Mind if we ask you a few questions, Madame Dubois?'

'Course. I want to help.' She smiled slightly. 'Fire away. But don't call me Madame Dubois – that's what *she* likes to call me.' She gestured over at the room where they'd met Mrs Coleman with her kitchen-towel-wrapped hand. 'That's what she called my mum too. I prefer Liz.'

'Short for Elizabeth?' Veronica said. *Yet another E ... ?*

An unexpectedly pained expression flashed across her face. 'That's right. Though not many people call me that.' As she leaned forward over the countertop, Veronica noticed a silver chain with a pendant slip from under her shirt. No – not a pendant. A key.

Liz tucked the key back inside her top.

'What was your relationship with Orson? You'd known him a long time?' Aaron asked.

The smile froze on Liz's face. 'We were friendly. Sometimes he would eat his breakfast in here rather than in the dining room, to have a chat – or just to read.' Her voice shook slightly.

'And when was the last time you saw him?' asked Veronica.

Liz paused before answering. 'Yesterday dinner-time. I brought him and the older Mrs Coleman their dinner in the dining room before clocking off for the day. Esteban arrived afterwards, his taxi pulled up outside as I was leaving – and the two boys ate separately, in their rooms.'

'You didn't see him after that?' she pressed.

Liz pursed her lips and shook her head emphatically. *She's lying*, thought Veronica. She glanced at the patio doors, which were filling up fast. They didn't have time to dance around the subject – not any more.

'Liz, we found a note on Orson's body, asking him to meet at the studio. It was signed "E". Sorry to be so direct, but, was it from you?'

Liz's lips trembled as they pressed together. 'No,' she said. But it was even less convincing this time. At the edge of her vision, Veronica could see Nate in the corner, gazing down at something in his hand – that thing again, whatever he'd been looking at in the porch. What was it and what was he doing?

Focus.

Veronica leaned forward, across the kitchen counter. 'Time is of the essence. Orson's killer is in this house – while the snow lasts, we've got them cornered. Your honesty is vital. If you were the author of this letter, you were most likely the last person to see him alive … Except the killer.

You might have Important Information we can use. There's no judgement here, not from us.'

Liz sagged. 'It's just … he said never to tell,' she whispered, her eyes darting around the room – but Rita was out of earshot. 'Not until everything was sorted.' The blood drained from her face and Veronica helped her sit down on one of the stools along the breakfast bar. 'We've been seeing each other for years, on and off. Since we were teenagers. I love him – *loved* him – I really did. And last night …' She lifted her eyes to look at Veronica and Aaron earnestly. 'Last night, he was just as always – better, even. Otherwise I would have said. He was happy. Talked again about leaving Grace. She's away in London. He thought she was having an affair. He said their marriage was dead. That our time was coming. He wanted to sell the business too. He said it was all part of him accepting himself – being who he really was, instead of the man everyone else wanted him to be. Truly, I was starting to believe him, starting to think we might actually have a future …' She shook her head, tears filling her eyes once more. 'I can't believe he's gone.'

So Liz *was* Orson's secret lover – and it sounded like he'd told her about his plans to sell the business too. Veronica was about to continue her line of questioning when she saw – *felt* – the world around her flicker. The house shook. She blinked, confused, as the ground shifted beneath her feet.

When she glanced up, she swallowed a scream. Liz's face had turned skeletal, ancient – zombie-like. Her skull glowed stark under strings of greasy hair. The cupboard door behind her was hanging from its hinges, revealing cobwebbed plates inside, and the knife on the surface was spotted with bloodlike rust, the half-chopped cabbage crawling with maggots. The rest of the room was trashed. Veronica's eyes darted towards the patio doors and her heart lurched – the snow had disappeared. Instead, the glossy surface of a dark, dark lake lapped at the bottom of the glass …

Aaron reached out for her – but by the time his hand met hers, everything had returned to normal. The whole house had shaken and, for a second, it had been *different*.

Dead.

'I can't believe he's gone,' Liz said again, with the exact same inflection as before, as if the glitch had never happened.

Veronica looked over at Nate. He shook his head slightly, his eyes wide. He'd seen it too. This wasn't just her. Veronica had the sense that the cardboard scenery of this world had been lifted away temporarily, revealing the true ugliness beneath.

Was that supposed to happen? Or had something gone wrong?

Aaron's hand was still tight in her own. He was seriously spooked.

'Are you two OK?' said Liz softly. 'You look like you've seen a ghost.'

'I-I'm sorry,' Veronica said, gathering herself together. 'Um … tell me more about when you met with Orson last night.'

'He was there at twelve, exactly as he'd promised – and he was carrying most of a bottle of champagne and two flutes. We drank, talked …' Her eyes dropped sideways.

'How much did he drink?' Aaron asked.

Good thinking, Veronica thought, smiling at him slightly.

'Oh – he had most of the bottle. I'm not a big drinker. When he left – would've been around one, one thirty – he was definitely unsteady. He might've had a drink beforehand too. I don't know. I basically had to stop him falling asleep right there in the studio. The little bed in there, it hurts his back.' Her eyes brimmed again. 'I keep thinking that if I hadn't urged him to go to bed, or if I'd helped him downstairs to his room… but he didn't want anyone to know …'

'Liz, this wasn't your fault,' said Veronica. 'You can't blame yourself. How could you have known?'

Liz sniffed and nodded.

'Can you think of anyone who might've wanted Orson dead?' Aaron asked. He still hadn't let go of Veronica's hand. Maybe he'd forgotten all about it. Veronica tried desperately not to shift her fingers – if she did, he might remember and let go – and willed her palm not to sweat. *Now, focus!*

Liz wiped her eyes. 'Look, the one person I can think of is Grace. If she had found out about our affair … well, she's a proud woman. She wouldn't take kindly to being deceived. But as far as I know, she hasn't found out. And even if she had, how could she have killed him? She was away in London last night – and she's not due back until this afternoon.'

'Yes,' said Veronica softly. 'Yes, that's right.'

Back out in the hall, Charlie and Yasmin were waiting.

Charlie's face brightened and a cruel smile flickered around her lips. 'Oh my god, you're actually holding hands! How *sweet*!'

Aaron had been holding Veronica's hand since the glitch – a fact which had produced a pleasant glow at the base of her spine. Now, he let go abruptly.

Yasmin giggled, hiding her smile behind her hand.

'V, darling,' said Charlie mockingly. 'I didn't think you had it in you. Bravo.'

Veronica felt her cheeks burn and bit her tongue. She turned her attention to the windows on either side of the front door, which showed barely a thin sliver of light above the snow. Based on how long the interviews in the kitchen had lasted and how much of the kitchen patio doors had filled, Veronica guessed they had fifteen or twenty minutes left, tops, before they'd find out what would happen when the windows filled up completely. To her relief, Charlie and Yasmin drifted away, giggling.

'You saw the … *thing* that happened in there, right?' Aaron asked in a low voice. 'That … glitch?'

'Yeah,' Veronica breathed. 'I don't know what that was – but I'm pretty sure Nate saw it too. Honestly, it reminded me a little of what I saw when I passed out before. Like I was suddenly in another place.' When she shut her eyes, Veronica could see the black lake water lapping against the window. She swallowed, her throat suddenly dry.

'But this time, it wasn't only you who saw it, so it can't be explained away with your headset,' Aaron said seriously.

Nate had wandered over to where Charlie was standing, gazing down at the body again while pinching her nose. Veronica was used to the smell already – she supposed hospital had prepared her for that; the scents of sickness and death weren't so far apart. Yasmin was on the other side of the fountain, bouncing on her glowy-heeled shoes.

'How did it go?' Nate asked the others.

Veronica frowned. She'd wanted to ask them, first, about the weird glitch they'd experienced in the kitchen – had Yasmin and Charlie felt it too? Why wasn't it foremost in Nate's mind?

'We went in the dining room,' Charlie said, 'and talked to some miserable old git polishing the silver.'

'The butler? Mr Inglesby?' asked Veronica.

'That's the one,' Charlie said. 'He barely told us anything. He was even more stuck up than *she* was.' She gestured her head at the door to the huge office containing Mrs Coleman. 'Sorry. If there was any information there beyond "I definitely didn't do it, you insolent teenagers", I don't know what it was. The old codger was in bed by nine and slept through, he said, and I gotta say, I believe him. He had a total holier-than-thou vibe.'

While Charlie spoke, Yasmin was wandering around the body.

'I even tried on my glasses,' Charlie continued, 'but there weren't any other clues in there either.'

Veronica observed as Yasmin lifted her foot, tapped the body's shoe and then the marble floor with her shoes. No footsteps led away from the body. *So he definitely fell*, Veronica thought. Her eyes lifted to the mezzanine landing above and, sure enough, she saw a faint glow – footsteps leading away into the gloom of the upper floor. Even as she watched, the glow faded.

Yasmin was gazing up there too, but she didn't say anything about the footsteps she'd seen.

She acts sweet, thought Veronica, *but it's not real. She's as competitive as Charlie is, deep down.*

'What about you guys?' Charlie said, though her voice sounded barely interested.

'We spoke with Ned, Rita and Madame Dubois,' Veronica said, turning her attention from Yasmin. 'Well … Aaron and I did. Nate,' she called over, 'what were you looking at all that time?'

'Just checking for any other clues,' he called breezily. He was already wandering again, doing his own thing – whatever that was.

Veronica clenched her jaw. Did he think they were stupid?

'But did you get the Information-with-a-capital-I? If so, we can go upstairs.' Charlie flipped her long dark hair over her shoulders. 'Check your tape thingy. I'm bored as hell of this level. Hopefully something more interesting will happen when we go up.'

Veronica slid the tape recorder out of her puffer pocket. She tried pressing the button marked *play*, but nothing happened.

Yasmin was now wandering around the edges of the hall, bouncing on and admiring her flashing shoes. 'Oh, guys,' she said suddenly, 'there's another door!' She pushed open a door tucked away under the staircase. 'Wow! It's a storage room and there's a fricking juke-box in here! Like, a CD juke-box! I didn't even know they made those.'

'Anyone inside?' Charlie called.

'Nope. I'm going to check out the juke-box.'

Charlie rolled her eyes affectionately. 'Literally ob*sessed* with music.' Then she called to Yasmin, 'Don't take too long, OK?'

'Try rewinding it,' said Aaron to Veronica quietly when he realised she was struggling to work the Walkman. 'Here.' He took the little machine and pressed a button to the left. It whirred, clicked off. 'Now plug in the headphones ...' He slid the little headphone jack into the hole. 'And *now* press play.'

Veronica's finger hesitated over the button. 'How'd you know about all this?'

Aaron shrugged. 'I have a lot of this stuff at home. Hating VR made me hate other modern tech too. Older things feel ... safer? I don't even have a smartphone.'

Veronica glanced up at him wide-eyed. 'Wow, that's ... extreme. You didn't care for that watch though?' She glanced down at the Casio.

Aaron snorted. 'Not because it's old. These were pieces of shit even back in the day.'

'Oh, he thinks he's so cool,' Charlie muttered, rolling her eyes. 'Bet you buy all this old crap from overpriced hipster shops, am I right?'

Aaron blushed – he clearly hadn't realised Charlie was listening.

'You don't have to answer that,' Veronica said, bolder in

defence of Aaron than she was of herself. 'She's just teasing.' She shot Charlie a hard glance. Aaron was only just starting to warm up – she couldn't let the others ruin it. She pressed play and the three of them stooped down around the headphones.

'But don't call me Madame Dubois – that's what she likes to call me. That's what she called my mum too. I prefer Liz.'

'Short for Elizabeth?'

'That's right.'

Charlie glanced up. 'Elizabeth. So what?'

'The "E" from the love note. She and Orson were involved,' Veronica said, frowning. 'That's the main information. But we asked her all about it and she admitted it. She told us everything and she really didn't know anything about—'

At that moment, a loud bassline thumped through the house from the direction of the staircase. Veronica jumped, nearly dropping the Walkman. The music was so loud Veronica could have sworn she could feel the entire building shudder, the bassline thrumming in her chest like a second heartbeat. Lyrics blared out in an upbeat male shout.

'Cut it out, Yaz!' yelled Charlie, her hands over her ears. 'Jesus fucking Christ!'

But the music didn't stop. It was loud enough to make Veronica's hearing aids ring. She covered her ears with her hands. She noticed the light was grey in here now, ghostly.

The windows were nearly full – they had a few minutes, tops, before they had to go upstairs. 'We have to go!' she shouted, the music refusing to let up.

'Where's Nate?' Charlie shouted back.

Veronica scanned the hall, the music reverberating through her chest as if it were trapped inside her. Nate was nowhere to be seen.

'I'll check the office and the kitchen –' Aaron jerked his chin at Charlie – 'you check the dining room?'

'And I'll get Yasmin,' Veronica yelled.

They nodded their agreement. Aaron set off in one direction and Charlie marched towards the dining room purposefully, her hands over her ears and her mouth tight with annoyance. Perhaps she was glad not to have to be the bad guy and get Yasmin to turn down the music, Veronica thought.

Veronica marched quickly towards the door under the stairs. She opened it.

The world swirled. Trees smudged up towards a white sky. The light was dim, but a fleck of blood-red danced in the forest ahead of her. Music thrummed around her. A house was glowing, bright-windowed, between the trees. Ivy crept up its walls. Dark water lapped at a small wooden structure by the lake.

No. Not now. Not here.

And then she was sagging against the doorframe, clinging to consciousness. She felt sick. The juke-box churned out its light and music.

She lifted her eyes. 'Yasmin?'

But the girl in front of her was not Yasmin. She was someone else. Wet hair dripping on to the dusty juke-box, her clothes sodden, her hands limp. An electric sizzle filled the air. She was gazing down at the juke-box, the music stuttering, repeating like a skipping CD.

The figure started to turn.

Not real. Not real. Can't be real.

Can't really be her.

Vision fuzzy, full of pixels. Head pounding.

'One, two, three, four …' said the dead girl as she faced Veronica fully, her eyes starting to lift, voice gurgling like she was underwater. 'Five, six, seven, eight …'

A giggle. The girl met her eyes.

'Em?' Veronica choked. Her throat was tight, a fist of fear squeezing her vocal cords.

'Ready or not …'

Over the music, no one could hear her scream.

7

The music had stopped, replaced by muffled silence and a frightened voice calling her name. *Max?*

'Veronica. Veronica!' Angel's face appeared above her. Bright blue eyes. Alabaster skin. But their face had lost its calm expression. They glanced over their shoulder. 'You have to get upstairs, all of you. Now.'

Veronica felt hands under her armpits, tugging her upward. Her head felt cold, tingly – was it possible to have pins and needles in your brain? What had happened? What was it she'd seen exactly? The feeling of terror and confusion lingered like a bad dream.

She must've blacked out again; another weird vision, her ancient headset playing up. That's all it had been, right? Because Em couldn't be here. Not really. That was impossible.

That was unthinkable.

She staggered, felt her cheek pressing into rough woollen material. Aaron was holding her up, his arms wrapped around her, pulling her into the warmth of his jacket. Heat flushed through her body, in spite of the lingering fear.

'What the hell is going on?' he asked, his voice rumbling in Veronica's ear. 'Is this supposed to happen?'

'No, this isn't supposed to happen,' Angel snapped, voice tight with panic. 'I have no idea what's happening. You should all get upstairs – and hurry!'

Veronica lifted her head from Aaron's chest, feeling a little stronger and a lot embarrassed. Charlie's tear-streaked face was glowing in the semi-darkness at her side – all her bravado disappeared as she gazed down … The darkness behind her shifted in the weirdest way – Veronica blinked. Maybe it was her head. Nate was there too, his own face blank with shock as he swallowed, his Adam's apple bobbing. And Aaron's eyes … they were grim. Sad. What were they all looking at?

She shifted her gaze around to the small room housing the juke-box.

Yasmin lay on the floor, a huge wound bleeding in the back of her head. Her cheek was pressed to the bare concrete, her eyes wide open.

Red dot. Dark forest. Invisible water.

Em had been there, standing in front of the juke-box.

She felt cold all over. 'Oh …' she said.

'Realistic, isn't it?' said Aaron.

'Deeply uncomfortable,' mumbled Nate, scratching behind his neck.

'No time for this, guys,' Angel said. 'You—'

'She's not really dead though,' Charlie interrupted suddenly, her voice tinged with relief, though still shaky and weak. 'This is realistic, but it's just VR. She's OK in real life.' She glanced down at Yasmin's shoes. 'Which means, we should probably get those. By which I mean, I should get those.' She crouched down.

'You're … you're going to loot your friend's dead body?' Veronica said, blinking.

'Not dead!' said Charlie, ripping open the Velcro and tugging off the sneakers. She tucked them under one arm, scooped up the axe. 'Yaz would want me to win, OK? Stop being so judgy, urgh.'

'Go upstairs. Now. All of you,' Angel said again, voice bright with urgency. 'I'll try to figure this out. But you shouldn't be here when the snow's filled the windows, either way. Go!'

Aaron tugged Veronica gently away from the juke-box room. She stumbled away from him by accident, fell to her knees. Her legs were like jelly. The floor felt unnaturally cold under her hands, icy. Charlie's free hand closed on her arm, her nails digging into Veronica as she pulled her up. She felt, again, the sting of Charlie's slap around her face – the sting of shame, years ago, resonating in her head.

Em had slapped her too, once. At school. She'd accused Veronica of stealing her stuff, and everyone had watched while she 'taught her a lesson'. Her glasses had been broken from the force of it, smashed on the ground. The other girls had laughed. The next day, Veronica had been kicked out of the bedroom she'd offered to share with Em when they were nine years old.

'You understand, don't you?' Nyra had said. Back then, she was nicer to Veronica – but things changed later on. Like mother, like daughter. 'It's been really difficult for Em, moving in here. She needs space. I know it's been years, but she's still grieving her dad. She's working through a lot of issues.'

Veronica had wanted to scream that she was working through issues too, and she hadn't turned into a sociopath.

Now, something in Veronica snapped.

'Get off me,' she said, tugging her arm away from Charlie, whose face twisted into a scowl.

'I was helping you, you psycho,' Charlie said.

Psycho. That's what Em used to call her too.

'Hey, calm down, we need to—'

Veronica cut Aaron off, her mind flashing red. 'Don't you dare call me that,' she growled at Charlie through clenched teeth. 'You *hit* me earlier. And you're the one holding an axe! If anyone here is psychotic, it's you!'

'I'm not *psychotic*. I just really need this, OK, and you were being ...' Her momentarily vulnerable tone turned quickly to outrage. 'How fucking *dare* you!'

Nate was ahead – now he called back, his voice uncertain. 'Guys, something's happening to the floor.'

He was right: the freezing cold floor felt odd under Veronica's high-tops – not quite solid, unsteady – and it wasn't just her shaky legs. Cold wetness was seeping over the edges of her shoes and into her socks.

'*I just really need this.*' What had Charlie meant by that?

But Charlie was tramping towards her, her beautiful face twisted in anger.

'Stop,' said Aaron, stepping between the two, 'now is not the—'

But Charlie dodged around him with surprising speed. She dropped Yasmin's trainers, using that free hand to push Veronica.

Veronica landed hard, backwards, in snow. One of her hearing aids partially dislodged, a whooshing, scratching noise filling her ear. She tried to stand up, pushing away from the ground.

Except, there was no ground. Instead of reaching a firm base, she pushed down into more cloying, freezing softness.

She tried to lift her head, but more snow piled down on top of her, heavy as earth. She spluttered, gasping for breath, panic gripping her lungs. The windows were glowing a ghostly grey, the electric lights in the hall flickering on-off, on-off, like signals in a storm.

The room was midway through transforming into … into *what*?

'Veronica!' Aaron was shouting. But it was like he couldn't get closer.

'Fuck,' Charlie cursed. 'I'm sinking!' She dropped the axe, creating an axe-shaped imprint in the deepening snow.

'I can't get up!' Veronica tried to shout – but the snow was pulling her under and suddenly her mouth was full of cold. She couldn't shout. Couldn't even breathe.

So this was it: her chance of saving Max's life disappearing like a dream.

Will I wake up now? she thought. *Next to Max in his hospital bed, nothing changed? Max still dying. Me having to face the rest of my life knowing I had a chance and I screwed it up.* The image twisted through her gut like a knife.

She forced herself not to surrender. She cast her eyes around. The stairs were close by, barely a few feet ahead – could they really be unreachable? Aaron was standing on the bottom step, extending his hands for her, real desperation on his face. She tried to move her arm – couldn't. Charlie staggered past her, somehow reaching the safety of the cold, grey-veined marble, and Nate was a few steps up, his face ashen as he stared.

Behind him, further up, was another figure. A girl. *Em.*

Haloed by the stained-glass window, her long dark hair was tangled and wet around her neck. Half plastered over her face. But Veronica could see enough of it to know she was smiling.

She tried to scream. Tried to thrash her way out. *I can't give up.* But the more she struggled, the more the snow pulled her under.

The last thing she noticed was Aaron jabbing at his digital watch before the world turned cold and white.

'Get off,' she said, tugging her arm away from Charlie's hand. The other girl's face twisted into a scowl. Veronica stared down at her hand. Why did this feel so familiar? Why was she suddenly so cold, right to the core? She glanced up at Charlie, anger sparking through her, warming her from within.

Charlie opened her mouth, but before she could speak, Aaron grabbed both their arms.

'We don't have time for this. We have to run, now, before it happens again!'

Veronica's eyes widened – this *had* happened before, and she remembered how it had ended. She remembered the flickering lights, the disappearing floor, the embrace of freezing wetness around her body – remembered Aaron jabbing at his watch … to reverse time.

She let go of her anger and allowed Aaron to pull her along, even as the floor grew cold and soft under her high-tops. Charlie staggered alongside her, clutching Yasmin's trainers in one hand and the axe in the other. They passed the body in the fountain, water freezing over and somehow tilting the corpse's face to stare towards Veronica – one blue eye fixing her as if pleading for help – and soon she was sliding on the transforming snow after Nate, who was the first to bound up the stairs. Charlie was next, then Aaron.

That was when Veronica remembered one last detail – the figure on the stairs – and her footsteps faltered. She glanced up, expecting Em …

But no one was on the staircase, this time.

Had she even been there before? Or had Veronica imagined it?

She slipped a single step from the bottom, cursing, both her legs sliding into the snow – it was happening again! – but Aaron caught her arm. 'Help me!' he shouted. The snow was sucking Veronica under, pulling on her legs like it was alive; like freezing, cloying quicksand. Aaron's hands felt tight on her arm and she grabbed on to him too, heartened by the determination in his brown eyes.

Nate lowered himself alongside Aaron, grabbing Veronica's other arm. Aaron and Nate pulled until she slid out, gasping but safe, on to the staircase. She whimpered, jerking her knees up, away from the snow – noting as she did her feet were bare, freezing and clammy. The quicksand-snow had swallowed up her shoes.

'Oh my god,' she said breathlessly. She scrambled a few steps up on her hands and knees, ungainly and panicked. Then, she paused to catch her breath and stared up at Aaron. 'Thank you.'

She tried to lock eyes with Nate too, but he glanced away. As if he was scared to meet her eyes. Uncertain.

Where has he been? Veronica thought, her heart pounding. *When Yasmin was killed, he was missing.* She stepped back from him. All along he'd been acting suspiciously – barely interested in the murder mystery. The device he'd been looking at. The distraction techniques. What game was he playing, if not this one?

I need to watch him.

'Come on,' said Aaron, already following Charlie up the stairs. He turned back to offer Veronica a hand. 'We're not safe here. Let's get to the next level.'

LEVEL TWO

8

Veronica followed the others up the right side of the split staircase. She paused near the top to wring out the legs of her jumpsuit as best she could, feeling shaky, cold and as bloodless as Orson's corpse.

Or Yasmin's.

The grisly scene by the juke-box flashed through her mind again – so convincing, she had to remind herself it wasn't real. Yasmin was alive. She'd have woken up back in the real world, reeling from her unexpectedly shortened adventure. Part of Veronica envied her.

But a bigger part of her was relieved it had been Yasmin, not her, who'd been kicked out of the Game so early.

She glanced over her shoulder at the place where she'd fallen before Aaron had rewound time. Now she knew what it would be like to lose, she couldn't face it – the vision of the future which had raced through her mind in that moment felt like some version of hell. She *needed* this prize. For Max. For her conscience.

She approached Aaron, who was sitting on the top step with his head in his hands. He lifted his head as she drew near.

'I wish it had been me,' he said quietly. 'I hate this place.'

Veronica leaned down, a bit timidly, and squeezed his shoulder. 'Alliance – remember? For Max.'

Aaron just nodded.

'I appreciate that you're still here,' she added, straightening up again. 'Even if you don't.'

He didn't reply, his head sinking back into his hands.

She reached a landing flooded with silvery daylight, the huge arched windows framing the snow falling over the gardens and the woodland beyond. The stained-glass window, round and rose-shaped, cast muted colours on the wall where a clock hung slightly off-centre. The second hand wasn't ticking and a thin crack snaked across the face.

It was a relief to see the daylight – even if it was all a digital illusion, shrouded in snow and coloured glass.

Veronica let her eyes roam around the small landing, which led off into two corridors with high curved ceilings and colourful hanging light fixtures, one on either side. The left-hand corridor had a dirty window at the end, barely penetrating the shadows of the long thin space. At the end of the right-hand corridor was a larger, full-sized window next to a glass-panelled door painted with a single golden word: STAIRS. More light filtered through the panel in the door, suggesting another window beyond. A more discreet staircase then led up to the next floor.

Charlie had collapsed on the worn carpet beneath the rose window on the landing, head on her knees, her chest heaving. Nate was wandering around again, frowning as he examined the walls, stopping to peer at a large oil painting of another house, set by a lake and shadowed by trees. Veronica felt her pulse quicken. The house in the painting was a bit like the one from Hide and Seek, the setting she'd played with Em. Ivy crawled up the walls and faint lights shone in the windows.

But didn't all old country houses sort of look the same anyway? She pushed the thought away.

She suddenly remembered there had been another person down on the ground floor – Angel. Where were they now? Were they OK? And would they return, like they had before, if Veronica called for help?

Veronica turned back to the banister – the only thing standing between her and the snowy darkness below. 'Angel?' Veronica called into the blackness of the floor beneath. 'Angel!' But their guide didn't appear.

What were they supposed to do now? Carry on playing? Was Angel in danger, were *they* in danger, or was this all how it was supposed to be, in spite of what Angel had said – a murder mystery in which the killer was still out to kill?

The story construction was pretty standard, Veronica thought. And the second murder had certainly upped the stakes. Could the players find the murderer before the murderer found their next victim?

Veronica heard a stifled sob and glanced over at Charlie, feeling her chest tighten as she realised the other girl was, in all likelihood, suffering from a full-blown panic attack. She was clutching the trainers she'd slipped from Yasmin's feet tightly to her chest and breathing super fast, short hiccupy gasps interrupting her inhalations.

Charlie and Yasmin had been close – as close as two people who'd never met in real life could be, Veronica thought. So, she felt for her on some level; even though Yasmin wasn't really dead, the scene had been shockingly realistic. The trouble was, Charlie was the kind of girl who scared Veronica. Yasmin had resembled Em, physically – and aspects of her character had echoed the Em that Veronica had once liked. But Charlie, she reminded her of Em after she'd changed, when she'd started caring about what she wore, learned contouring, woken at six thirty in the morning to curl her hair, kept her words sharp and her expression cold. Perfectly groomed. Perfectly cruel, when she wanted to be.

But Veronica had to remember: Charlie *wasn't* Em.

'Hey … Charlie,' she said gently, approaching Charlie and crouching down beside her.

'Fuck off,' the other girl muttered – though her obvious breathlessness stole the sting from the words. 'I'm fine. This is fine.'

'It's not fine.' Veronica forced herself to continue. 'Listen … I'm sorry about what happened down there. I shouldn't have blown up like that when you were only trying to help me up.'

Charlie sniffed, her breathing slowing. 'Yeah, you fucking shouldn't have,' she said, though her voice lacked the bite of her words.

'I don't really have an excuse. I was in a weird place mentally after finding Yasmin. And there's … some other stuff.' Veronica swallowed, her throat suddenly dry.

'Yeah, well. Same.' Charlie remained hunched over, though her back stopped quivering. 'Weird place. Stuff.'

'Down there … you said you really needed this. You mean, the prize?'

Charlie's shoulders visibly tensed. 'Yeah. I'm not going to tell you, because it's private, but all that stuff about spending the prize money on a big mansion with a cinema … that was kind of bullshit. You know, everyone's got their own "other stuff" going on. Even people who look as goddamn put-together as me.'

Veronica nodded, slowly, even though Charlie couldn't see her. 'You're right. So … can you forgive me?'

After a pause, Charlie said, 'I guess. And I guess I'm sorry I slapped you when we first met. That probably didn't help.' She was breathing easier now – and when she lifted her head, Veronica saw how tears had streaked through her make-up. Her vulnerability helped Veronica feel a little stronger.

'No, it didn't,' Veronica said gently, with a slight smile.

Charlie snorted. 'Right, well I'm sorry I did it. I was trying to be straight-talking. Focus you. Stop you from panicking. I like to think I'm such a bad-ass and it kind of … backfires sometimes.'

'Apology accepted.' Veronica offered Charlie a hand to help her up. Charlie allowed herself to be pulled to her feet.

'This doesn't mean we're friends, OK? I still don't like you. I mean, I don't like either of these other fuckers either. I only really liked Yasmin.'

For the first time, Veronica recognised Charlie's aggression for what it really was: weakness. Doubt. Fear. Realising this made her feel calmer. 'That's OK, you don't need to like us. We just need to trust each other enough to get out of here.'

Charlie exhaled long and slow. 'This whole thing is so

messed up,' she said, starting to remove her platform boots. But she stopped. 'You really think the Game's gone wrong?' she asked suddenly. 'Or could this be part of it?'

'I was wondering the same. I mean, what if Yasmin getting killed, then Angel saying it's not part of the Game is, well, part of the Game,' Veronica said.

'I mean, it definitely makes things exciting, doesn't it?' Charlie said. Her hands dropped away from her boot and she picked up the trainers, her expression serious. 'Huge plot twist,' she said in a quiet voice. 'The murderer is not only still in the house, they're still killing. Suddenly, there's even more at stake than we thought. Any of us could be removed from the Game next.'

'Exactly,' Veronica said, pleased Charlie was echoing her own thoughts.

'Here,' Charlie said, thrusting the trainers towards Veronica. 'These are too big for me.'

Veronica blinked. 'Really?' The trainers were a valuable asset – if Charlie truly cared about winning above all else, as she claimed, surely she would put up with shoes a size or two too large? Veronica guessed the truth: she felt weird about how she'd removed the shoes from Yasmin's avatar. Charlie definitely wasn't as tough as she acted.

'Yeah. Besides, they don't even go with my outfit,' Charlie said. 'And you don't have shoes, so ...' She stood up.

Veronica slid her bare feet into the trainers. They were a little snug, but they fit OK. 'Thanks.'

Veronica looked up to see Aaron approaching, smoothing down his jacket, running a hand through his hair again. He was shy. Veronica wouldn't have noticed the signs before, when he'd appeared so aloof and standoffish, but she did now.

'But I've been thinking,' he said. 'About this all being part of the Game. Angel seemed genuinely surprised ...' He frowned.

Charlie raised an eyebrow. 'Ever heard of, like, acting?'

'Hey ... where's Nate?' Veronica asked quietly.

The others were silent. Nate wasn't on the landing and he wasn't down either of the corridors.

'Fuck,' Charlie said. 'And he's the one with the damn phone. Let's look for him.'

'Wait,' Veronica said, her heart hammering. 'While he's not here ...' She glanced around, double-checking, then lowered her voice. She felt nervous, like she was betraying Nate, but the words rushed out of her even so. 'What's he been doing, sneaking around this whole time? It's like he's not even interested in the Game. Don't you think he's been up to something?'

'Yeah ... Where did he go just before Yasmin was found dead?' Aaron asked quietly. The question felt genuine, but nobody answered. He continued. 'When I walked into the juke-box room, Nate was already there – he was shaking your shoulder, Veronica. And Charlie arrived after me.'

'Shit … Now you mention it,' said Charlie, 'have you guys seen him looking down at something every now and then? If I didn't know better, I'd have said it was a smartphone.'

Makes more sense than a wallet, Veronica thought, the back of her neck tingling. 'So what we're saying,' she said, 'is that this could be part of the Game. But also that we need to find out what Nate's up to.' She met both of their eyes in turn. 'Just because Nate's been acting suspicious, doesn't mean he's the murderer though.'

There was a pregnant silence – then, suddenly, a loud bang rang through the landing. Another. Then, the door closest to them in the corridor leading to the staircase swung open.

'Almost got locked in there,' Nate said, as he stepped out. 'The door's super stiff – it's like this place has been uninhabited for—'

Aaron had marched forward and grabbed Nate's arm.

'Where did you go?' he said, his voice cold.

Nate's hands were empty, but Veronica couldn't help noticing how the pocket of his E.T. hoody drooped suspiciously.

'What? What the hell, man?' Nate tried to wriggle out of Aaron's grasp – but although they were a similar height,

Aaron was clearly stronger. 'Let go of me. I was checking out that room while you guys were busy talking. Don't you know we're on the clock – or do you want to go through the whole floor-turns-to-snow thing again? I was going to tell you if I found anything, but as it happens—'

'What's that in your pocket?' Aaron interrupted, his voice deadpan, his eyes fixed on Nate's hoody pocket.

'Nothing. Just that big dumb phone.'

'I can literally see the dumb phone in its holster, Nate,' Charlie said, peering at the rectangular lump at his hip.

'Let me go now. I'm warning you.' Something in Nate's voice – something suddenly older, meaner – convinced Aaron to let go. But he still stood close, half a step behind him, blocking off his exit down the corridor with the stairs leading up at the end.

Veronica stepped closer. 'Nate, we've seen you looking at something else. Something smaller – all three of us saw it. And you haven't been focused on the Game at all. You need to come clean – what's going on?'

'I …' Nate shook his head slowly. 'Guys, you're fixating on the wrong thing. We need to keep our minds on the Game.'

'Seriously, don't insult our intelligence,' Charlie said. 'How are we supposed to focus on the Game when one of our so-called team might be the one who killed Yasmin?'

'What?' Nate looked genuinely shocked.

'None of us can pinpoint where you were when Yasmin …' Aaron trailed off again, swallowed back the word. 'So – what's the story? What are you really doing here?'

'Hey hey hey …' Nate held up his hands. 'This is crazy, guys. I definitely, one hundred per cent did not kill Yasmin, OK? This place is full of NPCs – any one of them could have done it.'

'We need to rule you out, Nate,' said Veronica. 'We're not accusing you of anything.'

Nate swallowed, his eyes unsteady, but he didn't reply.

'Angel said Yasmin's murder wasn't supposed to happen,' Aaron said. 'They said it *wasn't* part of the Game. And I know we can't be sure, they could've been lying, but I trust them on this one. It feels different. Like something's gone wrong.'

'You trust Angel?' Nate smirked in disbelief. 'A complete stranger who shows up on the dark web claiming to be some kind of guide? The fact they *looked* shocked doesn't tell us anything.'

Charlie cocked her head. 'I'm with you on this one, Nate,' she said. 'V is too.'

They were losing sight of the issue. 'What's in your pocket?' Veronica asked again. 'Just come clean. We're not going to drop it. Even if you didn't kill Yasmin, we need to understand what's going on.'

Nate hesitated, sighed. 'Fine. Call your brute off me though, OK?'

Aaron's jaw tightened but, not waiting for Veronica to offer a signal, he stepped back slightly.

Nate reached into his hoody pocket and pulled out a smartphone. So, Charlie *had* been right.

'What the hell? How did you get that in here?' Charlie demanded. 'That's hardly fucking consistent with 1989.'

'Look, I need you to just listen while I explain, OK?' Nate's voice was suddenly different again, Veronica thought – harder. 'This is serious. And I'm going to be in a hell of a lot of trouble for telling you when I get out – but it's the only way to prove I didn't hurt Yasmin. '

Veronica shot Charlie and Aaron a glance. All three nodded in agreement. 'We won't interrupt,' said Veronica. 'Go ahead. Explain yourself.'

'Unlike you guys, I didn't come here by accident. I'm here on purpose.'

'What? How—' Charlie started.

'You said you wouldn't interrupt,' Nate said flatly.

Veronica nodded. 'Go on.'

'The Game is all sorts of illegal,' Nate continued. 'It draws people in without their consent and offers them insane and untraceable cash prizes. That's not OK. In short, I'm here to find out who's behind this and how I can take them down. I can't tell you more than that without putting myself in danger.'

The three other players stared at him dumbly.

'Who do you work for?' asked Aaron eventually.

'I'm not going to be able to tell you that. But I'm not with the police, if that's what you're asking.'

Veronica thought for a moment. 'Rival gaming companies then? Or some kind of national intelligence agency?'

Nate fixed his eyes on Veronica's. 'I can't tell you. That's a red line for me.'

'How did you get that in here?' Aaron asked, nodding towards the smartphone. 'Does it work? Can you get us out?'

'Yes, it works. And, no, I can't get us out. I was able to code this device into my avatar. It enables me to communicate with my real-world associates via the phone, yes – even send them images and soundbites. But I can't get us out of here. The only way out for any of us is to finish the Game.'

'Or get killed,' added Charlie shakily.

'Let's ... just try and stay alive for now,' Nate said. 'I don't know what Yasmin's murder means for us. I haven't seen this happen before.'

Veronica blinked. 'Wait ... you've played the Game before?'

'This isn't my first rodeo. In fact, this is my third time through. And before you ask, the mystery's different every time. Different time periods. Different settings. Different pieces of the puzzle. Even a different "moderator" each time – always called Angel though. And there's always a murder.' He glanced over at the rose window, which was starting to fill up. 'Never more. Never a player.'

Everyone was silent as they contemplated this new information.

'Maybe it's an upgrade,' Charlie said. 'The Game 2.0. It's been out for a while – perhaps they just wanted to shake things up.'

'Or do you think whoever's running the Game is on to you?' Veronica suggested, her voice fast. 'Maybe that would explain it – and the glitch …'

'When everything went all horror movie for a second,' Charlie said, 'the NPCs turning into zombies and the rooms all trashed? You guys saw that?'

'Yeah, we saw it,' Aaron said. 'So, Nate … could this all be your fault?' His voice was barbed.

Nate's jaw twitched. But after a moment of consideration, he shook his head. 'I don't know. Our system is pretty airtight. It's not happened before – why now?'

But Veronica clung to the idea, pushing Em from her mind. *Not Em. Nate.* Nate's meddling was responsible for the glitch. For Yasmin's murder – her *avatar's* murder. But Charlie was peering at her closely.

'Before, you said you were in a weird place mentally after finding Yasmin – and you mentioned "other stuff" too.' She air quoted the phrase. 'What did you mean by that?'

Veronica swallowed. 'A couple of years ago, my sister died … during a VR game.'

'Oh … shit,' Charlie said.

'But there's more. I … keep seeing her. In the Game.' She swallowed again, her throat madly dry. 'Has anyone else seen anybody here who just … doesn't belong?'

Aaron's body tensed slightly, but he didn't reply. Charlie shook her head, her expression worried. Nate spoke first.

'That's rough. I'm sorry, Veronica. I'm guessing the old headset doesn't help either. The brain can do powerful things – play tricks. But no, I haven't seen anyone else who doesn't look like they're part of the Game.'

Veronica allowed her shoulders to relax slightly. The headset. OK, yeah. What if the headset was interacting in some weird way with her subconscious? Em was playing on her mind because she was in VR for the first time since she'd died. Perhaps it was natural for her brain to conjure these frightening visions. If no one else had seen Em, she couldn't exist here in any place other than Veronica's mind.

'Besides,' Nate continued, 'there's the strong possibility that any mysterious, ghostly figure could simply be part of the Game. Remember the tale of the maid trapped in a secret passage when the old house burned down?'

Veronica nodded, surprised Nate had been listening after all when Rita told them the story. 'You could be right.'

Then, Nate glanced at the windows. Veronica followed his gaze. They'd wasted too much time talking – the thin arched glass was nearly a quarter full already.

'We need to get moving,' said Nate. 'You good, Veronica?'

'I'm OK. Yeah. Thanks, Nate,' Veronica said. She met his eyes, smiled gratefully. He returned the smile, confident and collected as ever.

'So … what do we do now?' Aaron asked.

Veronica stalked over to the banister and scanned the ground floor, feeling nauseous when her eyes met the impossibility of a twilit snowy interior, dim daylight falling from the first floor. 'I think we should just keep on playing,' she said. 'Keep trying to figure out what happened to Orson Coleman.' She turned to face the others, Charlie's pale face standing out against the dimming corridors like a sliver of bare bone. 'Something's gone wrong with the Game, but we were told the only way out was through. Surely that still stands.'

Charlie cursed under her breath but nodded. 'Maybe we should split up and search?' she suggested. 'For efficiency?' Her voice trembled.

'No,' Nate insisted. 'This time, we stick together. After what happened to Yasmin, it's the best chance we've got. Safety in numbers. Let's go. This way first, so we finish up by the staircase.' He stalked towards the corridor with the window at the end, Charlie close behind.

Veronica was about to follow when she felt the floor beneath her lurch and shudder. Her stomach twisted, pulse raced. She wondered if it was her headset – another faint? – But when Charlie dropped to her hands and knees, eyes widening in fear, she realised whatever was happening to her was affecting everyone else too.

The building continued to shake, a roaring sound filling the hall. Veronica was flung into the banister, winding herself, and found herself bent over it, staring into the darkness below. A figure floated there in the shadows. Suspended prone in the air, just as she had been in the lake – just as Orson had floated in the fountain. Except now, she was lifting her head.

Em.

Veronica felt a tugging ache in her throat, but when she blinked, the figure disappeared.

It's in my mind. All in my mind.

'What's happening?' Aaron shouted, clutching on to the banister where Orson must've fallen as the building rocked, a long diagonal crack appearing in the plaster between the windows.

Veronica watched in horror as a brown finger pushed its way through the wall … no, not a finger. A plant.

Leathery leaves of ivy sprouted from the slender brown spine, sending miniature chills down Veronica's spine, one after the other.

But as quickly as it had started, the shuddering settled and everything was still and silent again but for a plume of dust falling from the ceiling.

Veronica gazed around at the others.

'What the fuck?' Charlie looked at Nate, then at Veronica, as if expecting one of them to supply an explanation.

Veronica walked towards the crack that had just appeared, pressed a quivering finger against the new growth.

'Has this happened before?' Aaron asked Nate. He sounded shaken, but not as shaken as Charlie.

'No,' Nate said. 'None of this has. It's like the Game is literally breaking apart.'

But Veronica was only half listening, memories rising in her mind. Memories of the Hide and Seek mansion, spooky and abandoned, where she and Em had played their last, deadly game. A mansion covered in thick, glossy ivy.

It's not one game breaking apart, she thought with suddenly clarity. *It's two games, coming together.*

9

'There's something different about this floor,' said Nate, as they headed down the corridor with the small window at the end. 'Even before the quake, I mean. The wallpaper's peeling. And the carpet looks years old. Downstairs everything was tasteless but brand new.'

'Tasteless? I kind of liked it,' said Charlie, peering round the corridor with the aviator glasses perched on her nose. 'Reminded me of my dad's house.'

Veronica's eyes widened. Exactly how rich was Charlie's family? But Nate was right. She had the strangest sensation that something was off-kilter, that they'd been knocked forward or sideways into a different time and place.

'What's it been like before, Nate?' she asked.

Nate paused thoughtfully outside the single door on the

left side of the corridor. 'There's always been snow and a murder mystery, but the houses, characters and time periods are different. The last one was a classic 1920s affair. The one before was set during the 1950s. The décor has always been consistent to the setting and time period throughout, and there haven't been any earthquakes … or gamequakes.' He reached out and turned the handle cautiously.

The door opened into what had once been an opulent master bedroom. A huge round bed dominated the space. A geometric chaise longue upholstered in red velvet stood guard outside a mirrored dressing room. The dressing table yawned across a whole wall in shades of white and gold – and an enormous pair of double doors led out on to a balcony filling up with snow. On the left, an arched doorway led into an ostentatious pink en suite with a round sunken bath, gold taps and a fluffy green carpet.

On the wall over the bed was a huge portrait of a handsome man in a shiny tuxedo. Veronica recognised him instantly as Orson Coleman. Standing next to and slightly behind him with one hand resting on his shoulder was a beautiful, tall white woman with blonde hair and a cream dress.

'You think this was Orson and Grace's room?' Veronica asked, staring at the picture.

'Probably,' said Nate.

'Having a fuck-off portrait of yourself in your own room is a total power move,' said Charlie, with a note of admiration. 'But, like, what the hell happened here? It's trashed.'

Charlie was right. But it wasn't *just* trashed; it was like the room hadn't been occupied in *years*, rather than just for one night. This was more than the neglect and shabbiness of the corridor; this was destruction. The four players stared speechless at the wreckage. The bed was dishevelled and covered in a layer of dust. The chaise longue was ripped, innards of white foam spilling out – and the dressing-table mirror had shattered. All the drawers in the room had been opened, with stuff spilt out everywhere: expensive-looking but cracked bottles of cologne, underwear, even papers. There was hardly room to walk on the floor.

Veronica remembered the split second downstairs, in the kitchen, when the Game had glitched. The NPCs had aged years, the cupboards had been hanging off their hinges and the whole place had been covered in cobwebs. Maybe that's what had happened up here, except permanently. The conviction hardened in her mind.

The Game wasn't right.

Beside her, Aaron was nudging at a pile of old clothes with his shoe, frowning.

'I think this has turned into a cold case,' Veronica said quietly.

'Yeah, this feels totally different.' Charlie was searching through the detritus, her glasses pressed up on her nose. 'But I guess we carry on looking?'

'There's no other way out,' Nate said grimly. 'One clue. One piece of information. That's all we need.'

Aaron jumped as a mouse shot out from under the clothes, tearing its way across the floor and out into the corridor.

Veronica felt cold. There had been mice in Hide and Seek too. A trick by the game, designed to make it harder to hide, to stay quiet. She picked her way carefully across the room and into the en suite. She scanned the dead plants on the bathroom windowsill. The carpet had a damp, mouldy feel under Yasmin's trainers. She edged around the shards of glass from a smashed mirror above the sink.

Something moved in one of the broken fragments on the floor and Veronica glanced up, her heart suddenly hammering in her ears. She crouched down, picked up the largest shard carefully. Her own eye stared back at her. She was about to chalk it down to exhaustion when a shape sped across the glass. Her heart was pounding. She peered closer, shifting the piece of mirror to the right to glimpse the shadow now behind her.

She froze as the shard caught the bottom half of the reflection.

Someone was standing in the tub, behind the mouldy white curtain on its curved golden rail. The outline of a body.

She spun around, yanked the curtain to one side in one panic-fuelled movement.

No one. And yet ... goosebumps prickled over her flesh.

'Are you here?' she whispered.

The sounds of the others sifting through the trashed bedroom faded – instead, her heart hammered in her ears, a quickening baseline, a soprano *drip-drip-drip* laid over. What was dripping? The taps were dry and rusted.

Slowly, Veronica turned around and raised the sharp fragment of mirror in a trembling hand.

There. Someone really was in the bathtub. Her clothes were wet. Unmistakably, they were the clothes Em had died in, in the game. A short velvet dress. Tights tangled with pondweed. The black faux fur of her coat a mess of mud and grime. Her hair – her long, dark, beautiful hair – perfectly replicated in VR ...

Veronica tilted the mirror further. She didn't want to, but she had to see. Had to know. Emma's reflection was staring right back at her. Her face was bloodless. Her eyes burned. Veronica stifled a sob. She dropped the mirror shard and spun around.

Once again, the tub was empty.

'Everything OK?' Nate had entered the room.

Veronica jumped, stumbled away from the tub and sat down hard on a creaky wicker chair. Her eyes were fixed on the space where Em had been standing.

She swallowed. 'No.' She glanced up at him. 'Nate, she's really here.'

He frowned. 'Who?'

'Em. My stepsister.'

Nate shook his head. 'Veronica ... that's not possible. Take a deep breath.' He crouched in front of her. 'Come on. In for the count of five – hold – out for the count of eight. It always helps me.'

She breathed deep. When she spoke again, her voice was calmer. 'I saw her in the mirror. It wasn't a glimpse this time – there was nothing unclear about it.'

'I believe you. What I don't believe is that her ... spirit or whatever ... is really here.'

'You don't believe in ghosts?' Veronica said. The word sounded strange on her tongue. She didn't believe in ghosts either. Except, she was certain she had just seen one.

'I wouldn't say that, actually,' Nate said. 'But souls aren't digital, Veronica. They're made of stronger stuff. This isn't God's world. His creations ... they can't exist here.' He shook his head. 'It doesn't matter what I believe. What matters is that you need to recognise it's in your mind.'

'But I saw her,' Veronica protested.

'You didn't. I mean, you're not really seeing anything in this place – you know? It's VR. These aren't my eyes.' He pointed up at his eyes. 'This isn't really my voice, even though it sounds just like me. It's a digital reproduction – just like my body. See? It's all an illusion.'

Veronica nodded slowly.

'Besides, did this ghost actually do anything any of the times you've seen her?'

'No,' Veronica said in a small voice.

'Has anyone else said they've seen her?'

Veronica shook her head.

'See?' Nate smiled. 'Powerful brain, right? You saw her, Veronica. I believe that. But she's not really here.'

Veronica let out a sigh. 'OK. Powerful brain.'

Nate offered her his hand. 'Hey, I only came in here because Aaron was driving me insane … but, really, we should move on.'

She accepted his hand and he pulled her up. 'You don't like him much, do you?'

'Aaron?' Nate scratched his head. 'Yeah … no. Can't say I do. He's a bit of a … well … a spoilt brat, isn't he? Sorry.' He shot her a sheepish smile. 'I know you … like him.'

Veronica felt her cheeks colour. 'I don't—'

'It's OK,' Nate interrupted. 'He just … kind of has everything I want in life, and he's not grateful at all. Like, if my mom were around, if my family had that kind of financial security ... Man, sorry, you didn't ask for my sob story.'

Veronica smiled, but she privately wondered why – if Nate was working for a gaming company, or a security agency – he was worried about money. 'Aaron ... he's OK. Honestly,' she said. 'I know what you mean, but he's not as much of a brat as you think. I mean, there's a reason why he doesn't want to be here ...' She wished she could tell Nate the story about Aaron's friend – but it wasn't her place.

'Huh. Well, for you, I'll take it under advisement.' Nate started to turn, but Veronica jumped in again, urgency quickening her voice. She had to ask.

'So ... you're really here *just* to investigate who's behind the Game?'

Nate's eyes flickered. 'There's a pretty big payout for me if I succeed.'

'Bigger than the prize?'

Nate's smile tugged to one side, as if he was a little disappointed.

'I'm asking because I want to trust you,' Veronica explained.

'Look, I want to win as much as the next player. But what I told you is true. I'm here for the truth ... and to hold whoever runs this thing to account.'

He turned away.

'Nate?'

'What's up?' Annoyance tinged his voice now – but there was one last thing Veronica had to ask him, while they were alone.

'Can you … with your phone … can you find out if my brother's OK?'

He hesitated. 'I mean—'

'Max Moretti.' She rattled off the name of the hospital. 'He's in the children's ward. Please. It's life-and-death stuff, or I wouldn't ask.'

His eyes softened. 'I can't promise anything,' he said, but he was already drawing the phone from his back pocket.

'Thanks, Nate. I mean – really. Thank you.'

Veronica felt a small coil of relief unravel in her belly. But before Nate had a chance to place a call or send a message, Aaron's voice called out urgently.

'Guys, come over here. There's another room.'

Nate slid his phone back into his pocket as he and Veronica headed back into the main room. A door Veronica hadn't noticed before – concealed behind a set of shelves beside the bed – was wide open. Charlie was standing by the door, peering up a narrow spiral staircase – she led the way up. At the top was a small round room – surprisingly cosy compared to the rest of the house – with a curved glass desk arranged in front of the large windows. On the desk was a stack of dusty paper, a fountain pen, four or five dead bluebottles and an electric typewriter with a cracked display. Aaron was standing over a wastepaper basket beside the desk full of screwed-up balls of paper.

'How did you find the door to this place?' Veronica said, a note of admiration in her voice.

'Aaron was pulling books off the shelves to read the blurbs,' Charlie supplied, rolling her eyes. 'One of them must've triggered the door mechanism. Dumb luck.'

Aaron didn't protest – he was too busy peering at the couple of sheets he'd pulled from the bin and attempted to smooth out. 'They're letters,' he said. 'Well, the beginnings of letters.'

'What do they say?' Nate asked, leaning against the doorframe.

Aaron read aloud: '*Dear Grace, I don't deserve you* … Then it stops. And then this one starts, *Dear Grace, Things have been really tough* …' He peered at a couple of others. 'These ones are virtually illegible. I can see *you've done so much for me* and *I could never forgive myself*, but if he elaborated on why, it's unreadable now. Like he went crazy with the pen trying to cross out whatever he'd written.'

'Seems like Liz was right,' said Veronica. 'He really was planning to leave his wife.' The letter fragments reminded her of what her dad had said to her mum, before she left.

'*Deep down, I think we've known things weren't right for a long time.*' As if him cheating on her with Nyra had been somehow inevitable. As if he was being the mature one.

No wonder Mum had run away and never looked back.

'Unless there's something more to it,' said Aaron. '*You've done so much for me* … all that talk of forgiveness and not deserving her …'

'Because of his affair with Liz?' Nate questioned.

Charlie sighed impatiently, shifting her axe from one hand to the other. 'Whatever. We should press on. That might be a clue, but it's not glowing like the letter we found on the body did, so it's not the clue we need. And remember what Angel said? Some of this shit could lead us astray.'

The bedroom on the other side of the corridor must've belonged to Mrs Anne Coleman – another enormous space, this one decorated more traditionally with a lot of chintz but equally trashed and abandoned. Wind rattled the windows, sending the snow spinning outside.

Veronica passed through the door next to Mrs Coleman's bedroom, which opened into a bathroom with enough space for not only a roll-top bath but an actual sofa, mildewed and faded, and a library of books so mouldy Veronica could barely read the titles – the ghost of *Misery* by Steven King whispered from one of the spines.

As she peered up at the top shelf, she noticed a small crack near the ceiling start to creep down the wall like a strand of hair growing in fast-forward.

When they'd carried Em's body from the arcade on a stretcher to the waiting ambulance, Veronica had watched its progress when no one was watching her. The stretcher had unbalanced as they'd tried to slide it into the ambulance and strands of Em's dark hair had slipped out, as stark as an accusation.

Veronica was jolted out of the memory when the floor started to shake.

'Get down!' Nate shouted.

Another quake, Veronica thought. Then, a hand tugged her to the floor. She dropped to her knees beside Nate, watched another crack race up the wall, a blast of cold air snaking round her body. The quake was bigger this time – Charlie, despite clutching on to the sink, fell hard as the building lurched, and Veronica noticed how something fell out of Charlie's pocket and landed in front of Aaron, who'd crouched low and was sheltering against the tub.

But she couldn't see what it was. Couldn't even wonder. Dread, nausea and confusion converged upon her. She clawed her fingers into the floor, emptiness spiralling through her stomach as the whole world felt like it was disappearing.

She lifted her eyes. Ivy had pushed its way through the cracks again. She heard the sloshing of liquid – glanced in the tub to see the grubby porcelain full of water so dark it was nearly black. Waves churned on its surface, as if something was thrashing beneath. As she watched, wide-eyed, a mouse raced across the roll of the tub, scrambled to the floor and disappeared into one of the cracks.

Then, a face. A face pressed on the underside of the water, streaked with darkness.

Em's face.

Veronica shut her eyes. *It's all in my head. All in my head.*

Her hands were still burrowing into the old, damp carpet like claws when the quake stopped. When Veronica opened her eyes, the tub was empty again. She felt like she hadn't been breathing – but now, air was snaking into her lungs, slow and cold.

She lifted her eyes as Nate did, kneeling opposite her, the crumbled dust of fallen plaster greying his hoody.

'Is everyone OK?' Veronica said quietly, her voice trembling as she stood up. 'That was … worse than last time.'

'Sure, I'm great,' said Charlie, her eyes fiery. 'Thought I'd got the golden fucking ticket, but now Wonka's shitshow of a factory is literally falling apart around me. Anyone know what happens if this whole thing breaks apart with us still in it? Are we gonna get jolted out? I knew someone whose cousin got seriously messed up by that. Literal PTSD. Someone said you could die from a jolt.'

Aaron cleared his throat. He'd been quiet since the quake, his eyes wide.

'Aaron, are you OK?' Veronica asked.

'I saw her,' he said. 'Before, in the first quake. And just now. In the tub.' He shut his eyes for a moment. 'I didn't want to believe it the first time. I thought it could've been a mistake. But now ...'

Veronica's whole body tensed. 'You ... saw Em?'

'Long dark hair. Brown skin. Dark eyes. Right?' His voice was barely a whisper.

She nodded.

'I believe you, Veronica. She's here.'

Silence fell over the group.

'Are we saying,' started Charlie in a quavering voice, 'that Veronica's goddamn dead sister has followed her in here and turned this whole thing into a literal horror story?'

'That's not possible,' Nate said, his voice calm. 'That whole theory is just rumours and speculation.'

'There's a *theory*?' Veronica said. He'd acted, before, as if it wasn't even a thing.

Charlie turned on him, dropped her voice to something

close to a whisper. 'OK, smart-arse. So explain to me: how are we here now? We've been uploaded, right? Our actual consciousness, our sense of self – we're here. We even have real-feeling bodies. As far as we're aware, the other world, the *real* world, doesn't exist right now. So doesn't it make sense that when people die in VR, like *really* die, they're … well, kind of trapped?'

'Doesn't that mean Yasmin could be a ghost here too?' Aaron said.

Charlie's face hardened. 'Well no, doofus, because she's not *really* dead. And don't bloody interrupt me, OK? Can't you respect a flow when you see one?'

Veronica's heart was hammering. Nate opened his mouth, but no words followed.

Charlie's voice grew louder and more confident as she got back into her stride. 'Yeah, anyway, it kind of makes sense, right? Charlie isn't as much of a bloody idiot as you thought. VR doesn't work like the real world. Your code doesn't just get erased, you don't get buried and rot and disappear into the great expanse of the fucking universe. Like, a VR game still recognises you as a player – your code is there until you actually leave the Game. A part of you, then, lives on here – even if your body's dead and buried out there. It's like … like the detritus of social media accounts from dead people left on the internet long after they're dust. Get it? Except more.

Realer. I'm talking about actual motherfucking digital ghosts.'

'So, Em … she's really here?' Veronica said.

'Well, if Aaron's seen her too, she isn't just in your mind, is she?' Charlie glared at Nate as if daring him to challenge her.

He lifted his chin. 'I think what we all need to remember is that a haunting could totally be part of the Game. Remember the tale of the trapped maid? Glimpses of a ghostly figure with dark hair, dark eyes … You can see how Veronica could interpret it as her sister. But that isn't necessarily true.'

But as he spoke, Veronica noticed something else: Aaron's eyes weren't fixed on Charlie's face any more. Instead, he was staring hard at the item that had fallen from her pocket during the quake. A piece of paper, crumpled and folded but printed with stark courier-font writing. Belatedly, Charlie followed Veronica's gaze. Her own eyes widened and she lunged forward to scoop up the paper.

But Aaron was closer – he picked it up, Charlie's fingers missing it by inches.

'Is this the clue?' he said, his voice icy.

'I—' Charlie's skin had turned pink. She tried to snatch it back, but Aaron held it high, far out of her reach. He turned his back to Charlie, unfolded the paper.

'What is it?' Veronica asked.

'A bill for a psychotherapist appointment in London,' Aaron said. 'Addressed to Mrs Orson Coleman.'

'Orson's wife, Grace,' said Veronica quietly. Indignance overwhelmed her. 'Why didn't you tell us, Charlie?'

'I was going to,' she blurted, her hands clenched into fists at her side. 'I just—'

'You weren't going to.' Aaron cut her off, his voice icy. 'This whole thing is bullshit. Why are we even pretending to be a team when every person here is playing for themselves?'

Veronica's heart twisted. She had thought she and Aaron were a team, even if they didn't trust the others.

'You don't get it. I really need that prize,' Charlie said, her voice breaking. She slumped down on the carpeted step leading up to the tub. 'Daddy's in trouble.'

Aaron laughed sharply. 'Oh, Daddy's going to have to take away your state-of-the-art gaming console?'

'He might go to prison,' Charlie said flatly. 'This prize money would be enough to bail him out. I need it.'

'So your dad's a white-collar criminal scumbag, and you think he deserves this money? Veronica's brother is going to *die*,' Aaron countered, his voice cold with rage as his finger pointed in Veronica's direction emphatically. 'But you're too fucking self-absorbed to care.'

Veronica felt her hands shake. Hearing it like that, blunt

and loud and used as a weapon, felt like the worst thing in the world.

'Oh … I knew he was in hospital, but …' Charlie's eyes lifted to meet Veronica's but then slid away, down and to the left. Like most people, she didn't know how to react when she heard Veronica's brother was dying. Unlike most people, she didn't cover up her discomfort with empty platitudes.

'Don't use my brother like that,' Veronica said to Aaron, her voice trembling. 'Don't think it's your right to tell people. I told you in confidence!'

Aaron's face fell as he lowered his arm. 'I just thought … I thought—'

'You can't do that,' Veronica said, her voice warming as she stepped closer to him, her heart pounding for all the wrong reasons, heat coursing through her veins. 'You can't use stuff you were told in private, important stuff, to win an argument. That's selfish. Childish.' She thought back to how he'd pounded at the front door – how he'd sat there and refused to play when he hadn't got his way. 'You can't just have everything you want, Aaron, without caring about who you're hurting. Nate was right. You're just a spoilt brat.' Her cheeks flushed with heat when she realised what she'd said.

There was an uncomfortable silence. Then, Nate shrugged. 'I'm not going to deny I said that. Anyway, it's true.'

Aaron's jaw clenched in determination as his eyes darted between Nate and Veronica. 'Selfish. Childish. Spoilt brat. It's great to know what both of you really think of me.'

Veronica felt the anger drain from her body. 'I shouldn't have …'

Aaron dropped the letter on the floor between them. 'Forget it. I'm done with this. I never wanted to be here. I've got no interest in this dumb mystery or anything except getting out of here as soon as possible.' He turned away, started towards the bathroom door.

'What the hell?' Veronica said, starting to panic. 'Don't just walk away! Sure, Charlie shouldn't have hidden the letter, and I shouldn't have said those things, but it's done now. I'm sorry. We can get past it. We *have* to get through this together.'

'What do you care?' he asked in a quieter tone, his back facing them. 'Took you about five seconds to turn on me. You're just the same as everyone else.'

Her heart lurched.

Aaron continued. 'And you're the one who persuaded me to trust you all, to believe I couldn't get out of this alone. But all of this proves that I'm the only person I can trust.'

'Don't do this, Aaron,' Nate said, stepping in front of him. 'You're in danger out there, on your own. Trust me.'

'I don't.' Aaron pushed past him, sending Nate staggering

against the mouldy sofa. He turned at the doorway, though kept his eyes downcast. 'It's just a game and it's not like I'm quitting this time. If I get killed like Yasmin, then at least I'm out of here. I just want to get through it alone. Don't follow me.' And with that, he stormed out of the bathroom.

Veronica listened to his footsteps fade away.

She was hurt that he'd left. Guilty that she'd snapped at him – but mostly absolutely frozen in disbelief that it had taken so little for him to decide not to trust her.

The round bathroom window was a little less than half full of snow and she knew they had to continue to play. But she stood there, staring at the bizarre glossy green ivy in the cracks of the wall. She walked over to the window, not wanting Charlie and Nate to see the sting in her eyes.

'I feel like a piece of shit,' Charlie muttered, breaking the silence.

'You don't need to feel like a piece of shit for me,' Veronica said, continuing to stare out of the window. 'You didn't know about Max. I didn't tell you.'

Charlie nodded. 'Shouldn't have hidden the clue though. Should have known that wouldn't end well. But, I was thinking ... maybe Aaron being gone isn't the worst thing in the world. I mean, he wasn't exactly pulling his weight, was he?'

Veronica shook her head. 'Let's just …' She stopped, peered out of the window. 'Hey, guys … is that …'

Charlie and Nate joined her at the window. 'A car?' Charlie said, squinting.

'A Range Rover,' Veronica added.

The green vehicle hadn't been obvious at first. It had been abandoned off-road and was half buried in snow. One of the headlights appeared to have been smashed, having collided with a tree.

'So, Grace came back after all,' said Nate. 'That's the car the gardener said she'd taken to London.'

'Holy shit. The psychiatrist's letter. Do you think she's …' unhinged?' Charlie said. 'What if she came back unexpectedly, found Orson and the cook together and fucking flipped?'

'Liz didn't say they'd been discovered …' Veronica said. Even so, she remembered what Liz had said – how Grace was proud, and she'd have been so angry if she'd ever found out …

'She might not have known.' Charlie's voice was excited. 'Grace could have seen them but stayed quiet until Orson was on his own.'

Charlie and Nate drew back from the window, Charlie chatting excitedly, but something in Veronica rooted her to the spot. She peered over the snowy window ledge and narrowed her eyes. Some distance from the crashed car was the small woods from which she and Charlie must've first emerged – she recognised it from the shape of the path, the size of the clearing. The woodshed was a dark shape between the leafless trees ... except, it wasn't exactly the woodshed any more.

The building was larger – its shape different. A peaked roof overgrown with moss and a small, decrepit jetty pointing out into a thin sliver of dark water that faded into snow. Ivy tangled over the structure like a shroud.

The boathouse.

'Are you coming?' Nate's voice.

She puffed out a long, shaky breath, turned away from the window and towards the others.

Charlie was beaming. 'I think this is it, guys. I think we've solved it. The murderer has to be Grace Coleman.'

10

Veronica, Charlie and Nate walked across the hallway, heading towards the corridor on the other side of the main staircase.

'It all makes perfect sense,' Charlie enthused. 'She drove home from her therapist early, maybe she was hoping for support and, like, quality time with her husband. No one notices her come in. It's late – midnight – and the house is asleep. Except ... not everyone is resting. She's searching. The bedroom's empty. But in the studio, she peers through the crack in the door to find Orson and the goddamn *cook* in bed together. She doesn't disturb them, not there and then. She's seething. She's been so incredibly betrayed. And she's not well anyway. She's going through therapy. She needs his support more than ever, right? Why is he doing this to her?'

'You know,' Veronica interjected quietly, 'a lot of people have therapy …'

But Charlie appeared not to hear. 'She waits in the bedroom for a while, maybe she thinks of getting ready for bed. Like, what else is she meant to do? But she starts pacing. She ends up out in the corridor again, watching and waiting. Round about here.' As they passed the rose window, Charlie picked a shadowy spot against the corridor wall and stood there, channelling her imagined version of Grace. 'She's been seething for ages, waiting for him to emerge from the studio and come to his actual bed. The longer he takes, the angrier she grows. She wants to confront him. And then, finally, he's wandering down the corridor, and he's drunk. Clutching this bottle of Dom like he's *celebrating*. Maybe he doesn't even notice her, standing there in the shadows …' Charlie lifted her axe. 'She doesn't know what she's going to do yet, but there's a feeling coming over her. A feeling she's never felt before …'

Wind had started to moan through the gaps in the building. Veronica felt cold air coil around her bare ankles above her new trainers. She shivered. She remembered what Esteban had said – how even though this house was brand new, it acted like an old house.

Nate cleared his throat. They were standing right outside the door on the left-hand side of the staircase corridor now. 'Charlie, we should—'

'So he's leaning over the banister, drunk, probably about to vom up whatever delicious meal *that woman* cooked him right into that beautiful fountain that she, Grace, so carefully picked for their entrance hall.' Charlie's face snarled. She stalked quickly towards the railing, held out the axe in a dramatic finale. 'And that's the last straw. That's when she breaks. She reaches out and pushes him. Maybe it doesn't even take that much force. It's so, so easy. Almost like it was meant to happen. For a moment – euphoria. Then … she realises what she's done.'

'And she goes … where?' Veronica said. 'She crashed the car. It's freezing out.'

'Which means,' Charlie said, wriggling her fingers spookily. 'She's still in this house. And she's not going to stop killing. Not until her mad, mad brain is satiated …' She paused. 'Fuck, am I literally the only person in this house who doesn't have a therapist? Even Yaz had one.'

'Maybe you should get on that,' Veronica murmured. 'It might help with …' She waved her hands around Charlie as a whole.

Charlie snorted.

'Are you done?' Nate said, deadpan. 'Because we really should carry on. Remember the whole snow-floor thing? Those windows aren't going to wait while you do dramatic re-enactments of every suspect.'

'Whatever. Sorry for doing all the damn work in this investigation,' Charlie huffed. 'Anyway, isn't it pretty damn clear Grace is the killer? She's not just a *suspect*.'

'That's exactly what she is,' Veronica said. 'A suspect. The evidence is all circumstantial.'

'*The evidence is all circumstantial*,' Charlie parroted, rolling her eyes.

Nate placed his hand on the door handle. 'I checked this room out earlier,' he said. 'It's just a guest bedroom, by the looks of it, so maybe we should move on. We're short of time and there's—'

'We should check it,' said Veronica. 'Just quickly. Fresh pairs of eyes, right?' she added. They'd found the important clue on this level but not the information. 'Plus, there might be an NPC hiding in there.'

Nate offered a small, disappointed smile. 'Sure, why not?'

She felt bad ... but deep down she knew Nate wasn't telling the whole truth and had no intention of doing so. She had to play this her way and make sure he wasn't hiding anything.

She glanced over at Charlie. It wasn't like Veronica could trust her either. She had been so determined to win she'd hidden a vital clue. Even after the Game had started to go wrong.

What else were they willing to do to get what they wanted?

When Nate opened the door, Veronica felt unsteady, as if a rug had been pulled from under her feet. She stumbled, leaned hard against the doorframe, feeling the way her nails dug into the beds of her hands, grounding her. She breathed deep, smelling the tang of metal and electricity as she blinked, the room shifting into focus.

'What the ...' Nate said. 'It wasn't like this before.'

The light in here was thin and white, emanating from a series of long strip bulbs naked in the ceiling, several of them hanging loose and sparking on to the rows of metal shelving units. No windows. And the dimensions of the room were all wrong. It wasn't even a room, really; it was a vast storage space, a warehouse. No way this could've fitted inside a house, even one as big as Orson Coleman's. It was warmer in here too – sweat prickling across her upper lip as she took a step inside.

Where were they?

'This ... isn't the same game,' Charlie said. Then, she struck her hand against her forehead in realisation. 'Fuck, this is the warehouse on Planet 9 from Dead Stars. Which means ...'

A low, rumbling moan emanated from somewhere in the depths of the room. Veronica shivered.

'Dead Stars is a space zombie game, right?' Nate said, his voice dry.

Veronica shuddered, glanced over her shoulder at the door, through which a sliver of corridor was visible. 'Maybe we should just—'

The lights flickered. Suddenly, as brightness returned, a figure appeared, slumped on the floor amidst the piles of twisted metal shelving and broken tech, their back half propped up against one of the large metal bars. Alabaster skin, now ashen and sickly – black hair stuck to their forehead, boiler suit ripped and torn.

'Angel!' Veronica said. She hurried forward and crouched down beside them – their eyes lifted up to meet hers, but slowly, as if it took them huge effort to do so. 'What's wrong? Are you hurt?'

The lights in the room flickered again. That moan sounded again – a little closer now, accompanied by a scuffing sound. Someone or something was walking slowly between the huge shelving units. Charlie's knuckles whitened around her axe handle.

'The Game … it's fighting against me,' Angel gasped. 'It doesn't want me here. Had to … graft this game on to reach you. We … don't have much time.'

Nate crouched down beside Veronica while Charlie remained standing, scanning the spaces between the shelves.

'There's something you need … to know,' Angel continued. 'Yasmin … she's dead.'

Veronica blinked. 'We know. We were there.'

'No, you don't understand.' Even in their injured state, Angel managed to glare up at Veronica with something like frustration. 'She's *really* dead,' they said. 'When she was killed in the Game ... she was killed in real life.'

Veronica's heart was pounding loud in her ears, her hands trembling as she lifted her hands up to her forehead. *Not again ... Not again ...*

'Yasmin is dead?' Charlie said from behind them both. She held her axe limply now, her face bloodless. Her voice sounded small and very young.

'The Game killed her,' Nate said, and his eyes were angry as he met Angel's. 'This sick little game has actually finally killed someone.'

But Angel's eyes glinted. A moan sounded somewhere very close, the sound of a few things knocked off a shelf.

Can we die in this *game too?* Veronica wondered, though her mind was spinning. She clenched and unclenched her fists, trying to keep herself present. To focus on what Angel was saying.

'Oh, it wasn't ... the Game,' they said, struggling to force their words out. 'There's no way any of the NPCs are capable of this kind of drastic, unprogrammed action.'

'*So ...*' Nate started slowly, drawing the word out until he trailed off. 'What you're saying is, it's—'

Suddenly, the groaning was right by the small group. A figure dressed in a grubby space suit with a cracked helmet burst through the crates a few paces away from Veronica. She scrambled away, horrified by the bloodstains on the figure's torso, the ripped US SPACE FORCE logo on their arm revealing a rotten wound beneath. But before she could process what was happening, Charlie was charging past her with a shriek of pure rage. The axe sunk into the figure's neck, rose, fell again hard, foul liquid splattering over the nearby shelves, Charlie's suit, the floor, even across Veronica's cheek.

It was as if Charlie was channelling every bitter ounce of her anger and grief into the attack. And she had a lot of it.

The zombie reached out for her, but Charlie ducked under its arms, swinging her axe into its torso. Finally, while it was doubled over, she severed the helmet-encased head, which dropped on to the floor. The body slumped. Charlie was left panting, clutching her gore-stained axe, her hair dishevelled, her suit awry.

'And that, my friends, is why you always pick up a weapon,' she said. Then, something appeared to crumble inside her. The realisation, perhaps, of everything Angel had revealed. 'Fuck you,' she spat at the body, her eyes brimming with tears. Then she turned to Angel. 'And fuck you too.'

'I didn't do this,' Angel said, voice trembling. 'The Game didn't either. One of you did.'

'What?' Charlie said.

'So what you're saying is,' said Nate, turning back to Angel as if nothing had happened, 'Yasmin's killer is one of us?'

'Correct. And if they get you, you'll die too,' Angel said. They searched the group suddenly with fresh eyes. 'Wait … where's Aaron?'

The lights flickered. A bunch of low, eerily familiar moans sounded from the distant reaches of the warehouse.

'He went off on his own,' Veronica said quietly, feeling her gut twist.

'That son of a bitch,' Charlie growled, tears streaming down her cheeks. She swiped at them angrily. 'He fucking did it, didn't he?'

Veronica shook her head. Surely Aaron wasn't capable of that. She looked at Nate, who had infiltrated the Game with a shadowy agenda of his own – and at Charlie, standing over the corpse of the zombie with an axe clutched in her hand. Charlie's friendship with Yasmin aside, both seemed more likely suspects than Aaron, who hadn't even wanted to play.

'You … need to get out of here,' Angel rasped. 'And so do I.'

'Will you be OK?' Veronica asked.

'I'll … be fine. It's you I'm worried about. I can't help you. The Game's screwed up … everything's off-kilter.' Their eyes flicked briefly to Nate's, then back to Veronica's. 'You have to solve the mystery of Orson's death … It's your only chance of escape. You're stuck here, in danger, until you find the answer.'

Shuffling footsteps. Flickering lights.

'Guys, I don't think I can deal with this many zombies with just an axe,' Charlie said.

Nate stood up, his jaw set.

'Wait,' Veronica said. 'How are we supposed to solve the mystery when the Game is … I don't know – different? Warped? We haven't even seen any NPCs on this floor.'

'Ah, that.' Angel sighed. 'The Game's essential structure, the clues … and information, should still be there. It's not impossible. Might … even be easier.'

The zombies sounded close now. Charlie was already backing away, towards the door, which had been left ajar.

Angel lifted a trembling hand to their forehead. 'I can't return again. Now it's up to you.'

Their petrol-blue eyes were locked on Veronica's and she found she couldn't look away – her pulse thumping through her head in a constant rhythm: *Yasmin's dead. Really dead. She's dead.*

'Goodbye,' said Angel, 'and good luck.'

Angel flickered out of existence right before Veronica's eyes, but she couldn't stop staring at where they'd been lying. Yasmin was gone – this dream, this unreality, had been her last. People really died in this place. *She* could really die. She imagined Dad and Nyra at the cemetery, standing over the graves of their three children, and found her throat aching. She hated them, sometimes. But Em's death had been punishment enough. No one could take that much grief.

As she knelt, she noticed a slim metal shape half hidden in the shadows under one of the nearby storage units. She glanced over at Charlie and Nate – but they were busy scanning the shelves for zombies, while retreating towards the door. She clasped the cool metal of the object. A gun. Futuristic but absolutely recognisable. She slipped it in her pocket as she stood up. Maybe Charlie was right about weapons.

'Come on,' hissed Nate, as the unsteady footsteps grew closer. Somewhere nearby, a bulb blew, a shower of sparks falling into darkness. Nate darted forward, his hand closed around Veronica's arm and he tugged her backwards towards the door. 'Hurry!'

Nate and Veronica staggered away exactly as three space-suited zombies shambled towards them, arms outstretched. A fourth zombie was different, its movements purposeful – a woman, once, her eyes darted around with animal intelligence. But she wasn't a woman any more. Her eyes were surrounded with black veins of rot, and when she opened her mouth to scream, a maggot wriggled on her tongue.

'It's a runner!' Charlie shouted. She flung the door open, exposing the carpeted corridor beyond. 'Fucking go!'

Veronica threw herself through the door, tripping and rolling on the dirty carpet – Nate was right behind her, helping Charlie slam the door shut and holding it while the runner flung its weight against the other side. The door splintered under its supernatural strength and the zombie's unearthly moan sounded, loud and clear through the trashed house.

'What the hell?' Charlie said. 'I thought that place was supposed to be temporary!'

Veronica pushed down her fear and scrambled to help the others pin the door shut – but by the time she'd placed her hands against the chipped paint, the zombie had fallen quiet. The game Angel had grafted on to the other side had, she suspected, finally disappeared.

'Wow. Dead Stars is much less fun without a laser gun,' Charlie said, sinking to the floor. 'And with the possibility of actual death.' Her voice broke on the last word and she hung her head, as if the weight of it was suddenly too great for her neck to support.

They were silent for what must've been about a minute, but felt like an hour. Veronica felt nothing but the darkness pressing at the insides of her skull, heard nothing but her own breath in her ears. Her hands trembled slightly when she wiped the gore from the zombie attack from her face. The weight of the gun – the *laser* gun – was heavy in her pocket. What the hell was happening here? And where was Aaron now? She gazed up at the ceiling, imagining him exploring the floor above. He'd said he wouldn't mind dying in the Game – it would be a way out, at least. But he hadn't known it would be the end of his life for real.

'I think it's safe to carry on now.' Nate straightened up. 'Not that I want to open that door to find out for sure.'

Charlie remained on the floor, her back against the door, and buried her face in her hands. 'Yasmin's actually dead,' she said. 'Shit, she's actually dead. I really fucking liked her. Only person I really liked in the whole damn world, the only person who made me better, and now she's gone.'

'I'm sorry,' Veronica said gently. 'She was … a really kind person.' She immediately cringed at how anodyne it sounded.

Nate eyed both of them carefully. 'More to the point, *who* killed her? It wasn't an NPC, so it must've been—'

'Isn't it fucking obvious?' Charlie snapped, her eyes blazing as she lifted them up to meet Nate's. 'I wouldn't kill her, since she's my friend. Veronica wouldn't, since she's a total sad sack – and besides, "kind" Yasmin was fucking nice to her. You're not even here to play the Game, so what's your beef with Yasmin? No, it had to be fucking Aaron. Don't you see?'

'But … when I arrived in the juke-box room, Aaron wasn't there,' said Nate.

Charlie appeared both angered and stumped by the statement.

Veronica's mind spun. 'Theoretically … that doesn't matter. The killer could have done the deed, left the room, then come in again once we'd all arrived, acting shocked. The fact is, we were all separated at the time. There's no hard evidence – just one person's word against another's.'

Charlie's face hardened triumphantly. 'Exactly.'

Veronica frowned. 'But what troubles me is motive. Aaron … he had no interest in the Game at all. Why would he do something like that?'

'Because he's a spoilt rich psycho, V,' Charlie said, standing up smoothly. 'Even you said it, back when he left.' She must've noticed something in Veronica's face because she scoffed. 'Yeah, sorry to burst your pitiful little crush bubble, but it's true. Remember how he reacted when he found out he couldn't leave? He kicked that door so hard I felt the building shake. He's moody and hostile and thinks he's better than everyone, even you. What? You seriously think he liked you? Have you seen the guy, V? He's a Class A jock type with movie star good looks. And have you seen your-fucking-self?' She raised her eyebrows. 'I mean, you're fine, V – it's OK to be a nerd – but you're hardly the kind of girl someone like Aaron would be interested in.'

Veronica felt a mixture of shame and anger bubble inside her. That was exactly the kind of thing Em would have said to her, towards the end. *'You've got hearing aids* and *glasses,'* her sister had said once. *'Literally nothing about you works properly.'*

Veronica shook away the memory. 'I never thought ...'

'He just wanted you to help him get out of here,' Charlie continued. 'I can totally believe he'd do this to mess with the Game, to, like, undermine everything and everyone here who cares about it and have his twisted revenge. And then he just buggers off when the shit hits the fan.'

'He wouldn't do something like that,' Veronica said, her voice shaking. Her whole body was tingling with rage.

'Oh, sure, you've known him a couple of hours and you know exactly what he would or wouldn't do.' Charlie rolled her eyes. 'Give me a break.'

'Look, I'm not a fan of Aaron,' Nate said, stepping between them, 'but even if he did do it, he didn't know Yasmin would really die, did he? We only just found that out. So, we're not saying he's a murderer. If he did it, he thought he was killing an avatar.' He let his words settle, then said, 'We haven't got time for this. We need to find the essential information from this level and move on – because I for one sure don't want a repeat of whatever happened downstairs. The snow's three-quarters of the way up the windows already.'

Veronica let out a shuddering breath.

Charlie pressed the heels of her hands to her eyes. 'OK, I guess. But if Aaron killed Yasmin, even if he didn't know she would really die, it was still a dick move. He might not have known he was killing her for real, but he took away her chance of winning – that's a big deal. Yasmin wasn't rich. And she had dreams.'

'Yeah, it was a dick move,' agreed Nate. 'That's why we have to find Aaron and tell him what Angel said. Before …' He shook his head.

'You think he might kill again?' Veronica said quietly.

'He's angry. Really angry with us all. And what Charlie said makes a lot of sense. So … I don't know what he might do,' Nate said. 'But he needs to know this.'

'Fine. We'll find him,' Charlie said, raising her eyes. Her knuckles whitened around the handle of the axe. The weight of the laser gun in Veronica's pocket felt suddenly reassuring. Charlie had a weapon – it was good she had one too. 'There better be some fucking NPCs in this last room,' she said, glancing at the single door on the opposite side of this corridor. 'Once we're done, we're going to take my trusty friend here –' she lifted the axe, hefting it blunt side down into her palm – 'find Aaron, and give him a piece of my mind.'

Nate was reaching in his back pocket for the brick-like phone. 'Or ... I could just call him.'

Charlie let the axe slump. 'Err, yeah.'

Nate stared at the phone for a few seconds, then said, 'I guess I just type his name out,' under his breath. He jabbed the large buttons five times – 22766. Charlie and Veronica drew in close. A ringtone sounded.

And sounded.

And sounded.

Eventually, the line crackled. 'Aaron?' Veronica said, quietly. 'Is that you?'

A low keening noise sounded on the other end of the phone. A shiver ran down Veronica's spine, slick and cold as an ice cube – was the noise even human? Nate's finger hovered over the end-call button, but at that moment the noise stopped.

'Ready or not,' said a girl's voice, 'here I come!'

Then the phone clicked off.

'It's her,' said Veronica, after a pregnant silence. Her heart was hammering so loud she felt like her ribs might fracture. 'It's Em.'

'Oh my *god*,' Charlie said, her voice trembling. 'I already believed she was here, but ... holy shit, that was creepy.'

Veronica glanced over at Nate, who was staring down at the phone as if it were about to spontaneously combust in his hands. 'Nate, you were the last one of us who didn't believe it. But I don't think this is all in my head. I think … I'm sure … she's really here. Surely you must get that now.'

'OK,' he said, finally sliding the phone into its holster. 'I don't … I think—'

Charlie cut in with a short, ugly laugh. 'Holy crap. When even Nate's lost for words, you know you're in trouble.'

A cold silence breathed over the small group.

'The question is,' Nate said, at last, 'what does she want?'

11

The three of them trudged towards the next door in the narrow corridor, a cloud of dread hanging over the group. Veronica felt something else coiling in her mind like a waiting snake – the horrifying truth of what she had heard on the phone: '*Here I come.*'

Veronica had been seeking Em on the day it happened. Now, it was Em's turn.

Fear sank deep into her core, winding its ivy-like tendrils around each one of her vital organs and squeezing. The others felt it too: Veronica could tell. Charlie clutched the axe tightly in her hand, her body a visible knot of tension. And Nate was quieter than usual, his air of calm self-assurance clearly fraying. He reached out for the brass handle of the next door, breathed deep, then swung it open.

The room inside was messy, but it hadn't been trashed like the others – and it didn't look like it hadn't been lived in for years. On the wall was a huge, cleavage-heavy poster of Cindy Crawford. A glossy electric guitar was mounted nearby, expensive-looking and apparently untouched. Sports paraphernalia were stacked up against the wall: a lacrosse basket, hockey sticks, a rugby ball. A trophy cabinet, which smelt strongly of old socks, was the tidiest thing in the room. A boom box was pumping out cheesy pop on the desk where a boy was sitting hunched over a notebook and surrounded by textbooks with titles like *Business Studies* and *Economics for Beginners*.

Orson's youngest, thought Veronica. *He's studying, even on the day his dad died?*

Charlie knocked on the open door when the boy appeared not to notice his company. He turned around. Even though Veronica had only seen Orson dead, she could tell this boy was the picture of his father. Blond hair. Blue eyes. A cleft chin. Mrs Coleman had said he was thirteen, but he looked older, Veronica thought. He reached out and switched off the boom box, a mechanical quality to his actions that had been missing from the NPCs downstairs.

'Who are you?' he asked.

'You must be Simon,' said Veronica gently. 'We're here investigating your father's murder and I wondered if we could ask you a few questions?'

After an uncomfortably long silence, Simon stood up slowly and jerkily turned towards the bed. He took a few quick steps and sat down on the mattress.

Veronica, Charlie and Nate exchanged a puzzled glance. Angel had said the essential components of the Game should continue to work, but Simon was acting like a malfunctioning robot. Was he capable of answering their questions?

'Everyone says I'm like my father,' he announced suddenly. 'But I'm not.' He met Veronica's eyes. 'My father was a failure.'

Veronica blinked. 'He had a multi-million-pound media business—'

'The business was all down to Grandmother.' Simon spoke over her not as if interrupting, but as if he hadn't even heard Veronica's voice. 'Father wanted to be an artist. It's Peter who takes after Father, not me – he doesn't look like him, but he's the one with the comic books.' He smirked, an unpleasant expression for one talking about his brother.

Veronica felt a stab of anger. This was how Em had talked about her behind her back, when she'd thought Veronica was out of earshot. Sneering and superior.

'I would never fail like he failed. I would never make my family ashamed of me. I skipped a year at school. That's how smart I am.' Despite his unnatural manner of speaking, Simon's cheeks were flushed with something like rage. 'And last night Grandmother told me Father wants to sell the business. Before I've had a chance to show everyone what I can make of it. It's not fair.'

There was a protracted silence as the players waited to see if there was more – but Simon didn't continue.

'Where were you last night?' Nate asked softly.

'Footsteps woke me up. It was nearly midnight. Grandmother was going to bed. She told me about Father then, out there in the hallway. She said we couldn't let him do it.'

Veronica and Nate glanced at one another.

'How did she—' Veronica started.

'I was asleep,' Simon interrupted suddenly. He averted his eyes. For a second, Veronica thought she saw his body glitch, separating into pixels – but it was over in an instant. He lay down on the bed stiffly, like he was a thing of wheels and cogs, not flesh and bone. 'Asleep,' he said again. And he shut his eyes.

As they stepped into the darkened corridor, Charlie cleared her throat. 'Well, I still think it's Grace. This whole thing feels like a massive red herring.'

'I don't know,' said Nate. 'I know he was glitchy, but ... that kid creeped me out. Grandma's special little boy.'

'The golden child,' said Veronica. Like Em had been. Veronica had always achieved decent grades – even in the subjects she wished she could drop – but she'd had to work hard at it. Em was naturally good at everything. Naturally liked by everyone. There'd even been talk of Oxbridge.

'Feels like almost everyone here had a motive to kill Orson. Do you really think a thirteen-year-old boy could've done it?' Charlie asked, sceptical.

'Did we get the information?' Nate asked. 'That was the last room, right, so we must've done.'

Veronica slipped her Walkman out of her jacket pocket. She held the headphones close to her ear, jacked up the volume, then hit rewind and play.

'It's Peter who takes after Father, not me – he doesn't look like him, but he's the one with the comic books.'

Simon's voice was faint and tinny through the headphones.

'Uh, OK?' Charlie said. 'I can't really see how that relates to anything. Although … maybe this still relates to Grace somehow. Maybe she's pushy like Grandma, you know? Simon didn't really mention her at all – isn't that suspicious?'

Suddenly, a shrill pealing sound arced through the house's silence. Veronica jumped, her pulse racing, and Charlie lifted her axe in readiness.

'My cell,' Nate said, eagerly reaching into his back pocket. 'Thank god, they managed to get me some signal.' The rectangular screen was lit up with a single word – but Veronica couldn't read it before Nate angled away the phone.

But Nate didn't answer the phone.

'Why don't you two head on up?' he suggested, eyeing the large window at the end of the corridor, beside the glass door that announced it was leading to the stairs.

Veronica noticed the snow was maybe an inch or two from the top of the window.

'I'll only be a minute,' Nate added.

'Huh, I thought we didn't have any secrets now?' Charlie said. 'You told us what you're doing here. What've you got to hide?'

Nate's phone rang for a third time, shrill and piercing. 'I've got to get this,' he said, through gritted teeth. 'I told you, there's still some things I can't be open about, or I'll be in deep shit.'

The two stared at each other as the phone rang a fourth time. *There's no point in a stand-off*, Veronica thought.

'Come on,' Veronica said, touching Charlie on the arm and guiding her towards the glass-panelled door. 'We can't fight among ourselves. Not now.' She glanced back at Nate and said quietly. 'Find out about my brother?'

He nodded briefly.

Charlie puffed out an annoyed breath, but relented.

The staircase beyond the door was narrow and quickly

turned dark when they were past the window. A coil of tension unfurled in Veronica's stomach as she realised they had at least managed to avoid the indoor quicksand-snowstorm mash-up this time.

'What the fuck is up with that guy?' Charlie said. 'Can't believe he's still keeping secrets about his dumb work after all we've been through. Surely after Yasmin …' She gulped. 'The priority right now should be getting us out of here. Who cares what sick fuck is behind all of this? The police can deal with that when we're out.'

The stairs spiralled and creaked as they ascended – the darkness surrounding them felt like a physical thing, sewn of velvet and menace.

'Honestly, do we even need him? You've got that tape thingy and Yasmin's trainers. I've got the glasses. Between us we can find the clue and information on this level, can't we? I vote we ditch him.'

'Charlie, we can't. He's our only link to the outside world,' Veronica said quietly. 'Besides, that would be wrong. We're all split up too much already.'

'*That would be wrong*,' Charlie repeated in a whiny, mocking voice. 'Jesus, V, get a life. We do what we have to do at this point – right or wrong doesn't play into it.' Then she paused. 'Oh, I get it – it's because you asked him to find out about your brother, isn't it?' Her voice had softened a touch.

'I have to know if he's all right,' Veronica said. 'But I wouldn't ditch Nate anyway. I know what it's like to be left out – to believe you can trust someone and then be let down. I wouldn't do that to someone. Can we drop it … please?'

Just then, at the last turn, light flooded the stairwell.

The space they entered stretched for what must've been the entire length of the building. One side was comprised entirely of the arched windows that had become so familiar – the other was full of paintings. Portraits.

'Wow, this place looks like it's been abandoned for, like, a hundred years,' said Charlie. She stalked forward, swung her axe through a banner of cobwebs so thick they looked like they might've been sprayed there as Halloween decorations. 'Check out these windows – they're so fucked that there's literally snow coming in.'

She was right. Trails of wind-whipped snow were strewn across the floor. Veronica tested a patch with her shoe, tentatively … but, thank god, the floor beneath the snow felt solid.

She glanced over her shoulder at the staircase. Nate probably had five minutes, tops, before he would be in danger – but he knew that, right? He'd be up here in a moment, for sure. Perhaps with news of Max.

Veronica approached the grimy first portrait – which was of Orson's mother, Mrs Coleman. Steel-grey hair. Steelier gaze. Shoulder pads like something the villain would wear in a superhero movie.

'Looks like there's at least a couple of rooms on this level,' said Charlie, pointing out a subtle door disguised between the portraits. 'One of them must be Peter's room, right? He wasn't on the previous levels and he's the only NPC left that the old battleaxe said was here. The only levels after this are the two in the clock tower, and it doesn't seem likely there'll be a bedroom up there.'

'Let's wait for Nate before we start poking around,' Veronica suggested.

Charlie had already decided who the murderer was, but that was no way to tackle a mystery. She'd blinkered herself. To solve any murder mystery, you had to be open-minded, willing to be led by the information available to you – not the other way around.

Veronica glanced back down the stairs. 'Nate's taking a while. I think I should go and check on him. The windows down there have got to be nearly full.'

'Whatever.' Charlie's voice, which had been momentarily animated by the mystery, fell flat and uninterested again. Like she'd just remembered what she was supposed to be like. 'You check. I'll start having a poke around up here. We shouldn't waste any time.'

Veronica didn't have the energy to argue – besides,

Charlie was already putting on her aviators. Veronica turned away.

'Charlie?' she said, glancing back over her shoulder as she reached the top of the stairwell. 'No more hiding clues, OK? And be careful. Aaron is around somewhere and he doesn't know Yasmin's really dead.'

Charlie hefted her axe. 'Oh, he'll be more scared of me than I am of him.' She flashed a wicked grin.

12

Veronica found herself creeping down the spiral staircase, step by step, as if she were a naughty child afraid of waking her parents. The murkiness of the middle turn swallowed her. She tried not to panic, and the darkness lessened to a stormy grey as she approached the glass-panelled door at the bottom. She peered through the glass – the arched window next to the stairs had maybe a quarter of an inch of brightness left at the top.

Nate was pacing in the gloom. 'Are you sure?' he said. 'I can't believe …' He trailed off, then said, 'Shit.'

A chill ran down her spine. Was Max OK? What had Nate been told?

He walked away from the glass door before pivoting and turning back, his eyes fixed on the floor. 'What am I supposed to do with this?' he said now, his voice anxious.

He probably had a couple of minutes, tops, before the snow descended. Why was he leaving it so late? Veronica knew she should open the door, tell him not to lose track of time ... but still, she waited.

'I have to go,' he said. 'I'll figure it out. This may be a Plan C scenario.' He rubbed his forehead. 'I can't leave here without the truth. This is our last shot to avenge her – I'll do whatever it takes.' There was a pause. 'Yes,' Nate said, in a serious voice, 'even that.'

Veronica's chest tightened in fear.

As he hung up, his eyes lifted suddenly to meet hers through the glass of the door. For a moment, everything was very still. Then, she pushed open the door and stepped on to carpeted floor, glad to feel it was still solid under her feet.

'How long have you been listening?'

'About thirty seconds,' Veronica said truthfully – what was the point in lying? 'Long enough to figure out you haven't been telling the truth. *Avenge her?* That didn't sound like a call with a rival gaming company or a national security agency.'

Nate's face darkened. 'Those were your theories. I neither confirmed nor denied anything you decided to believe. '

'Just tell me the truth.'

Nate glanced at the stairs behind her. 'Or what? You won't let me upstairs?'

A cold silence lingered between the pair. The floor was starting to feel icy under Veronica's feet.

'It was my mom, OK?' Nate said. 'She was a detective. She started to investigate the Game, five years ago – back when it launched. The deeper she dug, the more determined she grew to find out who was behind it. She got close. Too close. They came after her. Made it look like an accident.'

'And you, a teenage boy, are going to take them down on your own?'

'Not on my own,' Nate said shortly, his jaw visibly tight. 'But I've already told you my secret. I'm not going to give away anyone else's.'

'Why did you lie?'

'If you thought I worked for the CIA, I figured you'd all trust me more than if you realised I was essentially a vigilante.'

Veronica accepted this with a nod. Nate should've told her the truth sooner – after all, she understood what it meant to do everything you could for the people you love. 'Did you find out about Max?'

'I found a lot of stuff out,' Nate said. 'Max is on life support.'

She felt the news like a gut punch, fear and uncertainty chasing each other through her body. She pushed both emotions aside – not now. 'Life support?'

He nodded, his face oddly expressionless. 'Look, Veronica. I *know*. I know why Em is here. All the things she did to you ... the bullying, the cruelty, the humiliations—'

'Stop,' Veronica cut in. She breathed deep, feeling shaky and on the verge of tears. She forced herself to think clearly. She looked up. In moments, the tiny chink of window light remaining would be swallowed up by snow. 'We need to go. We can talk more when we're safe.'

That's when the large snow-filled window next to Veronica flickered – as if it were an electric light – and then ... switched off. How was that *possible*? The hanging wall lights were dead too. Panic rose up inside her and she swallowed, pushing it down. The hallway was completely dark and suddenly airless; it felt as if the mansion were a doll's house and a thick velvet blanket had been thrown over the whole thing. She stood very still, though the ground felt like it was swaying under her feet.

'Come out, come out wherever you are ...'

A sing-song voice. Em's voice.

'Veronica?' Nate's reply was panicked.

'Stay very still,' Veronica said quietly.

The window and lights flickered on momentarily and in the half-light, she saw her. The figure was several metres away, floating up off the floor with the fake fur of her coat waving slowly like the wet tendrils of her hair – pale face, paler than a face ever should be, like the face of the moon but with none of its peace. The light flicked off and on again, as if a mischievous child were playing with a switch. As she watched, the edges of Em flickered into tiny, blurred squares. Pixels. A buzzing sound filled Veronica's ears – then Em re-formed, as real as she had ever been. Her dead mouth pulled itself into a wide grin and as it opened, dark brown pond water spilt out on to the floor.

Veronica glimpsed Nate standing in front of the huge arched window, his face a rictus of terror.

The light extinguished – Veronica stumbled away from the stairs, towards Nate, nearly losing her footing, the edges of her pitch-black vision crinkling brightly like paper catching fire, her hearing aids whistling.

'Nate!' she called out. 'Where are you?'

'Here!' he called.

She staggered towards his voice. 'We need to get upstairs.' She reached out but felt nothing but the thick, soupy air.

There was movement in the darkness as she held out her arms. A low giggle. Em.

A cold body passed very close to Veronica. Water dripped on to her shoes. Then, a pair of hands closed around her neck.

She couldn't breathe. She struggled, clawed at her throat – but in the darkness the grasping hands slid under her skin, buzzing with strange electricity.

How could a soul made of pixels possess this kind of strength?

Then, Veronica pushed out. She felt resistance, then heard crashing glass. 'Nate!' she screamed.

And suddenly, the light returned. The hands were gone. And a high ringing sounded in her aids.

Specks of cold landed on her face, a snake of frigid air. The hall was dim as twilight and her ears continued to ring. But *was* it her aids? A phone glowed on the dark floor, which had not yet transformed to snow, but was so cold she felt it was close. The ringing stopped as Veronica watched – but the screen remained lit up. Nate's phone. He'd dropped it. But where was Nate?

She pushed herself up, risked stumbling over to pick up the phone, but it wasn't ringing any more: *Missed Call* showed on the screen. She felt an icy draught and lifted her eyes. The full-length window in front of the stairs had been totally smashed – sharp jags of glass set like teeth in the window frame – and snow was drifting in.

Veronica stepped forward, glass crunching under her feet. Looked out. Down below, a body lay on its stomach, starkly outlined in the snow. Already a white shroud of new fall was covering it, but the face – half turned towards her – was unmistakable.

Nate.

Veronica staggered back. The floor felt as if it were sinking, and although she wasn't sure if it was the quicksand-snow or simply her own weakness, she stumbled backwards on to the stairs, lifting her knees up to her chin and shivering. *She killed him. She really killed him.*

The phone was hard and cold in her hand. A crack snaked across the screen, but the device appeared to be working fine. She touched the screen to stop it locking, on instinct.

'V?' Charlie called from above. 'Nate? I found the next clue already. Sleeping pills. They were in the butler's bedroom.' Her footsteps creaked on the top steps, as if she were hesitant to round the dark corner. 'Guys?'

'I'm here,' Veronica managed, her voice strange in her throat.

'What's wrong?' Charlie said. 'Where's Nate?'

'He's dead,' she choked out. She forced herself to stand up, leaning heavily on the banister as she slipped Nate's phone into the pocket of her puffer jacket, keeping her thumb pressed on the cracked screen. 'I'm coming up.'

LEVEL THREE

13

Back upstairs in the gallery, Veronica found Charlie with her back to her, shoulders visibly tense, staring out the nearest window. The snow was falling heavier than ever and was whipping up, lashing at the broken windows in long swathes of biting white. It wasn't just snowing any more – this was a storm. And Charlie was staring straight into it, as if in challenge, one hand holding her axe, the other resting on the rotten, paint-chipped windowsill.

'What happened?' she asked in a flat voice, without turning around.

'I went downstairs, found Nate. Then I saw Em – clearer than ever before.' She gulped. 'Everything went dark – it was like the window wasn't a real window, but an electric light. Flickering off. Next thing I know, the window is smashed,

Nate's lying there outside ...' Her voice trembled. 'She killed him, Charlie. And I think she killed Yasmin too.'

Charlie paused then, and Veronica watched as her slender fingers tightened around the handle of the axe. She shook her head slowly, tapping her perfectly manicured nails against the rotten sill. Her hair, which had been dishevelled after the zombie fight, was back in its perfect high ponytail. 'Your ghost killed him,' she said flatly.

The wind moaned outside, like a beast in pain, and Veronica felt a chill run down her spine. She replied with a steady voice, despite how her heart was racing. 'Yes, I think so. I think Em's the murderer. I think ... I think I saw her in the juke-box room – but at the time, she wasn't clear. I didn't know it was her. She's clear now. Stronger.'

'But she's *your* ghost. She's haunting *you*. The rest of us, we're just collateral damage.' Charlie glanced back at Veronica. 'Don't you think?'

'I-I don't know.' She felt numb at the accusation – she hadn't expected Charlie to react like this.

'*I-I don't know*,' Charlie mocked. 'That's how ghosts work, V. Why would she care about the rest of us? Both times someone's died, you've been there. Can't you see it's you she's trying to get to?' She pushed a strand of perfect ponytail over her shoulder. 'Maybe she's even trying to hurt you by hurting us.' Charlie sighed, turning towards Veronica and looking her up and down. Regret flickered across her face, then hardened into determination. 'Logically, the best thing I can do for myself is get as far away from you as possible.'

Veronica shook her head slowly. 'Charlie, we have to stick together.'

'Seems to me, that's not working. Maybe Aaron had it right. Maybe we should try something new.'

'No. This is a bad idea.' Veronica's heart pounded harder. 'Alone, we're more vulnerable.'

Charlie cursed under her breath. 'I want to believe you. But this is all so fucked. Nate didn't get killed until you went down looking for him, did he?'

Veronica felt herself flush. Why was she doing this? Why was she making everything worse? Charlie was just like Em. Always blaming everything on other people – especially Veronica. No more. She was done with taking it. Done with not talking back. 'You do what you want, Charlie. You always do.'

Charlie shot her a barbed glance. 'I will. I don't need your damn permission.'

Veronica started to shake her head, but a whooshing sound started up in the gallery and goosebumps prickled over her skin as the cold breeze tickled her hair. She caught sight of movement over Charlie's shoulder, reflected in the glass.

'Charlie …' she whispered.

Charlie's face fell and Veronica spun around. A flickering figure was walking down the gallery. A trail of blood trickled down the side of her face, as if from an untended wound. She was a woman who looked to be in her late thirties, dressed in a once-smart white suit, which had a patch of blood on the shoulder. Her hair was a tangle of loose, glossy curls pinned behind her ears.

'Grace Coleman?' Charlie whispered.

The figure was faint, ghostly. It stared at Veronica and Charlie, its face a red-eyed, twisted nightmare. Ghostly Mrs Coleman was crying.

'Orson,' she said, her voice oddly computerised, glitchy, like it was carrying through a poor connection. She had stopped in front of the portrait of the older Mrs Coleman, facing Veronica and Charlie. 'My love. I rushed home as soon as I realised, but I was too late …'

'As soon as you realised what?' Veronica said softly.

'What was about to happen,' Grace said, her eyes fixed on Veronica's. 'What had been uncovered.' She lifted a mechanical hand to her wound, which was now gushing blood. As she did so, her voice changed, growing purer and younger, the accent shifting. Her arm raised up, up, until it was pointing towards Veronica. 'What did you do to me?' she said slowly, her face pixelated, fading and flickering.

Then it started to reassemble. Except it was different this time. Younger, the skin a darker tone. The eyes …

Yasmin? Veronica's eyes widened in horror.

Charlie shrieked in a mingled cry of shock and grief as Yasmin's mouth opened wide in a scream, her extended finger pointing straight at Veronica. Charlie threw the axe in panic, which spun right through screaming Yasmin and into the portrait of the older Mrs Coleman, lodging itself deep in her painted head.

Veronica backed away, her hands trembling, but as the two girls watched, the ghostlike figure shrieked out a strangled, sob-like metallic sound and then melted into thin air.

Charlie crumpled on to the floor, her shoulders shaking.

'Are you OK?' Veronica said, her voice as weak as her body felt. 'The NPCs … they were going wrong downstairs,' she said breathlessly. 'I think Em might be messing with them. They must've … I don't know … screwed up completely.' She reached out, but as her fingers brushed Charlie's shoulder, the other girl violently shrugged her off.

'Don't touch me!' she shrieked. She smoothed her hair, her back turned towards Veronica, still. When she spoke again, her voice was quiet but full of horror. 'What if that was Yasmin, really? Is part of her really trapped here forever? Like Em? She died, *really* died, while playing this game …'

Veronica felt cold. Tears prickled at the corners of her eyes, panic shook her fingers. *It's not true. It can't be true.*

Charlie raised herself up, approaching the axe where it was lodged in the painting. 'She was pointing straight at you. *"What did you do to me?"* I think she heard what we were saying. How you're responsible for bringing Em here. How she kills when you're around. It's you. You're cursed. Now Yasmin's trying to help me by telling me to go it alone.'

'That wasn't Yasmin, Charlie,' Veronica realised, her voice sounding oddly loud. 'It was Em. She's got control of the NPCs, or what's left of them. She's messing with us. Trying to separate and weaken us.'

Charlie hesitated, as though turning the idea over in her mind. But eventually, she shook her head slightly. 'It doesn't matter,' she said, her voice firm now, as she ran a finger over the handle of the axe. 'The fact is, when you're near, people die. I don't want you hanging around me any more, capiche?' She scowled at Veronica over her shoulder. 'I never liked you anyway.'

Veronica felt her heart racing inside her ribcage but tried to keep her voice steady. 'Charlie, I'm sorry you don't like me, but it doesn't matter – the fact is, we can't solve this apart—'

But Charlie had gathered momentum; she turned fully towards Veronica now. 'Wrong. You need my glasses, but I don't need your dumb tape. The NPCs are so screwed they're basically handing us the information on a platter. I've already got the clue from this level.'

'Sorry, but how's that going to work? How would we—'

'Also, stop saying sorry when you don't mean it. It's passive aggressive. "Sorry you don't like me" isn't an apology, OK? You're such a snake.'

Veronica felt herself flinch, her face burning. Even now, even after all she'd said and done, Charlie still had the power to hurt her with a casual insult. Just like Em had. *You're so slow. You're so clumsy. You're so weird. You're so negative. Why can't you just be normal?*

'As for how it's going to work, here's how.' Charlie turned and pulled the axe emphatically out of the portrait, which slipped and fell off the wall with a *thunk*. Dust clouded up from the floor. 'You're going to wait in there –' she jabbed the axe at the closest door, nestled between the portraits – 'until the windows are three-quarters full, OK? It's the butler's room. I already searched it when you were downstairs getting Nate killed. That way, I get a head start. By the time you get to the next level, I'll have solved this goddamn mystery, claimed the prize, and got me, you and even bloody Aaron out of here. That's fair enough, considering what you've brought into this place.' She was shaking with anger. 'And don't you dare follow me.'

'I didn't ask for this,' Veronica said, feeling real panic now. 'I didn't bring Em here on purpose – she followed me. Why are you punishing me? This is insane.'

'Well, at least it's my kind of insane now. Get inside.' Charlie stepped beside the butler's door and opened it up for Veronica.

She didn't walk in. 'No. If you don't want to play together, fine – but you can't stop me playing too.'

Charlie hefted her weapon. 'Seriously, V? You're arguing with the girl with the axe?'

'You wouldn't—'

The axe swung towards her, full speed. Veronica leaped out of the way – only just in time to watch it lodge into the doorframe. Her heart pounded as Charlie hefted it out. 'Wouldn't I?'

Veronica felt the weight of the laser gun in her pocket … but she didn't. Couldn't. Instead, she backed shakily into the butler's room.

'See you never,' Charlie said.

And she shut the door in Veronica's face.

Even worse: a turning, clicking sound.

She was locked in.

14

Veronica immediately tried the handle. But sure enough, Charlie had locked it. She must've found the key when she'd explored the room earlier.

'Charlie!' she screamed. 'Charlie!' But steady footsteps walked away.

The windows would fill up. The floor would turn to snow.

If Charlie didn't solve the mystery in time, Veronica would die when the snow pulled her under … if Em didn't get to her first.

She fell to her knees and buried her face in her hands, breathing deep. How had it come to this?

Nate's phone thunked out of her pocket on to the floor. Somehow it was still unlocked. Veronica snatched it up, swiping her finger over the cracked screen to keep it active. Trouble was, the battery was now down to its last three per cent. She brought up the call list again. A missed call was highlighted in bold. A call from …

… Angel.

Veronica felt the back of her neck tingle as she scanned the call list, showing how Nate had tried to call Angel several times, but the call had failed, and how he had then received two calls in a row. She switched into the messaging app. There wasn't much there that Veronica understood. *Must be code,* she thought. Whatever it meant, it was clear Angel and Nate had been working together. The last few messages were Nate asking for help.

A message flashed on screen as Veronica watched, her heart lurching.

Angel: I can't get in and can't get you out. I've tried everything. Sorry. Make it worth it, I love you.

She remembered what Nate had said about his mother. He and Angel must've been trying to avenge her death together. She remembered too the lingering eye contact between them beside Orson's body when Angel had first appeared. How had she missed it?

Veronica exited the messaging app with fumbling

fingers. A warning flashed up on screen – battery down to one per cent. She clicked on the phone icon to dial Angel's number – they had to explain what the hell was happening – but the screen shut down a moment later, before it had a chance to ring.

Dead.

The word triggered the memory of what Nate had said about Max. Life support. That was bad – really bad. He'd never been on life support before. If Max died … being here … going through what she was going through … it would all have been for nothing.

She thought about the first time he'd been really sick. It'd been around two years earlier. Not long after Em had died. Veronica couldn't ride with Nyra and Max in the ambulance and she'd had to follow in the car with Dad, attempting to keep the blue flashing lights in sight as they wove through traffic on the motorway. Veronica remembered clutching the underside of the car's leather seat so hard that one of her nails had bent and snapped.

Something about what happened to Em had made her determined never to let Max go. The fact he was Veronica's half-brother helped: she felt closer to him, bound by blood. Pieces of her, the best of her, were reflected in him. Besides, he was just a good kid. He didn't deserve this.

When they'd arrived at the hospital, she'd sat in the hard plastic chairs in the waiting room for hours on end, drunk scalding hot coffee, walking the worn route to the vending machine and back bringing food she couldn't eat, the news on repeat on the TV mounted on the waiting-room wall. She'd been there so often now she could conjure it whenever she closed her eyes – the smell of scrubbed lino, disinfectant and sour coffee. And then she realised, maybe, that was the first time she'd heard about the Game. On the TV, the newsreader in her red suit leaning forward across her desk.

'"*You'll know it by the snow." This mysterious phrase has been spotted across the UK and beyond – but what does it mean? Reports suggest an elusive VR world known only as the Game has been luring players in at random, offering big cash prizes. But who—*'

Yes. That was the moment Veronica had been pulled away by Dad to the room with the bed. Max's drawn face was resting on its white pillow – at once older and younger than it should've been, full of shadow yet vulnerable, oddly unformed. Tubes had snaked into his nose and he had been so, so small, his normally brown skin pale, dwarfed by the bed and the whiteness of it.

She thought of Em too. Because Max had looked like her in that moment. There'd been an open casket – and Nyra had insisted each of them gaze upon Em's face one last time. Tradition, she'd said. The creamy white coffin lining. Black hair. She'd been beautiful; ridiculously beautiful. Veronica had tried to cry but couldn't – she'd felt as frozen as the moment she'd seen Em, dead, in the VR arcade. As the moment before, in Hide and Seek, when Em had plunged under the water, her hair drifting around her face in a dark halo ...

Veronica hurled the dead phone now against the wall with a strangled cry of frustration, feeling sobs rise up in her body.

She folded down, her head pressed into the tops of her thighs, and let grief overwhelm her.

He'd better be OK. Or else.

There was a soft creak.

She lifted her eyes. The phone had hit one of the wooden panels set in the wall, which swung open to reveal a slice of darkness. Veronica's crying stopped abruptly, leaving her sore-faced and empty.

She stood up, stalked towards the panel, dust pluming into the air as her feet hit the floorboards. She eased open the panel door further, the hinges creaking as if she were in a comedy house of horrors. In the thin light cast from the snowy window, Veronica could see a passage snaking between the panels and the wall, quickly trailing into the deepest kind of darkness. The passage was waist-height – a crawl space, she assumed, connecting the rooms along the corridor.

'There really are secret passages then,' Veronica murmured. Rita had mentioned how, even though the house was new, it had been rebuilt according to the old Victorian plans. Perhaps the passages had once functioned as an alternative escape route, in case of emergency. *Or a way to listen in on secret information*. She shuddered, remembering the tale of the maid who was trapped in the passages when the original house burned down. What had she been doing in there?

Charlie had told her to stay here until the windows were three-quarters full – but the secret passage might contain something vital, some clue to solve the entire mystery and get them all out of here. She couldn't simply ignore it – and she couldn't sit around while time ran out. Charlie might not want to be anywhere near her, thanks to Em, but deep down Veronica thought if anyone was going to figure this puzzle out, it was her.

She searched the small bedroom for a torch. Instead, she found the stub of a candle and a mostly empty box of matches, which would have to do. She lit the candle and ventured into the passage on her hands and knees. Wary of Rita's trapped maid, she left the low door to the butler's room ajar.

She thought about the layout of the gallery – the rest of its rooms would be to her right. To her left would be the staircase to the level beneath. Veronica held out her candle in that direction, expecting the passage to end – instead, she could glimpse the top of a step and the shadow of the next one down, descending into deeper darkness.

These passages might run through the entire house, she thought, like dark veins through a body. But she couldn't go down to the lower floors again – that way, only snow remained.

She started crawling to her right, the candle trembling in her hand – it was difficult to hold the light steady while progressing over the filthy floor with just one free hand, her palm quickly caking in grime. A faint smell of burning reached her nose. She couldn't shake the sense of Em crouched on her hands and knees a few paces ahead of her, barely out of the ring of light cast by the candle, waiting for it to blow out. A strong draught whooshed through the passage, teasing the flame and sending the cobwebs overhead into a frenzy. Veronica jumped at a rumbling sound before realising it was thunder.

The storm was worsening.

Every couple of metres, she tested the panelled wall. Before too long, she sensed the something different – cold air, cold light. The outline of a doorway. A beam of daylight shot through the darkness at Veronica's eye level. She blew out her candle hurriedly, attempting to ignore the close darkness, and pressed her eye to the peephole.

Beyond was a child's bedroom. The surfaces were covered in dust in the spaces between the grubby dolls and toys. How old had Mrs Coleman said Peter was – sixteen? Veronica was surprised: the room appeared to belong to a much younger child.

She remembered though how Em's side of their shared room had been stuffed full of plush animals until she was nearly fourteen. 'I can't bear to give them away,' she'd say. 'I know it's silly, but they've always been there for me.' Half a year later, they were taped up in cardboard boxes and sent to Oxfam.

When it came down to it, Em's sentimentality only ran skin-deep.

A figure lay propped up in an ergonomic single bed with a sitting function like Max's hospital bed. Veronica felt a tug on her heart as she imagined Max like this too – hooked up to a machine to keep him breathing. She pushed the image away.

There was no sign of Charlie; she had probably been and gone. She pushed on the panel and it clicked open.

The figure on the bed didn't shift as she crawled out into the room and stood up.

The curtains over the windows were partially shut and it was dark enough that Veronica couldn't make out the face of whoever lay in the bed. The room smelt of plastic and synthetics and dust and a smell Veronica knew so intimately it nearly felt like coming home – the smell of sickness.

'Hello?' Her voice was very small and the figure in the bed remained motionless.

Was he asleep? Veronica edged closer towards the bed as if drawn by an invisible string. She had to step carefully now – the floor was messy. A number of rainbow-haired trolls sat around a tea set, and a pair of dirty trainers lay askew on the floor beside the bed. She glanced down at her own shoes. Yasmin's shoes. The grey of ancient dust smeared over the tops of the discarded trainers was very similar – and, like hers, the shoes were tangled with cobwebs.

She tapped her shoe to the discarded trainers and then on to the floor. An unsteady line of glowing red footsteps led back to the panel in the wall, the heel-toe footsteps clearly angled towards Veronica … Interesting. So, the last steps he walked were from the panel door to his bed, which meant Peter had entered the secret passage too, perhaps from another room. She was about to follow the footsteps to check which way they led down the corridor before they faded when a voice said, 'Who are you?'

241

Veronica spun back towards the bed, her heart fluttering and light.

The boy was awake, his eyes fixed on her, unblinking. He had a comic on his chest – upside down – as if he'd dropped it when he'd fallen asleep. Veronica remembered Simon saying, derisively, that his brother liked comics. Peter had sharp features that bore little resemblance to his father's or Simon's – unlike them, he was not classically handsome. He appeared too a lot younger than his sixteen years.

'Who are you?' he said again, in an oddly bright voice that didn't feel quite natural. Then, without waiting for Veronica to reply, he said, 'My name is Peter. I'm Orson's son.'

The Game, Veronica thought, had preserved this room and this character because they contained the key information that would allow them to progress – just as Angel had said might happen. But like his brother downstairs, Peter wasn't unaffected. He didn't seem as realistic, as human, as the NPCs they'd met on the ground floor. It was almost like he had some fixed phrases programmed and was eager to spill them out whether it was appropriate or not.

'Where were you last night, Peter?' Veronica asked directly, deciding there was no point in not cutting to the chase.

'Last night I was right here, where I always am,' Peter

said. 'I'm sick. Bedridden.' His voice was chirpy. 'I go to the bathroom and back here. Not much further unless someone helps me. Chronic fatigue, that's what it's called.' His face glitched, the expression freezing, then he barked out a strange laugh.

'Did you—' Veronica started, wanting to ask about the footsteps into the hidden passage, but Peter interrupted.

'No, I wasn't close to my father.'

Veronica waited, but he didn't continue. 'Your brother said you were more similar to your father,' she said slowly.

'My brother thinks anyone who doesn't have a sports trophy cabinet is a loser,' Peter said, suddenly sharp.

'I had a sister,' Veronica said softly, sitting on the side of the bed. 'She was better than me at some things too – the things that other people care about. I know it's not easy. But we have our own strengths, don't we?'

He glanced away. When he spoke again, it didn't relate to Veronica's question, but at least he sounded more natural. 'Besides, even if Father and I were similar, that doesn't mean we were close. Father was never here and even when he was, he didn't often come and see me. I think my illness made him uncomfortable. He always seemed like he wanted to leave.' He fingered the comic on his lap repetitively. 'I'm much closer to Mother, but she's not here right now.'

'She is here. I saw her car outside,' Veronica ventured,

deciding to press while the NPC appeared to be functioning relatively normally. 'And I spoke to her, in the hall. She was worried.' *About what had been revealed*, Veronica thought.

'I'm sure she's not here.' Peter smiled. 'If she was here, she would've come to see me. She always does. N—' He paused, his face pixelating, the consonant stuck on his tongue.

Veronica waited. Sure enough, the next statement followed – no questions required.

Peter's pixelated form coalesced. 'N-no, I don't know who could've done this. But you should question the butler. He's always had something against my father. And he's up all hours. Sometimes I hear him, pacing. His room's right next to mine, see.'

'What do you mean, the butler had something against your father?'

'He worked for my grandfather too,' Peter said, a little too quickly after Veronica had finished speaking. 'To him, Father lacked class. He never liked him.'

Veronica frowned. She was unconvinced – not liking someone, or thinking they were classless, was hardly motivation enough for murder. But Peter was definitely trying to lead her towards the butler as a suspect. Was there something to it? By all accounts, the man had given nothing away to Charlie and Yasmin. Or could Peter be trying to protect his mother, who had the strongest motive? When nothing else was forthcoming, she gently probed. 'Is there anything else you can tell us about last night? Did you hear any sounds, or wake at an unusual time?'

But the boy stared blankly into space, then – almost robotically – lifted his comic and started reading. The comic remained upside down.

'Peter?' she asked. 'Did you go into the hidden passages?' But the boy carried on staring at the bright pictures, his eyes unmoving.

Veronica had wanted to check out where Peter's glowing footsteps led, but it was too late; they had faded. Veronica tried tapping her shoe against Peter's discarded trainer again, but this time, nothing appeared. Perhaps it had never been designed to work multiple times – or perhaps it was a result of the Game going wrong.

She returned to the secret passage anyway, to check for further clues – but though she found another door at the end of the low passage, it was jammed or locked, and there was no spyhole into the room beyond. Her candle was burning low, so she returned to Peter's room and tiptoed across it over to the door into the main gallery.

'You'll find him, won't you?' Peter said, as she reached for the handle.

Startled, Veronica spun around to find Peter staring directly at her, bolt upright in his bed. 'What?'

'You'll find whoever killed my father.'

Veronica nodded slowly. The way he said it, it sounded like a statement of fact. 'I'll find them,' she whispered.

He lay down again and shut his eyes as a mouse scuttled out from under his bed and shot past Veronica, under the door.

She peered through the keyhole. No sign of Charlie. No sign of Aaron either. And no sound out there except for the howl of the wind. She eased the door open.

The light out here was dim and silver, the windows around three-quarters full. If it weren't for the footprints in the dust and the patches of snow, Veronica would have thought no one had been here for centuries.

She walked along the gallery, close to the side with the portraits. The wind was raging, the remaining windows with their cracked geometric arches rattling and bowing so alarmingly she was afraid they would shatter under the pressure. Tendrils of ivy were pushing their way through the cracks and around the window frames like desperate fingers. Mice rustled and disturbed the dust, and, somewhere, Veronica was sure she could smell water – the dank, green, rotten smell of damp, which had pervaded the other game, so unlike the crisp scent of winter on the ground floor.

Along with Em, Hide and Seek had crept in like a sickness. Now, this house was rotten – exactly as the old mansion had been, the dusty multitude of rooms and abandoned cubby-holes perfect for hiding, the sheeted furniture and the overgrown garden and the rickety boathouse by the lake. But Hide and Seek had been set on a calm, cloudy day; here, the broken structure of the Game was sighing and groaning and Veronica was sure she could feel the floor gently sway, as if she were walking the deck of some huge and ancient galleon.

She searched fruitlessly for a third door between the torn and dusty portraits – but there was none. Where, then, was the room with the locked door that she'd found at the end of the secret passage? Suddenly, she heard a noise – a low, slippery keening, separate from the howl of the wind and the rattle of the broken panes.

'*One, two, three …*' a voice sang.

She stopped, listened. Glass crunched under her trainers as she spun around to face … nothing. 'You can't scare me,' she said, her voice low and calm, even though her heart was pounding. 'Just leave me alone, Em. Move on. Follow the light. Do whatever the hell you have to do to get out of here.' Despite her determination not to show fear, her voice had turned shrill, strangled with panic.

The voice giggled. '*Four, five, six …*'

She wiped her sweaty palms on her jumpsuit and swallowed. *Focus.* Being here alone was different, scary.

'*Seven, eight, nine, ten!*'

She felt vulnerable … but somehow she had to keep her head. If she was ever going to get out of here, she'd need it.

'*Ready or not, here I come!*' said the voice.

Veronica clenched her fists. 'You're dead, don't you get that?' she called out. 'You need to let go.'

She started to walk again, approaching the staircase leading upstairs, when the creaking, slippery sound she'd heard before started again, louder this time. Veronica felt something cold and wet wrap around her neck. She yelped and struggled instinctively as the thing tightened, not understanding what was happening. She grasped at it, trying to loosen its grip as it pulled her back towards the wall of portraits – it felt freezing, wet and sinewy, like a river vine.

Or cold flesh. Wet skin.

Through pure determination, Veronica lifted the thing – the *hands*? – for half a second, forcing her fingers under its grip. She gasped out a breath and a strangled shout, but then the thing slipped from her touch, before redoubling its efforts.

As it pulled her harder, she staggered against what was – should have been – the surface of a painting but somehow wasn't. Somehow she could feel the cold – smell a smell that was half paint, half pondweed – and her arms shot out barely in time, grabbing the sides of the picture frame, knuckles white.

Now she understood: Em had taken control of the painting. Em's arms must have erupted from the image at Veronica's back, closed around her neck and started to pull her backwards. Sucking her into the picture's depths. She felt the painting behind her, how the dark surface of it had turned liquid and rippled like a lake. Her eyes bulged, teeth gritting as she fought to breathe.

Was it really game over, after all this time? She'd been so close.

Her vision started to fade – her hands weakening.

Suddenly, liquid arced over her head and hit the painting – and Veronica – and a sharp, unpleasant smell hit her nose. A shriek rang through the gallery – not a human sound, but similar, like a voice twisted and distorted as if it were a poor-quality digital recording played too loud. As if in reply, Veronica's aids sent a high ringing piercing through her ears, and she landed on the wooden floor in a puddle of foul-smelling liquid, gasping and clutching at her throat.

Then, wheezing, she lifted her head.

A dark figure was outlined against the windows, against the churning clouds beyond, the raging snow, where a flicker of lightning licked the sky. Veronica's eyes widened. It was hard to believe it had only been a matter of hours since she had last seen him. His varsity jacket was torn and covered in scorch marks, his once perfectly styled hair nearly as wild as his brown eyes. There was a huge rip in the left leg of his jeans, exposing a grazed knee as he stepped forward and offered Veronica a hand.

'Aaron?' she said, in a half-whisper. Her throat felt terrible.

'It's OK. That thing is gone … for now. But we should hide.' His voice was husky, as if he hadn't spoken for ages.

She gazed at him, speechless for a moment. Then, finally, she accepted Aaron's hand and allowed him to pull her to her feet. He had helped her. Saved her life, in fact. A warm glow spread from her heart as she realised she wasn't alone, not any more.

'Are you OK?' he asked her.

She nodded dumbly, her mind scrambled. At last, she managed, 'How did you …' Veronica glanced down at the empty bottle in his hand and noticed a pungent smell in her soaking wet hair.

'It's turpentine. Good for dissolving stuff that's made of paint, or so I've heard. There's a whole bunch of it in the room at the end.'

'You found the last room?'

He smiled slightly in reply. 'Come on, we can go there now and talk.' He glanced at her jumpsuit, now stinking and wet. 'There are some dry clothes in there too. Where are the others?'

Veronica adjusted her hearing aids, which, somehow, had survived the attack. But a long crack ran down one lens of her glasses. She slid them off and folded them in her pocket. She blinked at Aaron to refocus.

'Veronica … the others?' His voice was gentle and Veronica thought about all those romantic movies where the nerdy girl takes off her glasses and suddenly everyone realises how pretty she is.

Then, Veronica remembered everything with a jolt. 'Aaron, Yasmin's dead,' she blurted. 'I mean, *really* dead, in the real world.'

'What?' He blinked at her. 'That's not …'

'Angel found a way to contact us. I think it's for real. And if Yasmin's really dead, Nate is too—' Her voice hitched – she felt the sting of tears and blinked rapidly.

'What the hell happened?' Aaron whispered. 'How … What about Charlie?'

'She's OK. Or … she *was* OK when I last saw her.' Veronica shivered as a gust of wind curled around her wet clothes.

'Never mind,' Aaron said. 'You can tell me everything – but you should get dry first.' He gazed down at his feet, suddenly seeming shy. Veronica could understand why. They hadn't exactly left things on a positive note …

'Thanks for saving me,' Veronica said, breaking the silence.

'Look, I'm sorry I left,' blurted Aaron at the same time, colour rising in his cheeks. 'That was dumb. I have … trust issues. Charlie stealing that clue, it was bad, but it wasn't your fault. Or Nate's. You were … totally within your rights to call me spoilt. I'm sorry for telling everyone about your brother.' He was bright red now and clearly deeply uncomfortable – but he did meet her eyes.

Veronica felt some of the tension drop from her shoulders and she nodded. 'Thanks. But I shouldn't have said what I did either. I lost my temper and I'm sorry too.' She glanced at the windows. 'Let's hurry. We don't have long.'

15

Clutching his empty turpentine bottle, the glass whorled and greenish, Aaron led Veronica further down the gallery to the foot of the spiral staircase, which Veronica assumed must lead up to the clock tower. A large landscape painting hung on the wall, curiously straight compared to the other paintings in the room. Aaron pushed on the painting, which clicked and swung open. Veronica peered in. The left-hand wall of the room beyond was entirely windows, which met a bank of skylights nestled in the eaves. Lightning flickered in the corners, lighting up the cobwebs as Veronica stepped through and Aaron carefully shut the door behind her.

There was a single bed, the mattress stained and torn, the old sheets crumpled. But this was more than just a bedroom. Against the walls, multiple empty canvasses were stacked, offering up their possibilities. Half-finished paintings suggested the artist might've been responsible for a few of the portraits in the gallery – ghostly outlines in pale colours against dark backgrounds, the remnants of sketches scattered on an angled table.

'I think this was Orson's studio,' Aaron said.

Veronica nodded. 'So this is where he met Liz last night.'

A long storage unit was ranged in the darkest corner, stocked with multiple tiny paint pots and several other huge glass bottles like the empty vessel of turpentine Aaron now set on the floor by the windows. On the surface of the unit sat jars of brushes, spatulas and other implements, though they were all broken and scattered now, and a hi-fi set-up with several components damaged, the buttons missing, as if someone had smashed it with their fist.

Veronica glanced at the wall facing the doorway, searching for where she was sure the entrance to the secret passage must be hidden. She shifted a half-finished canvas – the outline of a naked female form – to find a familiar line of panelling.

'What are you doing?' Aaron asked.

Veronica pressed on the panelling, feeling a slight give in the old wood. Then, there was a click. 'I found the secret passages. But I couldn't open this door from the other side.'

Aaron crouched down beside her. Together they examined

the door. 'There's a keyhole.' He pointed to a small hole at the top of the door.

'There wasn't any lock in the other doors I found,' Veronica said. 'Orson was clearly particularly determined no one disturbed this place.' She frowned. 'Hey … wasn't Liz wearing a small key on a chain around her neck? Did you notice that?'

Aaron frowned but nodded slowly. 'I didn't think anything of it at the time … but yeah. So if you're right that it's the key for this door, I guess that means she could sneak in here, if she wanted,' Aaron said. 'He really trusted her.'

Snow was creeping up the studio windows, but they had some time – perhaps half an hour, Veronica guessed. Enough time to tell Aaron what he had to know. But as she watched, he opened the busted, creaky doors of a small wardrobe, retrieving an old sheet and selection of paint-spattered boiler suits.

'Here, get changed … One of these should fit you. You'll need whatever comfort you can get for upstairs.'

'You've been upstairs?' she asked.

'I thought I might be able to guess the solution – end this whole thing, even though I didn't have all the pieces. Didn't work, so I came back down.'

'And you didn't see Charlie?'

Aaron shook his head.

He turned his back while she stripped, leaving her ruined multicoloured jumpsuit and red puffer in a heap on the floor. She dried herself with the old sheet, coughing at the dust rising from its fibres, before dressing quickly again – all the while painfully aware of Aaron's presence barely a few metres away. Finally, she slipped the Walkman, her broken glasses and the small laser gun into the generous trouser pockets of the pale blue boiler suit, fastening the buttons with trembling fingers. 'Done,' she said, allowing Aaron to turn around while she fastened the Velcro of her trainers. 'Now, we need to talk,' Veronica said, feeling warmer already. 'You missed a lot.'

'OK.' He ran a hand through his movie-star floppy hair. Although he was grubby, his jeans torn and his jacket frayed as if he were at the end of a disaster movie, he remained unbelievably, totally gorgeous. She shook her head – she had to push any feelings she might have aside and focus on the facts – the bare minimum. She was good at that, wasn't she? 'So … Angel told you that Yasmin really died?' he prompted, when she didn't continue.

She felt heat rise in her cheeks but nodded. 'It's me … my sister. Em. She's here – for real. She's polluted the Game, twisted it – and she's killing us off, one by one.'

Aaron sat with this for a moment. His face was pale.

'You saw her, before,' Veronica said.

'Yeah. But I haven't seen her since I left the group. I was starting to think Nate was right – maybe it was the Game itself … the ghost of the maid who was trapped in the walls.'

'I wish it was,' Veronica said in a small voice.

'What happened to Charlie?' Aaron asked after a pause.

'She's so scared of Em, she insisted on leaving me – she thought she'd be safer on her own. And maybe she was right.' Veronica swallowed. If Aaron hadn't seen Em since he'd separated from her, there was a good chance Charlie wouldn't have either.

'Even *Nate* got killed.' Aaron ran a hand through his hair again, something Veronica was starting to recognise as a nervous gesture. 'He understood VR. He knew what he was doing. How the hell did you and I survive and he didn't?' He paused, breathed deep. 'So … you all really agreed it was Em? Not just … I don't know … the NPCs gone wrong? They're acting pretty weird …'

'According to Angel, Yasmin had to have been murdered by a player. The NPCs don't have enough agency for that.' She shook her head. 'Em is … sort of a player. Or perhaps would be recognised as such by the Game. She's not part of its coding. She has some kind of agency. So, to me, that makes sense. And she's getting stronger. I think she can take control of the remaining NPCs whenever she wants … like how she took hold of the painting.' She glanced up at Aaron.

'There's more. Nate … he dropped his phone before he was killed. Em pushed him out of one of the windows.' She swallowed, remembering the darkness of his body on the snow far below. 'He hadn't told us the whole truth. The only messages and calls on that phone were from Angel.'

Aaron blinked. 'Angel and Nate were working together?'

'Looks like it. Before he died, Nate said his mother had got too close to the truth about who was behind the Game and was killed. I think they were trying to finish what she started.'

'On their own?'

Veronica nodded grimly.

'If Nate and Angel were working alone, not with the FBI or something, no one on the outside except Angel knows we're here.' Aaron bit his lip.

'We really should go,' Veronica said as she glanced at the studio windows. But she had to make sure they hadn't missed anything from this level, first. 'Aaron, did you find anything on this floor? I spoke to Peter, but I've not listened back to the tape yet …' Veronica found herself suddenly trembling at the memory of the cold slippery hands around her neck.

'I can show you, actually. It won't take long. Come and look at this.'

He led her towards a telephone on the bedside table.

There was a landline in every room, of course, but this one also had a small machine at its side, which looked practically brand new compared to the general desolation of the room. A sign, Veronica thought, that it might be important to solving the mystery. Aaron was now pressing down the clunky, clicking buttons and making the small machine whir.

'Is this another tape player?' Veronica asked – the controls looked and sounded like the ones on her Walkman.

'Sort of. It's an answering machine. The phones may be out, but there's a message saved on here. Listen.' He pressed play.

Darling, it's me. I've had my appointment and I talked to Dr Perkins about Peter. She thinks it might be beneficial for him to have some therapy too, to talk through everything he's feeling. We have to take his behaviour very seriously, Dr Perkins says, so I've booked him in for an appointment next week. Peter's trying to understand who he is, now that he knows … well … the truth …

There was a pause.

I do love you, you know. I'm sorry. We will get through this – we've gotten through so much already …

Another short silence, then:

I'm at my hotel, but I think I'll just come home tonight, snow be damned. I'm worried about him – about you all. I'll see you later.

Then the message clicked off.

'So let's get this straight – Grace was seeing a psychiatrist in London yesterday and she asked her about Peter's behaviour?' Veronica's mind was spinning. 'I wonder what he'd done to make her worry?'

'I don't know. I couldn't get much out of him,' Aaron said. 'The Game's really done a number on that kid.'

She rewound the tape in her Walkman, pressed play. Peter's stilted voice chirped out through the little headphones, Aaron leaning in to listen.

'Father was never here and even when he was, he didn't often come and see me. I think my illness made him uncomfortable. He always seemed like he wanted to leave.'

Veronica frowned. 'Simon had said his father and Peter were similar – but Peter makes it sound like Orson didn't like to spend time with him.' She tried to untangle it all: Grace had been the number-one suspect, Charlie had thought. But the voice on the answerphone hadn't sounded like the voice of someone who was going to kill her husband – even if she had discovered his affair. She had sounded measured. Kind. Long-suffering.

She hit play on the answering machine again. But instead of Grace Coleman's voice emanating from the small speakers, as before, interference buzzed through the player. White noise. The volume turned up, up and up until it was louder than any tiny speakers had the right to be. She jammed her fingers on to the stop button, but the noise kept spewing out, except now there was a voice. A girl's voice.

One, two, three …
Four, five, six …

'Make it stop!' Veronica cried out, covering her aids, which sang out a high-pitched note. But the voice pounded through as if it were inside her mind, bringing with it a dark swirl of memories.

Seven, eight, nine, ten!
Ready or not, here I come!

Aaron pulled out the power cable, but still the sing-song voice continued.

I'm coming to get you!
I'm coming to get you!
I'm coming to—

Aaron dropped the machine on to the floor and rammed the
heel of his sneaker into it three times, hard. The answering
machine busted into a million pieces of plastic and metal,
fizzing with sparks, and finally the voice fell silent.

Veronica lifted her hands from her ears. 'Thanks,' she
breathed.

'What the hell was that?' Aaron said, his breath fast from
the exertion. He glanced up at Veronica. His voice was low
and serious when he asked, 'Em?'

She nodded, glanced up at the window – they had to
hurry. She shivered, wringing her hair to try and expel the
last of the turpentine. 'It's true, Aaron. She's really here,
really after us.'

Finally, he nodded in acceptance of the facts. 'Here,' said
Aaron, removing his jacket and slinging it around her
shoulders. He stood close as he fastened the top snap fasteners
and he didn't step away when he was finished. 'Veronica,' he
said, his voice close enough to feel warm on her cheek.

'Yes?' Her voice was hoarse. She felt herself leaning in
slightly, subconsciously, so they were barely a fraction apart.

'I …' His fingers remained on the collar of the jacket, his

warmth surrounding her. Something about Aaron made her feel safe. 'I guess I'm trying to understand … why would Em want to haunt you? What happened between you?'

She shrugged slightly. 'We started off OK. Friends, really. We actually got pretty close. But then when we got older, things deteriorated. She was cool. I was … not. Honestly, I was jealous of her. She didn't like me either, if that makes it any better. She tormented me at school. It was like living with your worst enemy. We were the same age, lived in the same house for six years, but we couldn't have been more opposite.' Veronica swallowed. 'When we played Hide and Seek, it was important to her to win against me. Like, she had to prove herself. And she was super competitive. If only part of you remains when you die in VR, I guess it's going to be that part, since that's the part you were tapping into when you were playing. My guess is she's still determined for me not to win – even beyond death, beyond the point that it makes any sense. Not only that, she wants to take everything away from me. My friends … even my life.'

'*Friends?*' Aaron quirked an eyebrow. 'The other players here, we're friends to you?'

'I …' Veronica cheeks burned. 'You don't know what it's been like these past two years. All my old friends said I'd changed – they didn't know how to be around someone whose sister had died. They didn't know how to support me.

My therapist advised a fresh start. My dad put me into a private school, but it's been hard – even harder in some ways. Being here … it's the first time in years I've felt like I could just be myself, you know? So yeah, I guess you … you *all* mean something to me.'

Aaron held her gaze – and Veronica felt her whole body fizz with some kind of alien energy, her lips tingling. She had never felt like this about anyone before. She leaned towards him, ever so slightly … But then, the house rang with a low-keening rattle, the windows shifting in their frames. Lightning streaked outside behind the snow-covered windows and thunder crashed so loud Veronica thought part of the roof might've collapsed.

Then, bizarrely, music started to play. A thumping bassline punched through Veronica's gut.

They were out of time.

Aaron grabbed her hand wordlessly, and they ran together out of the studio and into the gallery. Here they stumbled to a halt at a sight – illuminated in a ferocious slash of lightning – which nearly stopped Veronica's heart mid-beat.

Every single NPC they'd encountered so far stood in the gallery, expressionless and unmoving – the elder Mrs Coleman; Esteban; the butler; Liz the cook; Ned the gardener; Rita the maid; Simon; Orson himself; and Peter, who sat in his grubby shoes in a wheelchair pushed by Grace – all standing in front of the portraits along the gallery as if lined up for a ceremonial occasion. They were silent and still – like they were hewn of flesh-like painted stone or ghoulish wax.

Orson stood closest to where they'd emerged from the studio. He was dripping wet and when Veronica peered around in horrified curiosity, she saw the huge head wound on the back of his skull. His clothes were ragged and as Veronica watched, a large black spider crawled out of his collar.

She stumbled backwards and right into something hard. She spun around. The glowing CD juke-box sat beside the spiral staircase to the clock tower, pumping out an upbeat melody. The one Yasmin had been messing with downstairs before … before …

'What the …' she breathed. 'How did this get here?'

Aaron grabbed her arm. 'The Game's fucked. You'll see upstairs – it's even worse. Nothing is where it should be any more,' he said. 'Come on.' He tugged her towards the stairs, but Veronica couldn't move.

'We have to go,' Aaron urged.

Veronica nodded and her legs shifted into gear at last. The stairs were only a few metres away.

But then, when lightning flashed, the NPCs transformed into ghoulish, cobweb-strung skeletons – the juke-box was a burned-out wreck, wires exposed, churning out the endless music, which now sounded as though it was playing underwater, and two additional figures appeared by the door leading up to the clock tower in the lightning's temporary glow. Aaron stopped dead in his tracks as he too stared at the newcomers.

Yasmin, the wound on the back of her head trailing blood over her shoulder.

And Em. The drowned girl. Her hair wet. Her eyes darkened by rage.

They disappeared when the lightning flickered out, but Veronica stayed stationary, mute and frozen with fear.

Aaron kicked back into motion first. 'Come *on*,' he said, his voice loud with urgency. He grabbed her hand tighter and pulled her towards the stairs. In a few moments, Aaron had his foot on the bottom steps.

That's when cold hands closed around Veronica's shoulders and arms. She screamed as she was jerked backwards, pulled from Aaron's grasp. She fell on her back, striking her head against the floor, which felt cold, so cold through Aaron's sports jacket.

All the NPCs were gathered around her now, peering down with puzzled disinterest, as if she were a stain on the floor they'd forgotten to clean.

'Veronica!' Aaron shouted. 'What are you doing? The floor ...' His voice was desperate now.

Sure enough, the floorboards were turning to snow under her back as they had done on the first level, a dark, freezing sensation creeping in and curling around her bones. She scrambled up, but the NPCs didn't clear a path.

The bassline continued to thump, resonating in Veronica's chest like a heartbeat, discordant, unravelling as if some thread of the music had been pulled away and the notes were drifting apart.

Darkness bled into her vision as Em's face appeared among the crowd of NPCs. Veronica smelt water, murky and black, the green-rotten scent of pondweed – Em loomed over her and opened her mouth, as if to speak—

A hand punched through Em's body, grabbed Veronica and pulled her forward by the arm, lifting her roughly. *Aaron*. She'd expected to jostle into bodies as he dragged her behind him – instead, she watched as Aaron barrelled through Orson's body as if it were nothing but a human-shaped cloud. Pixels floated in the air, the colour of blood, as Orson disintegrated. Aaron stumbled on to the steps a second time, this time landing awkwardly on his wrist with a crunch like broken plastic. And Veronica tumbled half a beat afterwards, her knees hitting the stairs painfully.

The music cut out.

Lightning flashed … The silence that followed was deafening.

Veronica lowered her head into her arms, Em's gleeful face imprinted on the insides of her eyelids.

'Veronica?'

She lifted up her head reluctantly. The aftermath of terror was rippling through her body. All she wanted to do now was curl up and disappear.

'I know you feel like you want to stop,' Aaron said. 'But you can't, remember? I already tried that.'

'Yeah, OK. I'm OK.' She glanced at his wrist. 'Are you? You fell pretty hard there.'

'Wrist is all good. Watch, not so much,' Aaron said, staring at the digital face, which now had spider cracks running across it and a dead screen. 'Too bad, but hopefully we won't need it again. We're so close.' Then, he lifted his eyes to hers. 'I'm glad you're OK. For a moment there, I thought …'

She opened her mouth, hoping for words, but instead she felt herself leaning forward – lips slightly parted in invitation. His eyebrow quirked, questioning, but something in his eyes softened and he leaned forward too.

When their lips met, Veronica thought she could feel her stomach literally flipping somersaults. The kiss lasted perhaps three seconds, but as Aaron pulled away she could feel her whole body tingling.

'Uh …' She bit her lip. 'Sorry, I … shouldn't have … I didn't think you would …' Charlie's words burned through her: *Have you seen the guy? And have you seen your-fucking-self?* She wished the staircase would open up and swallow her.

'Hey … You don't have to apologise,' Aaron said gently. 'I think it was sweet. It was me who shouldn't have. I just … I see you as more of a friend, you know?'

Veronica's ears were so hot she was surprised her hearing aids weren't melting. 'I guess I'm feeling kind of mixed up about everything,' she tried, gazing down at her trainers. 'I … know I shouldn't be focusing on stuff like that right now. I'm just …'

It wasn't like she hadn't kissed a boy before. First time, she'd been fourteen though and it had been a dare – on the boy's part. Like she was a gross-out challenge instead of an actual person. Then next time, not long before Em had died, it'd been a boy in her study group. Tom. She hadn't really liked him – but there were some things you were expected to do as a teenager, so they'd made out in the library until Veronica's lips were sore. His technique had been pure washing machine. *This* had been different. Crazy, spontaneous, kind of beautiful when, just for a couple of seconds, he had actually kissed her back. She lifted her eyes to Aaron's.

'Hey, it's OK,' he said. 'It's been a while for me, to be honest.' He blinked. 'One thing I didn't tell you about my friend Zara … we were close, you know? Maybe a little more than friends. I haven't really let anyone in since she chose her VR life over me.'

'That must've been hard,' Veronica said softly, feeling a little calmer. 'It's all right. I get that this timing is all screwed. I'm sorry.'

'Yeah, it was hard. And yeah, maybe the timing is off. But you know what? It feels like maybe I'm starting to trust again.' He smiled, slightly lopsidedly. 'Or at least, to trust *you*.'

16

Veronica glanced over her shoulder, back towards the gallery, her mind spinning. The terror of Em's gleeful smile, the sinking floor, followed by the strange, giddy elation of the kiss, followed by Aaron's gentle but crushing let-down – all of it churned in her stomach like an over-rich meal.

The long gallery was now all silent snow and shadows, empty of NPCs, the portraits so dark you could barely see the outlines of people within their frames. More snowflakes drifted from the ceiling like a crowd of silent miniature ghosts. No storm raged against those cracked old windows – though she could now hear it up above, rumbling like a wild beast in a cage.

No music. No juke-box. It was like none of it had ever been.

She turned her gaze upward, past Aaron. The staircase to the clock tower was steep and narrow – Veronica squinted into the darkness. Was Charlie already up there? She must be. But if so, why hadn't the Game ended?

She mustn't have figured out the solution yet, Veronica guessed. Who knew if she had found the studio containing the additional information for Level Three? Even if she had, the solution would require piecing together. Simply because you had the puzzle pieces, didn't mean you could make them fit.

Or else Em had got to her – but Veronica didn't want to think about that.

'You really didn't see Charlie up there?' she asked Aaron.

He held her eyes for a little longer than felt natural, then shook his head. 'I didn't see her. But it's different up there. Confusing,' he said quietly.

'Things down here are pretty screwed up too,' Veronica pointed out.

'No,' he said. 'It's even worse. How do you think I wound up looking like this?' He pointed to the scorch marks on his jacket, the tears in his jeans. 'You'll see. It's like the whole place is trying to fight us off.'

'Maybe it is,' Veronica said quietly. 'Maybe the Game can't distinguish between us and Em any more. We're all foreign bodies who need to be destroyed.'

The storm threw itself against the shuddering walls – it felt as if the entire building was at risk of whipping into ash-like snowflakes and disappearing into digital oblivion.

Aaron looked suddenly anxious. 'We have to get moving.'

'Wait,' Veronica said. 'We've got all we're going to get from this place. Three clues. Three pieces of vital information. And a few extras. We need to work it all out before we go up. Sounds like we don't want to hang about on that floor.'

'Yeah, OK. That makes sense. But … I'm hoping you can help there. It's all murky to me.'

Above them, a scuffle and a creak echoed down the staircase. Veronica glanced up, shook her head. Was the wind playing tricks again?

'Luckily, I'm pretty good at this kind of thing,' Veronica said, sliding the Walkman from her pocket as she climbed up to Aaron's step and sat beside him under the staircase window. 'Let's go through it piece by piece … The ground floor: the clue was the love note, and the vital information from the cook placed Orson with her at midnight.' She rewound and played the tape. Liz's voice rang through the staircase. When the clip ended she said, 'We also found out from Esteban that he had a relationship with Orson and that Orson wanted to stop running the business, which really pissed off his mum.'

'Second level,' said Aaron. 'Charlie found that note

placing Grace Coleman at a psychiatrist's appointment in London yesterday evening. There's no way she could've got back here in time.'

'But after you left we saw a car out of the window. Grace's car. And Grace definitely had a motive.'

Aaron raised an eyebrow. 'Right. She said she was coming home in her answerphone message on Level Three.'

'Which Orson might never have received, since he was in his meeting with Mrs Coleman and Esteban,' Veronica said. 'And then he was with Liz.'

'Do you think Grace did it?'

Veronica frowned. 'Honestly, no. It feels almost *too* obvious.'

'I'm already confused,' Aaron said. 'Doesn't it seem like *everyone* so far has had a motive?'

'Exactly. Let's review the suspects. I think we can probably discount Ned and Rita, who didn't appear to know Orson well at all – I can't see that either would have a motive. And Liz loved him, so she wouldn't have done it unless she was turned down – but that's not where the clues were leading us, like Orson's discarded letters to Grace. In fact, she was hoping they would finally be together for real. And Esteban. He was too honest with us to be the killer. I think they're all nos. Mrs Coleman … she was cold, but it seems unlikely she'd kill her own son, even if it would have given her control of the business. Let's chalk her down as a maybe to be ultra-careful. The butler too, since apparently he was really cagey.'

Veronica was forming mental lists. 'After we saw the car, we spoke to Simon. He was a dick, basically, who didn't seem to like his father at all – or his brother. He said something about how Peter was more like their dad than he was – a weird statement, but that was the key information. I don't know. I'm going to put him alongside his grandmother in the *maybe* column. He was really angry about his father giving up on the business. And though Simon's only thirteen, he's definitely tall enough to have pushed a grown man over that banister.'

'OK,' Aaron said, blinking at her. 'Then what?'

'Level Three. The key information was from Peter – Orson and Grace's oldest son.' Veronica pressed play on the Walkman and the two of them leaned over the headphones. Peter's stilted voice told them how his father always seemed uncomfortable around him. What was it about that clip? Something was niggling at her ... but she tried to think systematically.

'We haven't discussed the butler,' Aaron pointed out.

'The only suspect I never saw,' said Veronica. She frowned. 'Charlie and Yasmin didn't really get anything out of him, though he said he slept through the night.'

'That could be suspicious in itself,' said Aaron.

'Or, it could be a red herring,' Veronica said. 'See, there's the Level Three clue – Charlie found it really quickly – sleeping pills in the butler's room.' She paused. 'That seems to corroborate the butler's story – that he slept through the night. I'd have liked a look at the pills to see exactly what they were and how many had been used.'

'And there's the extra info on the answering machine,' Aaron said. 'The message from Grace about the psychiatry appointment she made for Peter. Something about processing what he had found out.'

Veronica played the tape.

'Grace said he needs to "talk through everything he's feeling",' Aaron said. 'What do you think that's about?' Then he sighed. 'Wait, are we really saying Peter could be a suspect? He's bedridden. How could he possibly have done it?'

Veronica shook her head. 'There was another thing – not an official clue, but something that seemed off to me: a pair of shoes by the side of Peter's bed. He said he only ever goes to the bathroom and back, so it felt strange to me that he had an easily accessible pair of shoes – and they were dirty, you know? They looked like … like …' Veronica bit her lip. 'Well, like my shoes did after crawling in those secret passages. Scuffed and covered in cobwebs. So I tapped them with these.' She held out Yasmin's trainers. 'The trail of footsteps led to his bed from the secret passages.'

Aaron's eyes widened. 'Did you see where they went?'

'No. I was interrupted and the trainers didn't work a second time.' Veronica frowned. 'Just because he can't walk far, doesn't mean he was in bed the whole time ...' Her eyebrows shot up. 'Aaron, what if Peter saw, or heard, or discovered something? Whatever Grace was talking about in the message.'

'So what we're saying is we think Peter found out something terrible that led him to kill his father,' said Aaron. 'By pushing him over the banister?'

'That's where the clues are leading us,' Veronica said. 'But why? What had he found out?' She answered her own question. 'The affair? Could he have heard Liz and Orson in the studio? Even if Orson mostly kept the door locked, that doesn't keep out voices ... sounds ...'

Aaron started to speak quickly. 'An affair is one thing, but Grace said Peter was asking questions about his identity.' Both of them thought for a moment, then Aaron continued. 'Peter had obviously spoken to his mother about whatever he'd discovered and was angry – angry enough for her to seek psychological help on his behalf. Veronica ... do you think ...'

'Perhaps Grace wasn't really his mother? But Liz was?' Veronica supplied. She let out a long, ponderous breath. 'Liz and Orson had known each other since childhood.'

'Peter could have been Orson and Liz's son? Or perhaps Liz's son with someone else?'

'Either way, that's huge. Orson and Grace obviously agreed to raise him as their own, with Liz able to watch over him too. That would explain why Simon's comment about how different they are was important – perhaps he even knew, or suspected. And it would also explain why Orson avoided Peter or was uncomfortable around him. Because he *was* different.' She blinked. 'Plus, why it felt as if, even when she was apparently telling us everything, Liz was holding something back.'

As she thought about Peter, Veronica felt a sympathetic anger swirling inside her. She had an inkling of what he had felt – at least in terms of discovering the affair. She remembered the first time she'd realised Nyra and Dad were seeing each other. He'd left his iPad unlocked, face down on the sofa, but she'd tilted it up, skimmed through the exchange. Nyra worked with Dad at his publisher, but this wasn't work chat. This was different. Veronica may have been nine years old, but she wasn't a fool.

Mum and Dad had been having problems, but they were trying to work it out – that's what they'd told Veronica anyway. Mum's eyes had been full of tears as she apologised for arguing at night, for waking Veronica up. '*I'll be better,*' she'd said. '*I promise I'll be better.*'

'We'll *be better*,' her dad had said, taking her mum's hand.

But she knew the secret she'd discovered was the end of that. No more trying. Dad hadn't tried anyway – he'd only been pretending. That was the first time Veronica realised someone could wear a kind face but be different underneath.

When Dad had walked back in, white-hot rage had coursed through her body and she'd thrown the iPad at the wall. The screen had shattered. Mum had left that night and Veronica hadn't seen her since. The only contact had been occasional and via Dad, who assured her she was checking up on Veronica, she still cared, but she couldn't cope.

Peter must've felt what she felt. Mum and Liz had both walked away from their child, let other people raise their own blood. Watched from a safe distance, as if their children were barely more than characters on a reality TV show.

Both Veronica's parents had betrayed her. Both Peter's had betrayed him.

'I think this is it,' Veronica said quietly. 'This is the solution. It's a motive big enough to make Peter want his father dead – or at least to confront him about it. Orson had been drinking – remember the champagne bottle in the fountain? Even a sick boy could have toppled him over the banister.' She paused. 'You know …' Veronica nudged Aaron gently. 'We make a great team.'

'I mean, you worked it out,' mumbled Aaron. He was blushing again, avoiding her eyes. 'But thanks.'

She smiled to herself. 'We should go up. We have an answer we can try.' Veronica stood and offered Aaron her hand.

'You got it,' Aaron said as she pulled him up to join her.

The clock tower was broader than it had appeared from the outside – its staircase less a tight corkscrew and more a long, winding climb. Veronica felt her heartbeat rise up as she started to walk. This was the final level.

The way out.

LEVEL FOUR

17

Darkness swallowed them – a thick, viscous, malignant darkness like none Veronica had ever felt. Where was the window she had heard rattling? Where was the light? Was Em up here? Aaron's hand reached for hers, held it tight, and they continued to climb side by side up the broad steps.

She felt a small twist of annoyance even as she appreciated the comfort of his hand in hers. He said he didn't feel that way about her ... but didn't he realise his attentiveness had been sending a signal? Still was, in fact?

Sometimes it felt like people never stopped lying.

As they climbed, the sounds of the storm distorted in the strangest way – Veronica's hearing aids shrieked and whistled, sweat pricking on her lip in a sudden heat, which quickly disappeared into a damp, blue freeze.

'What's happening?' she said, but her voice was so quiet it was like she was speaking into a pillow.

'Just keep going,' Aaron said, as if from very far away. 'We'll get through it.'

Veronica felt as if they'd been climbing forever. As she lifted her foot towards the next step, she was certain the staircase had extended itself, an extra turn added in the impossibly long upward spiral.

She stumbled, forcing Aaron to grip her hand harder, holding her up.

'Don't fall,' he said, glancing over his shoulder with fear in his eyes. And as she too glanced backwards, confused, she realised that the staircase behind them had disappeared completely into a snowdrift the colour of dusk – grey and sparkling, glowing with a dim light all of its own.

There was no going back.

Finally, when Veronica felt she was close to collapsing, the muscles in her thighs burning with a vicious heat, the staircase ended. At the top was a door, swinging soundlessly back and forth on its hinges as if moved by a breeze, *or an invisible hand*, but never quite banging against the frame. A gentle *creak-creak* sound caused Veronica to stop in her tracks, holding Aaron back from the door – it didn't sound in time with its fluctuations. Had it been a floorboard? Or was it simply one of the many sound effects that had become dislocated from the Game, drifting in a digital world without an anchor?

'Come on,' said Aaron. He reached out and opened the door.

A flash of silver.

Veronica didn't know what possessed her, but she pushed Aaron forward, as hard as she could – he cried out in shock, landing hard on his shoulder with a nasty crack. But the silver flash ... the axe ... had missed his head, where it would've landed, and instead now buried itself deep in the top of his leg. Veronica rushed inside.

Charlie had been waiting behind the door. Now, her face was set with determination as she heaved the axe out of the gruesome wound – Aaron cried out again, this time in pure agony, a hoarse, broken sound, which caused Veronica an almost physical jolt of echoing pain. She felt her body kick into action, nearly totally divorced from her mind. She ran at Charlie, barrelling into her and smashing her against a set of large, overstuffed bookshelves. The sleeve of Charlie's yellow check suit – as battered and smudged with grime as the sports jacket around Veronica's shoulders – ripped as she tore her arm free from the shelves and wrestled Veronica backwards.

Books fell down around her in a hail of hard spines and flapping pages – and a luminescent, shimmering disc hit

Veronica square in the face, sending pain arcing through the bridge of her nose. Distraction – for a second. But that was all it took: Charlie's knee was in her stomach and Veronica was doubled over, winded. Another silver flash. Veronica lurched out of the way, stumbling, as the axe lodged itself in the floor beside her – a moment later, and it would've been buried in her back. One of her hearing aids had fallen out, but she couldn't see it in the confusion – everything on her left suddenly felt muffled, like someone had stuffed cotton wool in her ear. Her sound–spacial awareness lurched off-kilter and suddenly it felt as if the storm were inside her head, while the sounds of Charlie cursing under her breath nearby were flung into the background.

Charlie must've swung the axe hard because she couldn't lift it up this time – the sharp blade was lodged firmly in the floorboards.

'Fuck!' Charlie shouted, casting her eyes about the room, presumably for another weapon.

'Charlie – stop!' Veronica yelled, her voice panicky. 'Just stop.'

'You can't fool me!' Charlie screamed. 'You deranged piece-of-shit ghost!'

Veronica spun around wildly, looking for Aaron. He was lying near the doorway, his face tight with pain. Oh god – he was really badly hurt. She hurried towards him, noting as she did the cavernous, ruined library surrounding her. The library contained mouldering books with leather spines and once-gold titles, festooned with cobwebs and even ivy trailing in through cracks from the outside, and Veronica realised with creeping horror that this room was likely a melding of the Game's original clock tower and a location from Hide and Seek. Because in addition to the books, she noticed cassettes, CDs, records and video tapes strewn around the space too – even broken and smashed devices Veronica was sure were old-fashioned gaming consoles and computers. A boxy TV fizzed and flashed somewhere nearby, half-hanging from a buckled shelf.

A silent, ferocious wind whipped through the space, stirring the fallen books.

Aaron was conscious, his eyes wide with pain and anger. Conscious was good, conscious meant he might be OK, Veronica thought dimly. And he was pinching together the gaping sides of his wound, so he knew he had to stop the bleeding. Then his eyes widened further as he glanced over Veronica's head. 'Duck!'

She ducked.

Something whizzed past her head and smashed with a thunderous sound against the doorframe, narrowly missing its target, amber glass shattering over the floor. *A paperweight.* Veronica turned around. Charlie had stopped searching for other deadly missiles and was trying to dislodge the axe from the floor again, her jaw tight.

'Just fuck off and leave me alone!' Charlie shouted. 'It's Veronica you want, isn't it?'

'Charlie, please. It's us,' Veronica said, imploring the other girl with her eyes, her voice, every cell of her body to believe it.

Charlie was gritting her teeth. 'Why should I believe you? You pretended to be Yasmin to get to me, in the gallery. And again up here – twice. You were quite quite convincing … though not convincing enough.' Triumphantly, she pulled the axe from the floorboard. 'Besides, I locked Veronica in the butler's room. So you'll have to prove it. Prove you're really Veronica and not Em.'

Veronica's stretched out her hands, holding up her palms. The quiet wind whipped her hair, sending a tendril over her eyes, but she held Charlie's gaze. 'I'm the one you slapped out by the woodshed, remember? Trying to knock some sense into me. I think that was before Em even entered the Game. You know, when I passed out in the entrance hall—' Her voice broke. Charlie hesitated, doubt clouding her face. Veronica's mind raced. 'You talked about some kind of wardrobe you couldn't access – you had loads of expensive stuff in there …'

'My NFT wardrobe,' Charlie muttered quietly. Tears

trembled in her eyes. She had stopped walking towards Veronica and Aaron, the axe frozen in her hand. Her face was a picture of relief. 'It's really you.' Charlie's hand dropped to her side, the axe hanging limp and useless. Her shoulders lost their fighting stance. 'Fuck.'

Veronica felt her own shoulders sag too. Charlie finally, actually believed her. Veronica knelt back down at Aaron's side. He was conscious but quiet, focused on pinching the sides of his wound together, his jaw set in determination. 'Do you have anything we can use as a tourniquet?' she asked Charlie.

'Yeah, that's the least I can do. Sorry, Aaron,' Charlie said, her voice weak.

'It's nothing. Just a scratch,' he joked, a smile flickering over his lips.

Charlie snorted and pulled the brown leather belt from around her waist. They looped it tightly around the top of Aaron's leg to slow the bleeding. He winced as Veronica fastened the gold buckle. She lifted her head then, and took in her surroundings. The room bore little resemblance to the dimensions of a tower, except that it too was round. And it was tall too – taller than the clock tower could possibly have been based on the outside view Veronica remembered, the upper echelons of the shelves disappearing into darkness. Two fireplaces spat orange flames up howling chimneys.

'Where's the way out?' Veronica asked.

Charlie pointed to a small red door on the far side of the huge round room. Painted with glossy red paint and set with a large brass knocker, it was out of place, like the door Veronica had opened to enter the Game in the first place. Veronica felt her heart stutter, like she'd missed the last step on a staircase, her foot descending into thin air. They were so close.

'Have you figured it out?' Charlie asked. 'The mystery, I mean? Because I stood there for-fucking-ever, guessing every solution I could think of.' She glanced over at Veronica. 'Sorry, by the way. About leaving you.'

A sudden gust of wind rattled the windows between the bookshelves.

'I think we've got it figured out,' Veronica said. 'And it's OK, Charlie. All the stuff that happened between us before we got here – it doesn't really matter now.'

'Cool,' Charlie said, straightening her battered suit jacket. 'Listen up. The NPCs here … I've found through long, hard experience that it's best if they don't notice you.' She clutched her axe tightly. 'They're pretty dopey, so it's not too tricky. I'll go ahead and keep an eye out. If I see one, I'll hold out my arm like this.' She held one arm towards them, hand flexed upward in a kind of *stop* gesture. 'Just stand very still and don't make a sound until the NPC passes, OK?'

Veronica nodded, feeling a fizz of mingled nerves and excitement.

Together, Charlie and Veronica helped Aaron to his feet. He tried to bat them away but swayed unsteadily as he attempted to rest weight on his injured leg, a sheen of sweat across his forehead. He surrendered when Veronica slung the varsity jacket back over his shoulders and looped his arm firmly around hers.

The library was lit by several of the familiar arched windows, slowly filling like hourglasses – but the natural light in here was dim, a fact not entirely attributable to the snow-heavy storm clouds flickering outside. Veronica realised daylight in this digital world was fading, glimpsing a slice of sky the soft purple of dusk. A few wall lights had glowed to life, sending upward arcs of yellow between the bookcases – but they served only to multiply the deep grey shadows.

The floor was covered with broken, scattered stuff – which made it difficult for Aaron to navigate with his injured leg dragging.

They hadn't been walking long when Charlie froze, holding out her hand in the agreed *stop* gesture.

A figure wandered out from between the shelves. The cook – Liz. She was still holding the kitchen knife they'd seen her holding earlier, and blood was dripping from her thumb on to the floor. Her hair was wild and her once-white apron was grimy and torn – her expression vacant. Her lips were moving though.

She wandered across the floor towards the group, appearing not to notice the junk crunching under her sensible shoes. She passed Charlie – and then she was close enough for Veronica to hear the phrase she was whispering, over and over.

'Ready or not, here I come. Ready or not, here I come. Ready or not, here I come.' She was close now – perhaps a metre away from Veronica and Aaron – her eyes fixed at some point in the middle distance. She stopped. Close enough for Veronica to feel the whisper on her cheek. Then, she stopped speaking.

A *drip-drip-drip* sound. Wetness through Veronica's shoe. Blood dripping from the cook's hand.

Veronica held her breath, her muscles starting to judder from holding Aaron's weight so long. The impulse to step backwards was overwhelming … but she resisted.

Liz turned away slowly, robotically. She carried on walking, finally disappearing between the shelves on the other side of the room.

Veronica let out a long breath – feeling Aaron's muscles relax. She felt a wave of nausea as she noticed the red stain on her left trainer.

'Come on,' said Charlie. 'That was too fucking close. We shouldn't hang about.'

Ivy pushed its way through the bookshelves in real time as they walked – like green fingers – dislodging books and other paraphernalia from the shelves. Mice bubbled up through the rubble. Here and there, Veronica spied a patch of damp on the floor, fizzing with sparks from broken TV sets and old consoles. The air smelt of pondweed – the two virtual worlds of the Game and Hide and Seek combining into a bizarre hellscape.

But, for now, Em didn't appear. And Veronica allowed herself to hope that, somehow, they'd defeated her on Level Three – when Aaron had punched through her to lift Veronica to safety, perhaps that had been the end of it.

Perhaps, if they could just reach the red door, she'd really be free.

A few paces further, Veronica was certain she heard the echo of footsteps somewhere in the dark corners of the room, where bookcases projected pools of black shadow on to the floor. Charlie gave the hand signal. Orson Coleman wandered across the library. As he passed, Veronica noticed the wound at the back of his head was like a gaping cave, sloshing with water that spilt down his back.

When he was gone, they continued.

Veronica's one remaining hearing aid wasn't helping

matters. Wearing only one was probably worse than not wearing them at all – she felt off balance, unable to distinguish background from foreground. But she was afraid of missing something – that one higher-pitched noise she might otherwise gloss over.

The red door was suddenly barely a few paces away. They covered the last bit of agonising ground and Veronica heaved a sigh of relief. She and Charlie helped Aaron down to the floor. Blood was soaking through his jeans and a sheen of sweat was on his brow. The smell of iron was overpowering.

She and Charlie exchanged a worried glance. If they didn't escape the Game soon, Aaron might die. For real.

Veronica's muscles were trembling. She pressed her hand against the door, the painted glossy wood cool against her skin. Finally, they were at the end.

'Fine,' said Charlie suddenly. She swallowed, as if struggling with words that were hard to spit out.

'Fine what?' asked Veronica, surprised by the outburst.

'Fine. You can fucking have it. The prize. For your stupid sick brother.' She tossed her ponytail – which was somehow still perfect and glossy. 'I mean, I'll let you say the solution. I won't, you know, try to jump in.'

Veronica blinked. 'Thanks? I mean, you said you'd already tried every solution so … I sort of already assumed …'

Charlie glared at her. Then, she rolled her eyes. 'Anyway,

here's hoping you have enough cash left over to buy me a drink sometime. Or, like, a whole fucking bottle of Dom Pérignon so I can stagger around like Orson Coleman in a badass suit, swigging a hundred pounds per sip. Though, like, without the grisly death part.'

'Of course,' Veronica said. 'Thank you, Charlie.' She guessed this was as close as the girl was ever going to get to a genuine friendly gesture, so she'd take it.

'Aren't you going to put up a fight, A?' Charlie said, peering down at Aaron. 'You're going to let this sap walk away with the prize, huh?'

He grinned through his pain. 'Just. Say it,' he said, nodding at Veronica. 'Go on.'

This was it. At last, Veronica would be out of here – and with enough money to pay for Max's treatment, assuming he was still alive. And Em ... she would be trapped here forever, unable to reach her outside of VR. And there was no way, this time, Veronica was ever playing a VR game again.

She rested her hand against the red door but hesitated, glancing over her shoulder at the room behind, at Charlie and Aaron, who smiled at her shakily. They'd all been through so much already; now, she had to seize the moment. Reveal the answer. Win the Game. She cleared her throat.

'The killer was—'

A black shape rose in the nearest window, off to the side

of the door, and the words died in Veronica's throat. Something started to thump loudly, violently against the glass.

A fist.

Charlie stepped forward, her axe raised, her jaw set. 'Some kind of psycho NPC? Knew we wouldn't get through without a fight.'

The fist broke through glass, fumbled with the latch.

'Wait,' said Aaron, squinting. 'I think it's …'

The window swung in, bringing with it a gust of wind-whipped snow and a familiar face.

Nate.

18

'Stand back,' said Aaron. 'Could be a trick.'

Charlie held her axe in readiness as Nate tumbled in through the window, heaving on the floor. 'I don't think so,' she said, under her breath.

Nate lifted his head and stared straight at Veronica, who stood frozen in shock.

'Nate …' said Charlie. 'Is it really you?'

Ivy snaked through the window where he'd entered. The walls started to crack. A freezing wind blew through the library, raising the hairs on Veronica's arms. Nate staggered to his feet. A trail of blood had frozen between his nose and his lips and he was cradling his left arm. His fingers were bloody, his whole body was covered in frost, and his eyes were burning with anger.

'Yeah, it's me,' he said. He jabbed a finger in Veronica's direction. 'No thanks to her.'

Veronica felt the world swirl around her.

'What do you mean?' Charlie said.

'She pushed me out of the Level Two window,' Nate said. 'I've had to claw my way up the damn clocktower to tell you. It's been her all along. Veronica is the killer. She killed Yasmin. She thought she killed me. And I'd hazard a guess she's planning to kill you too.'

Snow swirled in through the window as Charlie turned to face Veronica. 'Is this true?' she whispered.

'Of course not,' Veronica said, keeping her voice steady. 'Charlie, you know me.' She trained her eyes on Nate. 'I don't think this is really Nate at all. Em has taken over his body like she did to Yasmin, back in the gallery.'

Nearby, a black TV lying on its back sprang to life, white static searing across its screen in a blare of noise and stuttering light. The players stared, transfixed, as a shape outlined itself in the static. The shape of a face. And where once had been white noise, a single word hissed from its mouth in a distorted, ugly shout: 'LIAR.'

Now, the static ghost of images flickered across the screen, eventually hardening into grainy black-and-white footage. Veronica realised she was gazing down into the tiny room under the stairs – the one housing the juke-box – in

CCTV-style video. The door opened. The tinny sound of a voice emerged from the TV speakers as Yasmin shouted back through the door.

'*Wow! It's a storage room and there's a fricking juke-box in here! Like, a CD juke-box! I didn't even know they made those.*'

'That's Yaz,' said Charlie, her voice unsteady. 'This is gameplay footage, isn't it?'

'Don't trust anything you see,' Veronica said quietly. 'This is VR, remember? Everything can be manipulated.'

Even so, Veronica's heart hammered as she watched Yasmin play around with the juke-box. Yasmin jumped as music blared, pressing her hands over her ears – then jabbed frantically at the machine's clunky interface to find the volume.

The door of the juke-box room swung open.

Veronica's throat was dry.

'V ... that's you,' Charlie breathed. 'You were first in the room after Yasmin?'

'I told you,' said Nate.

Veronica shook her head. 'VR, remember? You can't trust this.'

On-screen, Yasmin hadn't noticed anyone enter – the music was too loud, synths and a thrumming bassline distorting through the TV set's small speakers. The Veronica on-screen was frozen with an odd expression, as if staring at someone not quite in Yasmin's position – someone slightly over her shoulder. Veronica squinted. A shadow, a staticky smudge, *was* hovering above the juke-box.

But it wasn't as clear as it had been at the time. *She* wasn't as clear as she had been.

'What is that?' Nate whispered. 'That …'

'Em,' said Veronica flatly.

'I thought you said this wasn't real?' Aaron said, his voice strained and breathy.

'Half-truths. Em's trying to manipulate us, don't you see?'

The Veronica on-screen reached down robotically and picked up a broken metal candelabra on the floor. When she lifted her eyes, her gaze was fixed firmly on Yasmin.

'No …' Charlie said softly, looking away.

Yasmin never turned around, even when the candelabra arced high over her head. The picture cut out the moment the candelabra reached her skull – but Veronica could hear the sound in her head. When metal met bone.

She'd told herself it wasn't real.

The screen cut to static.

'V, I swear to god you need to tell me if this is true, right now,' Charlie said, her voice tense.

'There's more,' said Nate, before Veronica could reply.

He was right. Now, a new scene fizzed to life.

The Level Two corridor. The light was flickering and Nate, facing the camera, stood in front of one of the huge floor-to-ceiling arched windows. A figure floated in the hall, between him and the camera. Like last time, the floating figure was indistinct – a white-noise shadow casting electric specks into the space. Veronica shifted into view at his side. Then, all the light blacked out.

'*Veronica?*' Nate's voice from the screen.

'*Stay very still.*' Veronica watched herself reply.

The window and light fixtures flickered on, off and on again.

'This is how it happened,' Nate said. 'This is real.'

On-screen Veronica's eyes flicked from the ghost, to Nate, to the window, her expression calculating. She took a purposeful step towards Nate as the light cut again.

'*Nate!*' she called out. '*Where are you?*'

Lights on. She staggered towards him, losing her footing slightly. On-screen Nate's face looked doubtful, suddenly. Veronica's back was to the camera.

'I knew what you were going to do in that moment,' Nate said now. 'You looked like a different person. Suddenly, I understood.'

'You didn't understand anything. I was confused, Nate – the lights. Em tricked me.' Veronica's voice was full of emotion. 'You have to believe me. Look!'

301

On-screen, Em's ghost was surrounding Veronica, a cloud of pixels obscuring her actions.

'It's as if … as if Em was trying to stop her,' said Charlie quietly.

'*Confuse* me,' Veronica corrected. *Em never was as strong as she thought.*

Through the cloud of pixels, the Veronica on-screen reached out – *pushed*. Nate crashed through the glass. Veronica glanced over her shoulder, up the stairs. There was a slight, nearly imperceptible delay. Then, '*Nate!*' she screamed.

'This footage – it's all a trick,' said Veronica. She met Charlie's eyes, Aaron's, Nate's. Her voice was high and panicky. 'I'm sorry, Nate. I didn't push you on purpose. Charlie, I should have been more honest. But I knew it looked bad. Can't you see? Em's trying to frame me. She followed me into the Game. She polluted it, turned it deadly. Now, she wants you to do her dirty work. She wants you to kill me.'

A loud bang rang through the library – Veronica jumped back as the TV set sparked and burst into flames, the air full of electricity.

Behind the burning TV, several books flew from the shelves, pages tearing out mid-air. One of them nearly hit Veronica on the head – she ducked, barely in time, the books crashing to the floor in a cacophony of spines.

'What the hell?' Charlie said.

Then, a small figure emerged from behind the nearest bank of bookshelves, their face lit up, ghoulish in the firelight. *Yasmin.* Her eyes burned, her body was taut with anger. As Veronica watched though, her face shifted. Her hair lengthened and curled. She grew taller by a couple of inches. Her leather jacket changed in texture and grew wet, dripping on to the junk at her feet, then darkened into the familiar velvet dress, the faux-fur coat.

Veronica held Em's gaze. 'You should have stayed dead,' she said, her voice trembling as she stepped forward to face her stepsister. Her hand slid into her pocket where she felt the reassuring weight of the gun she'd stolen from Dead Stars. 'But you couldn't even give me that, could you? You made my life hell when you were alive. Now, you're determined to ruin it from beyond the grave with your lies – and Max will pay the price. Your own brother.'

'You're a liar,' Em said, her voice glitching as she raised her hand to point at Veronica. 'You killed Yasmin. You tried to kill Nate. And you killed me too.'

Veronica's eyes shifted from Aaron and Nate – both severely injured – to Charlie, whose hand was tight around her axe. Charlie was staring back at Veronica, as breathless as if she'd sprinted up a flight of stairs. Only one of these players was a real threat.

'Don't believe her, Charlie,' Veronica said. 'You know me, remember?'

The other girl's face was doubtful, her eyes trembling with tears.

'You *don't* know her. None of us do,' said Nate, staggering forward and meeting Charlie's eyes, cradling his bad arm. 'I found out just before Veronica pushed me that her sister didn't die in VR due to an accident. Veronica held her underwater in the game and drowned her. It was because I found out that she pushed me. She knew the fact she'd murdered her sister in a VR game would look suspicious. None of us would trust her after that.'

'It was a game,' Veronica snapped. 'I didn't know she'd die for real, didn't know Yas—'

Charlie gasped as if she'd been punched. Veronica realised her mistake: she'd slipped up, admitted it.

Em started to laugh. Her voice echoed round the library, pierced through Veronica's head like a needle as black water spilt from her mouth. Charlie raised her eyes – and her axe.

'No more hiding,' Em said, her voice sing-song, distorted. Her body disappeared, reappeared a few feet closer. 'Found you!' She disappeared again, reappeared in a burst of pixels barely a few paces from Veronica. 'Found you! Found you!' Her arms reached out, her eyes eager.

Veronica had lost control of the narrative – but she had

one card left in her hand. There was nothing left to do but play it. Em disappeared again, reappeared, her hands closing around Veronica's neck.

In one breath, she pulled the laser gun from her pocket, trained it on Em's stomach.

'Finders keepers, losers weepers,' Veronica whispered, Em's face inches from her own, and pulled the trigger.

A bright flash of blue light burst from the weapon, a sound like an electronic *zoop* rang through the air. Em disappeared in a shower of dark pixels.

Charlie screamed. Veronica pointed the gun at her.

'Drop the axe,' she said calmly. 'Game over.'

Charlie was frozen to the spot with shock.

'Drop. The. Axe,' Veronica tried again. 'And shut up. Or I'll shoot.'

The hammer strikes the nail that sticks out, Veronica thought. *And sometimes, the nail strikes back.*

The axe thunked on to the wooden floor.

'Veronica?' Aaron's voice, low and trembling. 'What's happening? Did you really kill Yasmin ... and try to kill Nate?'

'Yes,' Veronica said, her gun remaining fixed on Charlie, the tremble in her voice the one sign of the emotion she was pushing down, deep inside. She glared at Nate before turning to Aaron. 'Get down, all of you. Hands on the floor in front of you.'

'You killed Yasmin,' Charlie whispered, her voice laden with hatred as she dropped to her knees. 'And I just … handed you the prize. I fucking *trusted* you.'

'Yasmin was collateral damage,' Veronica said calmly. 'I saw Em in that room, hovering over the juke-box – and I knew what I had to do. I had already killed my sister once in VR. So, I killed her a second time. It felt like a fair price for everything she did to me in real life. Except, Yasmin was standing in the way.'

'Collateral damage?' Charlie's face reddened, her whole body trembling with rage.

'But Nate?' Aaron asked.

'Oh, that was on purpose. When he found out from Angel about what I'd done to Em, I knew he wouldn't trust me again,' Veronica said. 'He wouldn't let me win.'

'It was stupid,' Nate said to Veronica, his voice hoarse with exertion, 'giving me your brother's name. A tiny bit of digging and it was all there.'

'Not as stupid as you telling me what you'd found out,' she said.

'Guess I didn't think you were actually psychotic.'

'I held my own sister underwater until she drowned, and you didn't think I'd push a stranger out of a window?'

'Touché,' Nate said.

A small choking noise from Charlie – a sound of horror

or disgust, Veronica couldn't tell.

'You know what sucks?' Veronica said, warming to her subject. 'I hate the lying. The cheating. I hate it more than anything. You know how Em's mum and my dad got together? They were having an affair. A sordid goddamn affair while my mum had an actual real-life mental breakdown trying to fix their marriage. The night she found out, she left and never came back. Even though she promised, *promised* never to leave me.' The laser gun was surprisingly heavy in her hand. She swiped it around the room – Aaron, Nate, Charlie. All staring at her. All at her mercy. 'And then *they* moved in. Nyra and Em. She started out nice. It's crazy to think now, but I actually thought we were friends. Max was born a year later and I started to think everything would be OK. He held us together. He made us a family, or something like it. Then a few years down the line, Em revealed her true colours. I've been surrounded by fucking liars my whole life –' she was shouting now – 'and the worst thing is, the one person who never lied to me, the one person who's actually fucking good in my life, is Max. And he's dying. In order to save his life, *I* had to be the liar for once.'

The wind roared. A smell of damp pervaded the air and when Veronica glanced down, she noticed she was standing in ankle-deep water, seeping in through her trainers. The lake.

A small distraction, but a distraction nonetheless.

Suddenly, a roar split the air, followed by rapid, splashing footsteps. Veronica raised her eyes and her gun towards the sound. When she squeezed the trigger, the *zoop* felt like it shattered the Game itself. The tower trembled; a high electronic noise rang through the air. The flesh of Veronica's hands, still wrapped around the gun, separated into pixels before coalescing once more.

Charlie was a few feet away from Veronica, her arm frozen in mid-air. The axe dropped from her hand and fell into the water with a splash. Charlie blanched as a red stain bloomed up from her stomach, and spread across the vest under her open blazer.

'You're wrong. Yaz was good,' Charlie whispered. 'She was worth ten of you.'

She fell, face down, into the rising flood.

The desperate howl of the wind was the only reply.

Veronica turned to Nate and then to Aaron, who had his back against the red door, his face ashen. Both were injured and exhausted; neither was a threat to her. But she couldn't have survivors. Not now. If anyone else emerged from this place alive, they'd know the truth – they could go to the authorities. The laws on killing in VR were murky, but she was pretty sure she could end up in jail for attempting to kill Nate when she'd known he could die in real life too – let alone Charlie. She had bigger plans for her prize money than bail.

She walked over to Nate. Held out the gun. He was shaking in the rising water, his hands bloody and broken from the long climb up the tower.

'You shouldn't have come back,' she said.

'You won't spare my life?' he asked. 'You've killed three times now. You don't have to kill again.'

'Not an option. You know that.'

'So what? You're just going to … live with this? With what you've done?' Nate asked. 'Four lives on your conscience.'

'Four lives to save Max's. I'll be just fine.' She rested her finger on the trigger.

Nate launched himself up, reaching for the laser gun. She kept hold of it, but when he knocked her hand downward, it discharged. A loud *zoop*, a splash and a scream.

Nate had been hit, a scorched, smoking wound had opened above his knee and he had fallen back down in the water. Veronica trained the gun on him again.

Suddenly, she felt something – Nate's shoe? – smash into her leg, and she fell backwards. She tried to keep the gun above the water, but it was deepening fast. She felt pondweed – hands? – pulling her down, the bottom of the lake mulchy and soft below her yielding as she struggled to keep her weapon dry. A shape shifted over her head. *Em?* No – it was Nate. The lake appeared to lift him up, even as it pulled her under. She aimed once again and discharged the laser gun before it was pulled out of her hands by the rushing current. She watched desperately as its bright shape sunk down into the mulch beneath.

But the gun had already done its final job.

Nate's lifeless body fell through the murky water, a wide wound in his chest pluming with dark blood. Dead – for real, this time.

She surfaced. The weeds grasped at her like fingers, but she was a strong swimmer; she wasn't weak. Not like Em. She wouldn't be held down.

Her remaining hearing aid stuttered and whined – damaged by the water. Veronica ripped it out, spat the water from her mouth, gasping as she tried to find her bearings. Lightning shot across the sky outside and somewhere nearby a radio blared out the Game's 80s soundtrack, distorted and off-key.

There. The red door.

And Aaron, floating on the surface nearby.

She swam over. He didn't shift – she wondered if he was already dead. But as she gazed down into his beautiful face, he met her eyes.

'I wasn't going to kill you, you know,' she said. 'Or Charlie, since she agreed to hand me the prize.' She pulled him close, his head supported on her arm. 'Not if I could avoid it anyway. I like you, even though you're a bit of a liar too. Charlie was honest, at least. Nate … he kind of ruined everything.'

Aaron's eyelids flickered. 'I like you too. You don't have to kill me,' he replied.

'Of course I do. I can't have what happened here getting out, can I?'

He frowned slightly. 'But Angel … don't they know anyway?'

Veronica shook her head. 'All they know is that I killed Em. I guess they might be suspicious. But that's hardly proof I killed anyone else. They were kicked out of the Game before anyone caught on to what was happening.'

Aaron blinked. He was struggling to speak – to cling to consciousness, Veronica thought. 'That … doesn't matter. The point is … I get why you've done … what you've done. I wouldn't tell.'

'Really?' Veronica felt her heart lift.

'Of course – you do what you have to do. I … respect that about you.' His voice was calm, despite the pain he must have been in. 'We're not like … the others. I would have done the same … to save someone who was important to me.' His voice was warm. 'When we get out of here … I want to see you again.'

She couldn't help the way her stomach flipped at the thought of being with him in the real world. 'I don't even know your last name … or where you live,' Veronica said, a little breathlessly. 'We don't really know each other at all.'

'It's Tan. And Scottsdale, Arizona – just FYI. And no, we don't.' He smiled slightly, through his pain. 'But we've … been through something unforgettable. Something … that will bind us together forever.'

She blinked slowly, trying to gather her thoughts. 'You are so full of shit, Aaron Tan,' she said, at last – and with that, she pushed him under.

'The murderer of Orson Coleman was Peter Coleman, his son.'

Veronica felt her whole body tense with nerves as she stood in front of the red door, chest-deep in water, hoping she'd landed on the right answer. 'His motive was revenge; he had discovered that he had been lied to his entire life. He, Peter, was Liz's son – not Grace's. And the method … He pushed his father over the banister of the first-floor landing. Orson's head cracked on the edge of the fountain as he fell. He was dead before he hit the water.'

The door to the clock tower's upper floor clicked open before the final words had even left Veronica's mouth, revealing a slender crack of light.

'This is it,' she said to herself. She'd done it. No matter what everyone else had thought of her, no matter how many obstacles Em had placed in her way, she'd reached the end of the Game – solved the mystery, saved Max. 'At last.' Her nightmare was nearly over. She pulled on the door. The water stopped at the threshold, as if enclosed by an invisible wall.

She raised her eyes and bright white light flooded her vision. Laughter bubbled up inside her.

In the whiteness, shapes shifted. A swirl of snow, the drape of a shroud – or the curve of a pillow. A white face, *Em's* face, eyes black as coals – then, it was swallowed up in the snow. Veronica's brain, expelling the poison that was Em forever.

The whiteness fuzzed, then exploded into pixels – a ringing started in her ears. No ... an alarm.

'She's waking up,' said a voice. 'Get Mr Moretti.'

Smells returned to her next. Disinfectant. Bad coffee. Scrubbed lino. Clean sheets.

She was in hospital.

'Let's get this thing off you, love,' said a woman's voice.

Then, someone lifted something off her face. The headset. Bright strip lights overhead caused her eyes to water and she blinked. She'd never seen anything so beautiful. Then Max's face appeared.

'Veronica! You're back!' he said. And he wrapped his thin arms around her neck.

19

Max's new clinic was in Northern California. One day, when he was resting after his treatment, Dad drove Veronica and Nyra to a trail up in the foothills where huge redwoods scraped the blue glass of the sky.

As Veronica stepped out of the car – the whine of its electric engine shutting off as Dad opened the driver's side – she breathed in deep to smell the clean, fresh scent of the trees.

'I'm glad you're here,' Nyra said to her softly, approaching. 'I know it's been tough, over the years. Me and your dad, we didn't start our relationship in the best way.'

'No, that wasn't great.'

Nyra's cheeks coloured slightly. 'I regret it. You've had loads to work through. I think sometimes I would forget that, before. There's no doubt I could have been kinder. And now with your mum being back in touch … well, it's a lot.'

'I know,' Veronica said, smiling. She felt especially benevolent today. 'But things are better now. It's all over. Everything's going to be fine.'

Nyra squeezed her arm gratefully.

'Hey, are you two coming?' Dad called. He was wearing his embarrassing exercise leggings again, a light jacket tied around his waist despite the thirty-degree heat.

Nyra and Veronica exchanged a small eye-roll and followed.

The three of them set off on the trail. The path was quiet – no sign of the passengers from the five or six other cars in the parking lot. A few deer raised their heads as they plunged further into the forest's shadows, darting away at the sight of company. The earth was dry under Veronica's walking boots and the faint smell of ash tainted the air.

'Nyra and I spoke to the consultant,' her dad said. 'They're really encouraged by your brother's stats. They're saying he may make a full recovery.'

'That's wonderful news,' Veronica said, her cheeks hurting from smiling so hard.

'You really have saved us, Veronica,' he added. 'All of us. Now, we're a real family.'

It was the kind of thing he'd never have said to her before.

Her whole life since winning the Game had felt like a dream. The mysterious and enormous transfer into her bank account. The press hounding her for comments – until she hired private security and flew the family to San Francisco. A whistle-blower who called themselves Angel showing up on the news. That had been the nail in the coffin for the Game – the linkage to four mysterious deaths of teenagers across the world. Veronica hadn't commented. And, naturally, the Game wouldn't be played again.

Everything was perfect. Exactly how she'd planned.

As they approached a fork in the trail, Nyra and Dad hung back, fussing over the water in their backpacks. Veronica gazed at the paths through the trees. The left one veered upward slightly – deeper into the forest. The right was wider, tamer. She felt drawn to the left, energised and enthused by the towering trunks, the low hiss of the wind, the steep path. These days, she relished a challenge. She tapped her new Bluetooth hearing aids. 'I'll head on,' she said. 'This way.'

'All right, darling,' her dad said. 'We'll be right behind.'

She hit play on her favourite playlist and started up the path, relieved to be alone for a while. Nyra and Dad had changed, now she'd won the money. No more therapy. No more school, even – Veronica was finishing her exams in her own time, at home. But however cool they'd turned out, they were parents, and Veronica had to find her own space – figure out how to be true to who she was.

An 80s synth track started up on her playlist.

She frowned, turned the music off. She didn't like that song. Didn't remember adding it.

The path turned and levelled out. The trees thickened and changed – nearly imperceptibly. The quality of light felt different ... deeper somehow. The air now was fresh and damp. None of the desert quality she'd smelt previously.

Ivy snaked up the trunk of one of the trees nearby, lusciously green with thick, finger-like stems.

Veronica swallowed, breathed deep. Amazing, how nature could shift and change.

A shape darted between the trunks at the edge of her vision. A deer, she thought. Of course it was. And yet, she stopped, feeling suddenly as if she were being watched. Cold trickled down her spine like a long, slow drip.

She should go back to Dad and Nyra, she thought.

The shape darted again through the shadows.

'Hello?' Veronica called, her voice shivering slightly.

A low giggle rose from the darkness. Or was it a giggle? Perhaps it had been the call of an unfamiliar bird. Or else ... someone was trying to frighten her.

'This is bullshit,' Veronica muttered. She marched off the main path into the trees. 'Hey, where are you?' she called.

'Stop trying to scare me! It's not funny!'

She walked a few paces further – but everything was silent. She spun back towards the path, suddenly afraid, but ...

Where is the path?

The sunny dirt trail had disappeared entirely – though she hadn't walked far at all. Instead, the tall trees fully surrounded her, trunks wrapped around with ivy. Leaves rustled on the ground nearby. Veronica started again, her footsteps crunching on the leaves. She tried to keep her breathing steady.

She had to stay calm. The path couldn't be far. In fact, the trees started to thin nearly immediately and Veronica felt a coil of tension unravel in her chest. It was OK. She was OK.

Except, the atmosphere felt different now in the clearing ... The golden California sunlight had disappeared and, instead, the sky was white with clouds. Footsteps sounded behind her – Veronica spun.

No one was there.

'Hey, stop this!' she said – but her voice had a definite tremor, this time.

When she turned back to the clearing, a small hut stood at its centre. She was certain it hadn't been there before ... Veronica felt a chill on the back of her neck. She lifted her hand, swiped to find cold wetness there ... Snow?

Horror rose up inside her as she studied the hut – no, the *woodshed* – now framed by the falling snow. It couldn't be … It wasn't …

A low giggle sounded again – a shape shifting nearby. Veronica started to back away from the shed, back into the trees, back into her real life, the life she deserved, the life she had fought for, the life she had *killed* for.

But when she spun around, Em's face was inches from her own – her cold hand closing around her arm. 'Found you!'

ACKNOWLEDGEMENTS

Let's Play Murder is a true pandemic book. I first dreamed up (or nightmared up?) the concept during spring 2020. After all, it was at heart a horror story about being trapped in a house! My first draft was torturously written during the following year. It was the worst first draft I've ever produced – no exaggeration. As such, the fact that you're holding this book in your hands is (a) a miracle and (b) the result of team effort, faith and determination.

My biggest thanks go out to my editors at Bloomsbury, Zöe Griffiths and Katie Ager. Both of you have dedicated so much time and passion into shaping this story on every level and I can't thank you enough. I'm so proud of the result.

Veronique Baxter, my agent, has been a cheerleader for my work from the start and this novel has been no exception. Special thanks for reading that second draft and telling me it wasn't too bad – I needed that!

All too often the full publishing team behind a novel isn't credited, so I want to ensure I say a huge THANK YOU to everyone else who worked on the book:

Editors – Zöe Griffiths and Katie Ager (for ... well ... everything!)

Copy-editor – Veronica Lyons (for sorting out my dodgy logic)

Proofreader – Sarah Taylor-Fergusson (for your exceptional eye for detail)

Sensitivity reader – Enisha Samra (for your thoughtful additions to the hearing-loss rep)

Managing Editor – Fliss Stevens (for ensuring the whole process ran smoothly)

Publicity – Grace Ball (for your enthusiasm and spreading the word)

Marketing – Mattea Barnes (for helping this book find a home on reader bookshelves)

Cover design – Tom Sanderson (for tapping into everything I could wish for in a cover – actual tears)

Production – Michael Young (for making my story into a real book ... i.e. making my dreams come true!)

Rights – Stephanie Purcell and all your amazing team (for introducing this book to the world)

A big shout-out to everyone in my wider bookish community – 'my' Chicken House authors (I learn so much from you every day!), my brilliant colleagues, fellow publishing people and anyone else I'm pals with IRL or online. Your presence on the other end of my smartphone is such a comfort.

Thanks as well to Natasha – your bottomless supply of Prosecco-fuelled writing advice is very important to me – and to Catherine and Tim (and Idris and Anaïs) for being true and loyal fans! Also to my parents, for supporting me in pursuing my dreams since forever, and for letting me play The Seventh Guest (and, less appropriately, Doom) on our 1990s family PC – they were huge inspirations for this book. Lastly, and most of all, a huge thank you to my husband, Jeff, who's always there with a hug when things get tough, and never loses faith in me.

And to you, my reader: I'm very glad that, like Em, I FOUND YOU!

Q&A WITH THE AUTHOR

1. **What inspired you to write this novel now? Is there a book or movie that provided inspiration, or a particular current event?**

   Let's Play Murder was dreamed up during the summer of 2020, and written and edited during the following two years – it's very much a pandemic book! I've found that writers reacted to the pandemic in one of two ways: either through escapist, joyous and fantastical work *or* by diving deeper into the horror and darkness ... You can guess which of those approaches was mine! At heart this is a book about a bunch of characters trapped in a house and a (VR) world falling apart – to me it very much holds a mirror to the world we were all living in during that time. In terms of books or movies, I was inspired by a mix of *The Seven Deaths of Evelyn Hardcastle*, *Ready Player One* and the video games of my 1990s childhood, particularly The 7th Guest and Doom.

2. **Each of the players has a strong (sometimes divisive) personality and their own secrets outside the Game. Was there a character that you especially enjoyed writing about? Who was the most gut-wrenching to kill?**

I loved writing Charlie – she of all the characters seemed to shout out to me with a clear and distinctive voice, and at various times she took over a scene in a way I haven't experienced with another character before. Writing her was really fun and refreshing! She's obnoxious, hypercompetitive and difficult, but she actually has a very big heart, so I was sad to lose her at the end. As they say, kill your darlings …

3. **You've written from the perspective of unreliable narrators before. What draws you to that particular viewpoint?**

As a reader there's nothing I love more than to be shocked by a big twist, and unreliable narrators are one of the best ways to disguise what's coming. In my first novel, *We Are Blood and Thunder*, I played with a dual narrative, exploring the story via one unreliable narrator and one reliable one. *Let's Play Murder* was even more ambitious because I stuck with the unreliable voice all the way through – a challenge for sure, but a LOT of fun!

4. **Your books have fantastic scenes of horror in them. For example, the zombie attack in *Let's Play Murder* is an all-out terrifying scene. What inspires you to come up with these scenes?**

My reading has developed a lot in recent years. As a teenager and up to my mid-twenties, I read loads of fantasy. I still love fantasy – but nowadays I read and watch a lot of thrillers and horror. The scary scenes in *Let's Play Murder* felt like they flowed naturally and added something powerful to the story. I think as readers we are desperate to feel something – and fear is a very heady, addictive emotion.

5. **What inspired you to set the Game in the 1980s?**

During the early months of the pandemic, when I conceived this idea, one of the ways I coped with feeling trapped was escaping into photos, videos, early computer games and other paraphernalia from my childhood. I was born in 1989, and after immersing myself in all this stuff I decided to set the Game around my birthday. Partly it was just for fun (anyone who knows me knows I love the 1980s aesthetic), but I also think there is a weird psychic link between nostalgia and horror – we are always looking back to some kind of 'golden age' (usually when we were young) but doesn't that mean we're less engaged with the real issues that face us? In *Let's Play Murder*, I stripped back my own sense of nostalgia to find the real horror underneath.

6. **As well as being an author, you are also a commissioning editor – another very demanding job. How do you balance the dual roles? Do you find that being an editor influences how you approach your writing?**

I feel so lucky to have two jobs I love! But balancing these roles is a constant challenge. At the beginning of my time as an editor I had a very strict routine of writing in a cafe for about an hour before work. The pandemic changed that and I am still trying to recapture something of that rhythm. Nowadays it feels a lot more chaotic – but somehow I'm still writing! I learn so much about writing and editing from both sides of the editorial desk – one generally inspires and enriches the other. But as for my approach to writing, honestly, it's not very 'editorial' at all – I tend to write a terrible first draft as I hate planning and annoyingly I don't seem to be able to use *any* of my editorial insight on my own stuff! It's like writing and editing come from two very different parts of my brain.

Have you read

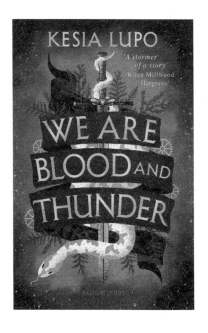

Turn the page for an extract of the gripping first
instalment of Kesia Lupo's stunning and original
YA fantasy world

ONE
The Hounds

Sixth year of the storm cloud

Lena ran until her lungs felt close to bursting, her feet thumping, sliding on the steep cobblestone road, down the peak of the city towards the walls and the forest beyond.

The Justice's words rang loud in her ears.

You have been found guilty of magecraft.

The storm cloud was all-encompassing, a thick, poisonous gauze clinging to her clothes, obscuring her path.

I sentence you to die.

Islands of muffled light trembled in the gloom – a lit window here, a patch of fading sunlight there. Her feet thumped into greyness, invisible.

The hounds will eat your flesh.

She could hear them – howling, growling. Had they finished off Vigo? Or had they grown tired of his old flesh, now lusting after hers? He'd bought her time, but it was all for nothing. Tears stung her eyes as she pushed herself faster.

1

Your bones will lie bare under the sky, banished from the sacred crypts.

She could never outrun them. Nobody could. At seventeen, she was far from the youngest to have fallen under the hounds' vicious teeth; you only had to see the chewed-up remains at the foot of the city walls to know that. But there was a chance – just a chance. She had to try.

Your soul will never join the Ancestors, will never feast on the glories of ages past, will never guide the fates.

Lena found herself down in the lowest tier of the city. The fog was thicker here. She stumbled to a halt, suddenly unable to breathe, a crushing pain in her side. Pulling up the neck of her habit to cover her mouth and nose, she felt tears welling behind the glass of her shield-eyes.

You will be dead, in this world and the next.

A howl broke the gloom, then a chorus of howls, swiftly followed by frenzied barking; the hounds were gaining. No time to cry. She turned and ran, harder than ever, hobnailed boots clacking against the pavement.

Soon the city walls loomed above, a small bone crunching under her foot. She felt sick, but pressed on round the curve of the wall, desperately scanning the base where the dark stone met the bone-littered ground. The gates had been locked for two years, bolted with broad beams of oak, ivy grown over the rusted locks – but nearby … Vigo had told her …

Lena scanned the rotted undergrowth for the outline of the old rose bush – and found it, her heart no more than

2

a hollow, fluttering thing in the back of her throat. She could so easily have missed it altogether, a tangle of bare thorns almost lost among the skeletal remains of its neighbours. Parting the branches with her thick leather gloves, she spotted a slight dip in the earth. So small.

I used it as a child, he'd said, in the few moments they'd had together before the hounds. *I would slip out into the forest to play when I was supposed to be at my lessons. It was before my ... deformity.*

She'd shaken her head wordlessly, clutching at his old arthritic hands, the hands which had first picked her up from the steps down to the cryptling cellars as a baby, wailing into the dawn. She'd been crying again, then.

Lena, I cannot run. But you might just be fast and small enough to escape.

It was her only chance.

Lena threw herself to the ground as the howls behind her grew in intensity – along with the clink and scratch of claws on the cobblestones. She pressed herself under the bush, the old thorny stems snagging at her habit and showering her with rot, and scrabbled into the musty darkness beneath the wall. Curling her fingers as best she could into the damp soil, Lena pulled herself forward, wriggling until her feet were almost concealed under the rose bush, the weight of the great thick wall bearing down over her head, dark and cold and ancient.

The gap was tight, her lungs constricting as she forced her shoulders further, her arms outstretched. She thought she could feel a wisp of air from the other side – but it was then that a bark came from close quarters, followed by a frenzy of growls, a snapping of teeth. Something closed around the tough leather heel of her boot; a surprising strength pulled her backwards. Panic fuelled her. She gripped on to the wall's slick underside with clawed hands. Her shield-eyes snagged on a root, the leather strap snapping. She let them fall, kicked out hard and redoubled her efforts, squirming frantically under the wall until she could see the light filtering through the other side. She squeezed her shoulders forward and, with more difficulty, her hips, ripping the coarse material of her habit. By this time, she had begun to sob – but somehow she forced her way out.

Lena staggered to her feet, half-falling into the forest. Her heart plummeted as she absorbed the sight confronting her. The forest was a picture of decay, the trees visibly withering. A grey residue veiled their bark and occasionally bumped outwards in a strange fungus. The storm cloud was as thick as it was within the walls of the city, flashing and rumbling between the trees. She thought of her shield-eyes, fallen under the wall – but where she had crawled, the hounds could surely follow: she couldn't risk retrieving them. She ran instead, stumbling over roots, slipping on wet leaves. Here and there, a rotted trunk had fallen across the path, or a branch half-snapped from a larger tree threatened her head.

Gradually, the howls and barks faded altogether, but it was a long time before Lena allowed herself to be certain she had not been followed – perhaps the dogs, penned for

4

so long within the city walls, had been spooked by the alien scents and noises of the forest. Or perhaps the houndmaster had assumed her dead and called them off, or perhaps he'd feared losing them forever among the trees, as so many travellers had been lost before. In any case, she was painfully grateful. She slowed down, rubbed her stinging eyes and caught her breath. She rested her hands on her knees for a moment, her heartbeat slowing – and then she reached for the brass butterfly she kept in the pocket of her robe. It was as big as the palm of her hand, warm from her body. Tracing the delicate filigree of its wings, she felt her breathing slow.

Whenever she held the butterfly, she remembered how she had felt the night she'd found it – or rather, the night it had found her. She had felt wanted. Calm. Secure in the knowledge that she was worth something, because she had something of worth.

Out of the corner of her eye she saw a shape – a human shape, hunched at the foot of a tree. Her stomach convulsed and she ducked behind a rotten tangle of undergrowth, pressing her hand against her mouth to stifle a rising scream. But the figure didn't appear to have noticed her. The cloud shifted, alternately revealing and concealing a long cloak, brown boots, large leather gloves. So still, so quiet, his hooded head resting on his chest. Sleeping? But she saw no movement, not a twitch, no rise and fall of breath. Slowly, Lena realised the man was dead.

She slipped the butterfly in her pocket, stood up and walked towards him, her whole body still trembling – but gradually calming as she approached the corpse. She wasn't afraid of the dead – not unless they … She shook her head, not wanting to think about it. No, it was the living who frightened her.

She crouched, examined a blade dropped near the body, glinting in the faint evening light filtering through cloud and trees. It was a short dagger, the hilt twined with a dragon motif in silver, its eye picked out with a green gem. Hardly thinking, she picked it up, slid it carefully into her belt. As she carried on, she realised the man had been resting on the edge of a small clearing. And she saw another body. A woman, her back turned to Lena, marked out by her perfectly preserved, long red hair, splayed in the mud. And another – a man curled up under his cloak by the blackened remains of a fire. Without meaning to, she glimpsed his face, decayed and ghastly.

These bodies had been here for a long time. Had they been trying to reach the city? They were strangers, surely. What had killed them?

She didn't want to wait to find out.

She returned to the narrow path and carried on at a stumbling run.

After a time, it grew so late that she could barely distinguish the trees from the darknesses in between – but soon she began to see other things, shapes in the fog twisting into suggestions of hands, eyes, mouths. She blinked, rubbing her eyes and cursing the loss of her shield-eyes. No one in Duke's Forest would step outside with their eyes unprotected – the toxic storm cloud caused visions if they were exposed for too long. Every now and then, larger shapes loomed from between the trees, and she could not prevent herself from starting backwards before they dissipated, even though she knew they weren't real.

She imagined the strangers' bodies in the clearing moving, rising up, following her. *Don't. Think.* But despite her stern thoughts, and the exhaustion screaming at her to stop, she quickened her pace.

Eventually, Lena could continue no longer. Her legs gave out, and she felt her fingers burrow into the mossy mulch of the forest floor. The hallucinations were worsening. She knew she was vulnerable out here – to *real* threats – if she wasn't able to run. She remembered Vigo's tales of the giant snakes and wild boar that infested the wood, and screwed her eyes shut against a wave of terror. She took a deep breath. She needed her wits now more than ever.

But the forest stretched in all directions, and she had long lost the road – how would she escape? And even if she were to find her way out, what fate could a girl like her expect in the wider world? She felt for the birthmark on her cheek, several shades darker than the brown of her skin. Even the people of Duke's Forest had regarded cryptlings – marked out by their various deformities – with a mixture of disgust and begrudging respect for their duties. Vigo had said the gods were cruel, their followers toying with dangerous magic. What would they make of her? What did they do to Marked people outside of Duke's Forest?

Would *they* try to execute her too?

Lena felt a sickly chill spread from her throat to her stomach as she considered the most terrible possibility of all: what if the storm cloud had swallowed everything, leaving the city of Duke's Forest the lonely centre of the universe? What if those people had been trying to reach Duke's Forest to save themselves?

No – she could not give up. Lena opened her eyes and dragged her exhausted body upright once more, determined to continue, but now she was surrounded, not by trees, but by a mass of people, each one of them turning towards her – each one of them familiar. These were the dead of Duke's Forest, the dead the Pestilence had taken, the dead she had helped to undress, wash and embalm, replacing their eyes with the painted stones and glittering gems that now bore into her.

She was a convicted mage, and an outcast, and the Ancestors were angry.

She stumbled back against a tree, touched her forehead, lips and chest in a silent prayer, her hand shaking. 'Please …' she managed, but the Ancestors' hearts were hollowed out. The world turned black.

And don't miss

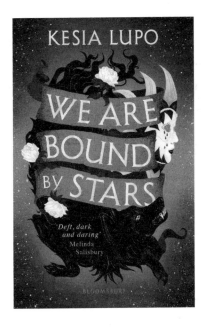

The second thrilling, plot-driven adventure set in Kesia Lupo's rich fantasy world that will keep you completely gripped until the very last page

AVAILABLE NOW

ABOUT THE AUTHOR

Kesia Lupo studied history at the University of Oxford and creative writing at Bath Spa. Now she's a children's fiction editor living in the USA with her husband. Her first two novels, *We Are Blood and Thunder* and *We Are Bound by Stars*, were fan favourites set in a highly original fantasy world. *Let's Play Murder* is her third novel published by Bloomsbury.